Windswept Love

Courtni Wright

Windswept Love

BET Publications, LLC
http://www.bet.com
http://www.arabesquebooks.com

ARABESQUE BOOKS are published by

BET Publications, LLC
c/o BET Books
One BET Plaza
1900 W Place NE
Washington, DC 20018-1211

All Kensington Titles, Imprints, and Distributed Lines are available at special quantity discounts for bulk purchases for sales promotions, premiums, fund-raising, and educational or institutional use. For details, write or phone the office of the Kensington special sales manager: Kensington Publishing Corp., 850 Third Avenue, New York, NY 10022, attn: Special Sales Department, Phone: 1-800-221-2647.

First Printing: June 2005

10 9 8 7 6 5 4 3 2 1

Printed in the United States of America

Chapter One

The sun beat down on their heads as nearly four thousand midshipmen from the U.S. Naval Academy marched onto the parade field for the last time that school year. For many, it was the last time in their lives. The nine hundred men and women who were graduating from the "boat school" would soon be commissioned junior officers in the navy or the marines, leaving behind the fast friendships, the demanding academics, and the dreaded parades that took place rain or shine. For four years, the seniors, who were called "firsties" at the academy, had donned the parade dress uniform, toted the old M-16 rifles, and marched from Bancroft Hall down the center of the campus onto the parade grounds. Now, their days on the campus yard had come to an end.

With each step, the distance between the two points on the yard seemed to grow, especially under the unusually scorching late-May sun. Joanne Crawford subtly shifted her hot, tired shoulders. As a company officer, she had to lead by example even if her shoes pinched and the collar of her uniform scratched her neck. She could not allow her shoulders to droop or her step to lag. Besides, her parents would notice any misstep. They were so proud of her accomplishments at the academy. She was one of only a few women and a member of an even smaller group of company officers. Joanne knew that she had made them proud. She could bear the heat and the discomfort one last time for them. Standing tall with green eyes that sparkled and medium-short brown hair, she was ready to join the fleet.

"This is our last parade, Joanne," Kingsley, the company officer to her left, said from the corner of his mouth.

"I never thought it would come," Joanne replied in a whisper.

"Four years, and we're free," Kingsley muttered in response.

"Almost. Only a few more activities and then graduation," Joanne added.

"It's been good knowing you, Crawford," Kingsley said.

"And you. We've been through some tough times, but we've survived," Joanne responded.

"Let's keep in touch," Kingsley said.

"Good idea. We've had good times," Joanne whispered.

"And bad," came the response.

"Here's to the good ones," Joanne replied as they saluted the flag at the intersection.

As she stepped onto the parade field, Joanne reflected on her life at the academy. She could have studied at almost any college in the country. Her high-school grades had been stellar and her SAT scores phenomenal. Ivy League and other prestigious colleges had courted her with offers of swimming scholarships. But she wanted to serve her country as a pilot and had chosen the Naval Academy over ROTC because she wanted to earn the coveted class ring under her spotless white gloves.

The Naval Academy only accepted the brightest and the best. When Joanne received her admission letter to the Annapolis, Maryland campus, she immediately accepted and put all other colleges and universities from her mind. Despite the hardships of life on the yard, Joanne had never regretted her decision.

Taking her place at the head of the company as the other midshipmen filed in behind her, Joanne reflected on the four years spent on the Chesapeake Bay and the friendships born from the hard work and endless study. She could not imagine living with more dedicated students. They had to be; low grades and behavior unbecoming a future officer resulted in dismissal.

They had worked and played hard, and in a matter of hours it would be over. Many of them had fallen in love with civilians or other midshipmen. Joanne was one of them. The separation caused by training and military assignments would be difficult but part of the life she had chosen. She was ready to embrace the challenges and give her best.

Standing at attention and looking straight ahead, Joanne saw the blur of colors and the mingling of people as they filled the reviewing stands. For most of the academy's parades, only die-hard enthusiasts occupied the stands. However, for big events like Parents' Weekend and Commissioning Week, people overflowed onto the grass for an opportunity to catch a glimpse of a beloved friend or relative.

Joanne's mind wandered back to the first parade in her freshman year. She had practiced her drills endlessly on the asphalt, learning the routine and surviving the heat. The trainer had barked instructions into her ears until she knew every step by heart.

"Pick 'em up, Crawford!" the trainer shouted.

"Sir, yes, sir," Joanne responded.

"Do it! Don't just say it!" the trainer barked again.

"Sir, yes, sir," Joanne yelled, stepping high.

"I'll make a midshipman out of you yet, Crawford," the trainer snarled in her ear.

"Sir, yes, sir," Joanne responded, thinking that he was really shaping a navy officer.

Joanne had followed instructions despite the effort and heavy uniform. The hard work had paid off. In the years to come, she had taken the trainer's place and helped other midshipmen make the transition from civilian to officer-in-training.

Although she could not see them, Joanne knew that her parents were somewhere in the crowd. They had taken the week off from their teaching jobs so that they would not miss a minute of Joanne's special week. They felt that her graduation and commissioning ranked among the most important events in her life, right behind marriage and childbirth. The demands of preparing detailed lesson plans and arranging for substitute teachers while they were away were a small price to pay to see their baby graduate with honors. Their daughter had made them incredibly proud.

Joanne had arranged to meet them after the parade for the obligatory photos on Stribling Walk near the chapel. Gathering at the statue in Tecumseh Court would have been more picturesque but much too congested. A few photos with the library in the background and maybe even Mitscher Hall would remind her of the long study hours and the openness of the campus. The chapel would forever bring to mind peace, meditation and solitary reflection. Long after the memory of hard work had faded, Joanne wanted to be able to see the beloved sight. It was inside the chapel that she had found solace and made so many important decisions. Many of them had been of little consequence, but some had made the biggest impact on her life. The ones that involved Mike Shepherd, her fellow classmate, were the most important.

Joanne would soon leave for places unknown. For the first time in her life, she would not have the comfort of familiar surroundings and faces to buoy her as she faced the real world. Her quasi-sheltered life of the Naval Academy would end tomorrow. With the tossing of the midshipman cover and the pinning on of ensign shoulder boards, the life she had led would end and a new one would begin.

Again, Joanne reflected on life within the Academy's gates. She had made many close friends with whom she had shared the good and the bad. The memories would live forever.

"Joanne, is my cover on straight?" her roommate had asked the first time they had been allowed to wear the midshipman's hat.

"Yeah, looks okay to me. How's mine?" Joanne had whispered as they stood in Tecumseh Court waiting for the drumbeat to signal the first parade of the academic year.

"I'm so nervous. What if I drop my rifle?" her roommate said.

"Keep walking. You won't be the first," Joanne advised.

"Aren't you worried?" her roommate continued.

"Sure. It's hot out here. I'm afraid I'll faint," Joanne replied.

"Don't mention fainting. I'm already sweating," her roommate whispered.

"It's time!" Joanne said as she swallowed hard.

"We're really part of the Academy now. Let's do it," her roommate replied.

Joanne and her roommate had walked proudly without stumbling, fainting, or dropping their rifles. Four years of marching had passed without a mishap. Now, they were ready for the next adventure. They didn't need to check their covers anymore. The uniform was part of their being now.

As Joanne listened to the steady beat of the drums for the last time, she reflected on her years at the "boat school" and the people who had helped her endure. One handsome midshipman in particular had enriched the last semester of her senior year. She would miss the place, but she would not miss Mike Shepherd. His laughing brown eyes, tall trim body, and reddish brown skin would remain in her life forever, or so she hoped. Mike had entered her life on Induction Day as a shadowy figure among the many plebes. However, in the last semester of their final year, he had taken possession of her heart and become much more than a friend and classmate.

Joanne and Mike Shepherd had already endured many hardships in their training at the Academy. But, despite the struggles, they both knew that it was the Academy that had brought them together. It was those memories that would support them during their months of separation after graduation.

Joanne remembered her initial reluctance in letting Mike into her life. As captain of the women's swim team, she wanted to show him that she was as strong as he was. She had been determined not to turn into one of those weak women just because a man was nearby.

"Let me help you, Joanne," Mike had said as she struggled with the laundry bag filled with towels.

"No thanks, Mike. I can manage," Joanne had stubbornly replied.

"There's no need to break your back. No one's looking. I can carry that for you," Mike had said.

"It's my job. I can do it," Joanne had insisted, shifting the heavy load on her thin shoulders.

"Suit yourself. I have liniment in my closet if you need some. Good luck in the meet," Mike had replied as he trotted toward the men's locker room.

"Wasn't that Mike Shepherd? Why didn't you let him carry that?" Tina, one of the members of the swim team, asked as she helped Joanne with the bag.

"I don't like for the guys to help me. Some of them think we shouldn't be here anyway. I don't want to give them more ammo to use against us," Joanne quipped, rubbing her sore shoulders.

"He's not like that. Besides, Mike can hardly keep his eyes off you. You should've let him help. He might have asked you out," Tina replied.

"Really? I hadn't noticed," Joanne commented, standing a little straighter.

"If you'd take your nose out of your books for a while, Mike would ask you out," Tina argued, setting the clean towels on the benches.

"You know the rules," Joanne advised.

"There's nothing to prevent you from dating someone in our class as long as you're discreet. You just can't date an underclassman," Tina commented.

"Technically, you're right. However, I don't want to take any chances. Mids get bounced all the time for just barely stepping over the line. I don't want to risk it," Joanne replied, finishing the last of her setup duties before the big meet against Maryland.

"I tried," Tina sighed and vanished into the pool area, leaving Joanne to think about the opportunity she might have let slip through her fingers.

Despite the Academy's strict rules against fraternization that made Joanne look the other way whenever she saw Mike's tall lean body at swim meets, she had fallen in love with him. She had taken furtive peeks at the muscles that rippled beneath the reddish-brown skin that covered his thin, angular, six-foot-tall body, the short wavy brown hair that glistened with droplets, and the laughing brown eyes that squinted into the pool as if assessing its depth. Even as the water dripped from his glistening skin following a meet, Joanne had only sighed and looked away. She did not have time for romantic entanglement, even if he shared the same thoughts.

Composing her face as she stood in the heat beating down on the parade grounds, Joanne remembered the first time she had seen Mike. They had been freshman and it was the first day of military training for plebes, who would join the rest of the brigade of midshipmen when the academic year began in August. He had looked nervous and intimidated with his new close-cropped haircut, baggy white uniform, and seemed unsettled by the squad leader's loud voice. She had felt the same way, especially with the constant barrage of orders.

Although they had not been in the same company, Mike's room had been just around the corner from hers in Bancroft Hall. Unfortunately, the blur of activity had kept them from speaking that summer and most of their freshman year.

Joanne had kept Mike in her peripheral vision.

She had seen him in classes and watched him as he performed his duties. If the Academy life had only allowed them more freedom, she might have broken the silence between them and not waited until their senior year to meet the man she loved almost from the moment she saw him.

Allowing her mind to drift, Joanne remembered the evening of their first real conversation. She had spotted Mike sitting across the restaurant with three of his buddies. Being seniors and only months from graduation, the midshipmen no longer had to wear their uniforms to town. At twenty-one, they had been able to celebrate their service selection with something a little stronger than ginger ale.

Mike picked his way across the crowded restaurant. As he had approached her table, she turned toward him. For once, Joanne had not wanted her reputation for being all business to scare him away.

"Hey, Joanne," Mike said, his voice sounding high-pitched to his ears despite the baritone range that he usually sang in the men's glee club.

"Oh, hi Mike. Join us?" Joanne offered as tears sparkled on her lashes.

"No, I'm with a couple of the guys. Just wanted to congratulate you on your assignment. I saw the roster. Is anything wrong?" Mike asked, feeling a little uneasy at interrupting the conversation at her table.

"No, not a thing. These are tears of relief. It's over. There's a light at the end of the tunnel. The four years are almost over," Joanne said, smiling happily.

"I'm looking forward to the change myself. Submarine school should be a piece of cake after this place," Mike grinned.

"Let's get together soon and talk about our future. We've known each other all this time and haven't really talked. I'd like to get to know more shipmates before our commissions separate us forever," Joanne offered.

"Yeah. Let's do that. I have a concert this weekend, but I'll get in touch," Mike agreed and returned to his table.

Sighing quietly as the perspiration glistened on her top lip, Joanne thought about that night and the romance that began with so few words. Initially, she and Mike had tried to keep their relationship on friendly terms. They met for dinner on the weekends and went fishing on the bay. Occasionally, they spent long evenings with each other's parents, eating dinner, watching television, and playing cards.

However, their love and passion quickly consumed them. They gave in, knowing that her career as a pilot and his as a submariner would soon tear them apart. They spent the precious moments they could steal from their studies and military commitment sharing each other's hobbies, walking down quiet paths, camping by trickling streams, and loving each other. The countdown to graduation changed from a prelude to liberation to a dreaded farewell. They had so much to share, so many memories to make, and so little time.

Mike meant everything to Joanne. He was the man she had always dreamed of finding and loving. Unfortunately, their last months as midshipmen had passed too quickly. Now, Joanne and Mike were on the brink of a new experience and life apart.

As a pesky fly buzzed around her face, Joanne remembered every date with Mike as if it had just happened. One in particular held a warm spot in her heart. They had eaten a quick dinner and then spent the evening talking about themselves and their plans. She could still feel the excitement of being close to his warmth and hear his voice.

"I've asked to be stationed in Norfolk. It seems like a good compromise. I'll still be able to visit my folks," Mike had said as they walked through the historic city of Annapolis.

"I'm headed to flight school in Florida for the same reason," Joanne replied, pulling her collar closer.

Turning to gaze into her eyes as they stood under a streetlight, Mike had said, "That's not my only reason. Norfolk's close to you, too. I love you and don't plan to let you get away."

"It'll be difficult," Joanne responded, leaning against him.

"Didn't they teach us that the best reward comes with the greatest effort? You're worth it," Mike had replied.

"Ah, Mike. Why didn't we fall in love sooner? We could have had years together instead of months," Joanne sighed.

"We will have years, just not right now. At the moment, we'll have to be happy with days and months," Mike said, holding her close.

"I guess that'll have to do. We'll have to cram every minute with memories so that we have something to keep us going while we're apart," Joanne had said, melting into his kiss.

Studying her face in the glow of the streetlight, Mike said, "There's no hardship that I can't survive knowing that you love me."

"Me too," Joanne had whispered as she tasted his sweet kisses again.

Walking into the chapel, they had melted into each other's arms as they stood in front of the midshipman's window. They had met there so many times, seeking solitude and solace. Whenever they had a problem, they had sat in the chapel and talked in the chapel until they had smoothed out all of the rough spots.

Holding Joanne's hand tightly, Mike said, "At lease we're not getting married immediately after graduation. The first years as ensigns will be too demanding, with practically no time for family. I don't want to put ourselves through the torment of being married and separated from each other."

"I don't envy my roommate, Beth. She and Calvin are getting married the day after graduation and then heading for training at different bases thirty days after that. I don't want that life. Separation is difficult enough without that," Joanne had agreed, watching the flickering candles.

Nodding in agreement, Mike said, "We'll just have to wait to start our future. We'll spend the rest of our lives together, later rather than sooner. Being apart won't make me love you any less. I love your smile, your laugh, and the cute way you wrinkle your nose when you laugh. I love the way you listen to me and make me feel important. Nothing will change that."

"You're right. We don't need a ceremony to symbolize our togetherness," Joanne replied, smiling happily into his eyes.

"You're the only woman I'd ever think of marrying. One day, when we've finished our training, we'll get married and settle down," Mike added.

"Or sooner if we find out that we can juggle marriage and the military," Joanne added.

"That's right. Sooner's good, too," Mike had smiled and pulled her closer.

"But only if we can get reassigned to the same

base," Joanne had sighed, snuggling against his shoulder.

"That won't be easy with me on a sub." Mike reminded Joanne of the men-only branch of the navy to which he had been assigned.

"True. I guess you'll have to transfer to another division," Joanne suggested in an off-hand manner.

"You know how much I've always wanted to be a submariner. I don't see myself requesting a reassignment. You could ask for a transfer to a job in Norfolk," Mike responded gently.

"You know that becoming a pilot is a passion for me. I don't anticipate doing that," Joanne replied, sitting erect and bristling mildly at the suggestion.

"Then we'll wait as planned," Mike had retorted. "A long engagement will give us plenty of time to get used to navy life and separation. You're part of my being. Thinking about you makes me feel good. I can wait."

"Good. That's settled. No marriage until after we've gained more experience or until one of us requests reassignment. I feel good about our decision," Joanne continued.

"So do I," Mike replied, holding her gently in his arms. The midshipman in the stained glass of the chapel window seemed to smile his approval.

"Do you really?" Joanne had asked with a touch of sadness in her voice.

"No, but that's the way it has to be," Mike replied, kissing the tip of her nose.

The change in drum cadence brought Joanne's mind back to the present. Squaring her shoulders and adjusting her saber, she barked orders to her company. Hearing the rattle of rifles behind her, she knew that they had obeyed. Feeling safe and sure, Joanne led her people in the last parade of her career as a midshipman.

With a salute, Joanne signaled that the life that she had shared with Mike at the Academy would soon come to an end. Their careers would start with the commissioning ceremony. Their love affair would become a long-distance romance. The somber drumbeat made her wonder if they would find "fair winds" or turmoil and heartache. Only time would tell.

Chapter Two

As Joanne hurriedly slipped into a pair of shorts and a well-worn tee shirt, she caught a last glimpse of the bedroom that had been hers while growing up in her parents' house. The wood floors gleamed in the sunlight, and a pansy-shaped area rug lay on the floor at the foot of the bed. The room was floral and inviting, a far cry from the battleship gray that covered the walls and floors at the Academy. It was also messy. She had been home for a week and had thought little of keeping it neat. Now that she had graduated, she no longer needed to set an example for the midshipmen. Soon, she would be the junior officer following the example of the instructors and senior pilots above her. For the time being, however, Joanne enjoyed being on a much-needed thirty-day leave.

Unlike most recent college graduates who had to rise early to go job-hunting, Joanne slept late, a real treat after four years of 0530 reveille. She lolled in the bathtub rather than rushing through her shower. She had even decided to allow her hair and nails to grow out a bit now that she had time for herself.

Life after the Academy would take on the hum of a leisurely routine. Joanne would have time for herself and Mike, until the demands of training separated them. Fortunately, neither of them had to report to their assignments until August.

Tossing her robe into the overflowing closet in a vain effort to restore order to the chaos, Joanne ran down the stairs as she always had before the demands of the Academy had taught her to slow her pace. She felt excited about the future in the navy's close-knit group of pilots. With Mike's love, Joanne looked forward to each day with renewed energy.

"Good morning, Mom!" Joanne bellowed as she entered her mother's carefully laid out kitchen.

"Well, it's about time you got up. I was beginning to think that the mess in your room had swallowed you," Angela Crawford said, accepting the hastily planted kiss from her only child.

"I was out late with Mike last night. I hope I didn't wake you when I came home," Joanne said as she poured a glass of freshly squeezed orange juice her mother prepared daily.

"Not a sound," Angela chuckled. "You know I sleep like a rock to block out your father's snoring. I certainly hope you don't marry a man who makes that kind of racket every night."

"I'll try not to, but there's no guarantee," Joanne laughed.

"Mike doesn't snore?" her mother asked without looking up from the cake that she was decorating. She had assumed that her daughter and Mike, who so obviously adored her, were sleeping together. Two people could not look at each other with such passion in their eyes without being intimate. Besides, unlike her mother who never discussed sex with her, Mrs. Crawford had been very open with her daughter and had talked about sex, having children, and practicing safe sex with Joanne.

"I haven't noticed, but I usually fall asleep before he does. I'm still really tired from school," Joanne replied, licking a glob of chocolate icing from her finger.

The sight brought back so many memories. "Will you and Mike eat dinner with us tonight?"

"No, thanks. We'll grab something in Baltimore. We're going to a jazz concert tonight. As a matter of fact, I'm on my way to his place now. I'm staying with him for the weekend. We have tickets to a play in Baltimore at the Morris Mechanic and the next day we're driving to Philly. One of his best friends from the Academy is getting married, and Mike's a swordsman."

"Oh, so I won't see you for a few days," Mrs. Crawford said, trying not to sound disappointed.

Hugging her mother, Joanne replied lightly, "You and Daddy will have your privacy back for a while."

"We don't feel that we've lost it . . . we just returned to the wonderful old days when the sound of your voice rang through the house. That's all. I know how it is to be grown and living at home. I'm happy to have a few minutes with you whenever I can get them. You'll be in Florida for a long time," her mother responded, placing her hand on Joanne's.

"I know," Joanne sighed sadly, "but you and Daddy can come visit me whenever you want."

"And we will. Don't you think you should get going? You don't want to keep that handsome ensign waiting," her mother said, aware that the sigh was not only in anticipation of missing home.

"You're right. I better go," Joanne said, picking up her bag and heading toward the back door. Turning, she asked, "You like Mike, don't you?"

"Oh, yes. He seems like a nice guy. Besides, he has the good taste to be in love with my daughter.

That shows that he's bright and discerning," she replied, smiling.

"Good, because I'm in love with him, too," Joanne stated softly.

Turning toward her daughter, Angela Crawford said, "I know. I've seen it in the way you look at him. It feels good to be in love with someone who loves you back."

Smiling, Joanne added, "Just like you and Daddy."

"Being married to your father and having you as a daughter have been the happiest parts of my life. I hope you'll be as blessed. Now go!"

Hugging her mother one last time, Joanne rushed to her car, all the while thinking of Mike. Although the Academy had consumed most of her spare time, she had dated really nice guys while in high school, but none as wonderful as Mike. Not only was he tall, handsome, and bright, he was athletic and witty. He enjoyed swimming and sport fishing, jazz and theater, and sitting by the fire. She could not have asked for a more compatible man.

Unfortunately, life at the Academy had prevented her from learning of his wonderful qualities until their tenure had almost come to an end. Despite the endless marching and studying, they had found each other amongst the battalion of midshipmen. The true test would come in holding on to each other while separated by their assignments.

Driving to Mike's apartment, Joanne again thought that Baltimore was a city of many contradictions. From the waterfront with its shopping mall and sports arenas to the center city with theaters and universities, the city offered just about anything that anyone could want. But as she drove, negotiating the one-way streets, all Joanne could thing about was how much she wanted to be with Mike.

Having grown up in the Maryland suburbs close to Washington, DC, Joanne had always enjoyed visiting Baltimore's diverse neighborhoods. The city's thriving Little Italy was populated with award-winning restaurants. The area around Peabody Heights and Johns Hopkins offered not only cultural enrichment, but academic opportunities at two of the country's most prestigious institutions. The residential neighborhoods themselves were colorful attractions. Neighborhood pubs sat on every corner. Painted front steps and stained-glass transoms added history and distinction to row houses, with local parks the dividing line between ethnic neighborhoods. Huge monuments forced traffic to skirt around them, while large markets selling everything from fresh fish to melt-in-your mouth donuts attracted crowds at lunchtime and in the evening.

Unlike Joanne, who was fascinated by the smells and sights of Baltimore, Mike had grown up in the area near the Meyerhoff Symphony Hall and took the city's cultural vibrancy for granted. As the only child in a household of a minister and an attorney, he had been too busy playing ball with his friends to see the city. Now that he was leaving for submarine school and eventually his assignment to Norfolk, Virginia, he let Joanne show him around the town, seeing it through her eyes. He enjoyed everything more with Joanne at his side. Baseball games, always one of Mike's favorites, became almost romantic as they held hands when not cheering for the Orioles. Sport fishing, one of their shared passions, took on new meaning with Joanne at his side. Everything about life felt richer now that Joanne had entered it.

"Hey, slowpoke!" Joanne shouted as she leaped from the car and watched Mike carry his heavy bag of golf clubs in one hand and fishing gear in the other.

"How about a little help here?" Mike countered, struggling to keep his balance.

"That's what I like . . . teamwork. By the way, you could wait to pack this fishing gear tomorrow, you know, or even tonight," Joanne replied, taking the fishing poles and tackle box.

"I considered doing that but decided to get it over with. I know how much you like me to organize and plan ahead. Besides, I have other more pressing things on my mind for tonight," Mike replied, placing the clubs in the trunk with hers.

"We're certainly prepared for anything. I can imagine your plans for later," Joanne quipped.

Planting a kiss firmly on her lips, Mike commented, "I love seeing you in the morning. We'll have to make a habit of doing this."

"Only in the morning?" Joanne teased, carefully placing the fishing gear across the backseat of her car.

"I wouldn't mind stretching it to encompass the entire day." Mike laughed, pulling her into his arms.

"That's more like it," Joanne cooed as she melted against his strength and inhaled the smell of freshly scrubbed skin. He never wore cologne or aftershave and did not need it. The scent of his body was intoxicating and heady.

"Do you really want to play golf today?" Mike whispered into her neck.

"It's definitely a toss-up," Joanne giggled as she pushed away. "Golf, fishing, Mike. Golf wins. We'll play golf today, fish tomorrow, and, ah, take care of the rest of our needs tonight."

"Only tonight?" Mike moaned, slipping into the passenger seat.

"Tonight and every night until we're too old to care," Joanne laughed, tossing her head back in delight.

"I like the sound of that," Mike commented, settling comfortably into the seat for the drive.

At first, as Joanne negotiated the maze of streets, she and Mike only listened to the mellow sound of a favorite classical CD. Having known each other for so long, they felt no need to fill the space with chatter. They often sat in silence while reading or watching television. Their hectic life at the Academy had trained them to enjoy downtime and peace and quiet whenever and wherever they could find it. Perhaps after they were away from the campus for a while, their lives would change. For the time being, however, they enjoyed not having to say anything.

An hour later as Joanne maneuvered the car into a parking space at the golf course, she broke the silence. "Wanna make a little wager?"

Carefully looking her over, Mike replied, "Such as?"

"Well, if I win, you'll buy dinner tonight," Joanne suggested.

"And if I win?" Mike asked, teasing her lips with the tip of his finger.

"If you win, we'll think of something appropriate," Joanne chuckled softly, pulling him into her arms.

"With those terms, I come out the winner either way," Mike replied before giving Joanne a kiss so deep that she almost forgot about wanting to play golf.

Reluctantly pulling away, Joanne added, "No, you don't. You won't destroy my resolve. Besides, this is a challenge rematch. You can't distract me from beating you. I want to finish what we started."

"You're the most singled-minded woman I've ever met," Mike insisted. "All right. If beating you on the course is the only way that I can get you into bed, let's go. We don't have time to waste."

"What are you talking about?" Joanne asked as she grabbed her golf bag.

"Our short leave . . . distance . . . school. I need all the memories I can make to keep me going while we're separated," Mike replied firmly.

"Oh, that! We'll have free weekends. There are flights from South Carolina and Virginia to Florida, you know," Joanne laughed.

"But it won't be the same, and we don't know our schedules. I've heard that there's practically no free time in sub school," Mike responded with a touch of sadness in his voice.

"I've heard that, too. But we'll find a way. I won't be able to beat you at golf on a regular basis if we don't work it out," Joanne teased, trying to brighten his mood.

"Is that the only reason that you'll miss me?" Mike demanded, pretending to be offended.

"Oh, no! I'll miss your sparkling eyes, your wit, and your kisses. I'll miss everything about you," Joanne replied seriously before adding with a wink, "But I'll miss a readily available and very beatable golf partner, too. Before I started playing with you, I had to buy my own dinner."

Trudging behind her, Mike muttered loudly, "That's all I am . . . a meal ticket."

"That's it. Keep that attitude. It'll make it easier for me to whip your butt all over this par-four course," Joanne laughed.

"You'll have to catch me to beat me," Mike declared, throwing down the gauntlet.

"Ohh, I like a good challenge," Joanne promised as she stretched and took a few practice swings.

Mike studied Joanne with a slow smile pulling at his lips. She was the best thing that had ever happened to him. Since meeting her, he had not only lost many golf games but discovered that he loved coming in second. He loved everything about her, from her easy laugh to her quick stride.

Comfortable with being together, Joanne and Mike chatted happily between shots while riding in the cart. Although their game had started out on friendly terms, it quickly became very competitive as soon as they each had a club in their hands. Despite the fact that Joanne had beaten him many times, Mike had a tremendous fairway drive that demanded Joanne's best effort to keep pace. She could not out-drive him, but she played a smart game that put her ball in good lie positions close to the green. Mike, on the other hand, often shanked the ball to the right into the rough. Joanne usually hit straight shots from the tee and fairway. Since their putting and chipping were about the same, Joanne had learned to lay back and let her short game prevail or wait until Mike lost his temper, which he often did.

Once Mike's temper flared, Joanne simply had to let his loss of concentration settle the score. She would continue to play her golf game waiting for the opportunity to pit her steely nerves against his frazzled ones. When his armor cracked, he would begin to slice the ball, sending it in the wrong direction. Joanne usually won their friendly matches on the heels of Mike's fury.

Joanne liked playing with Mike, not only because of the affection between them but because he challenged her to do her best. She had honed her competitiveness at the Academy and did not want to lose it. As a junior officer and leader of men and women, Joanne knew that she needed to remain razor-sharp to stay ahead of her crew. Golf provided that analytical edge that she needed. Besides, being a pilot and a woman meant that all eyes would be on her at all times. Although the navy let women become officers and pilots, little had changed. She would have to be better than all of the men to be considered just as good. Golf prepared her for that.

Watching Mike send another drive soaring into the air, Joanne thought about the many times that she had challenged him to a round of golf. The first time was especially memorable. Their relationship had been new but not at all tentative. Perhaps the years of studying, marching, and living together in the dorm had diminished the usual first date nerves. Whatever the reason, Joanne had not felt jittery about being with him. She had decided as they had sat shoulder-to-shoulder in the small golf cart that she enjoyed his closeness and his company.

From that day, Joanne and Mike had spent as much time together as possible. Although the academic and military demands often conflicted with their need for quality time, they had managed to study together most evenings and enjoyed free weekends doing nothing in particular. As their affection had blossomed into love, they had promised each other that they would spend as much of their thirty-day leave together as possible.

Both knew that juggling the distance and studies would make it difficult for them to find time to be together, but they had vowed to try. To their delight, they had been fairly successful so far.

Watching Mike stride toward the eighth hole, Joanne was glad that their plans had turned out so well. The more time she spent with him, the more Joanne loved him. She knew that leaving for Florida the first of August would be difficult despite her desire to become a pilot. She would miss him.

The beginning of the ninth hole found Mike ahead by two strokes, but not for long. The pressure of having Joanne so close caused him to send a drive off the tee that landed in the water. Muttering under his breath and sweating heavily, Mike took a drop shot and angrily sent his next ball into a sand bunker. By the time his ball dropped into the hole, Joanne was ahead by three strokes, and Mike was in a snit.

"Some days, a man just can't win," Mike sulked.

"Don't whine. Second place isn't that bad. Besides, you're good for my ego," Joanne reminded him, joining him in the cart.

"I'm glad you find pleasure in my infirmities," Mike said, chuckling dryly. "But you're right. Dinner with the woman I love isn't a bad consolation prize."

"If you're very good, I'll tailor my victory payoff to suit both of us," Joanne teased as she rested her head on his shoulder for a moment before driving toward the next hole.

"In that case, I guess I win after all," Mike laughed, feeling better about the muffed shots.

Riding in silence, Mike thought about the wonderful woman sitting beside him driving the cart. Joanne was an officer, a lady, a comedian, a lover, and a warm, sensitive person . . . everything he had always wanted in a partner. He was a lucky man, golf aside.

Back in the clubhouse, they sipped coffee and planned their day. Mike's defeat on the golf course guaranteed that they would eat well, since Joanne always managed to lead them to small, out-of-the-way restaurants that offered the best food. With dinner in her capable hands and a jazz concert that night, he could concentrate on showing the woman he loved a good time in his hometown.

Although his parents lived near the golf course, Mike decided not to stay with them while on leave. After four years at the Academy, he needed more freedom than living at home could provide and had decided to room with his buddies in a three-bedroom apartment in the Homewood section of Baltimore. His room in the apartment gave him a private place to share with Joanne.

Although Mike would report to submarine school at the end of his leave, his friends would be on temporary assignment at the Academy for at least six months. At first, he had hesitated in accepting their invitation, not wanting to leave them with extra rent to pay when he left for his assignment. But he changed his mind as soon as he learned that another of their friends would move in once he left.

Stretching, Joanne commented leisurely, "I guess I showed you a thing or two today. Dinner at Dante's Inferno would cap off my victory nicely."

"Sounds good to me," Mike replied, chuckling as he munched on the chocolate chip cookies and sipped coffee. "They serve great food and are close to the jazz club. As much as I like to beat you at golf, I can't complain about the loss. A witty, beautiful woman on my arm and good food in my stomach. What more could any man want?"

"It's nice to be appreciated even if I do have the feeling that you're only being PC by giving me top billing over the dinner."

"Not true!" Mike objected. "You're more important to me than anything else in the whole world, even food, although a good steak is a close second."

"You're so good for a woman's ego," Joanne said.

"Did I say something wrong?" Mike asked, pausing with his cup in midair.

"Not a thing," Joanne commented, laying her hand on his.

"Good. Let's go back to my place. I need to check my e-mail and take a quick shower," Mike said, paying the tab.

"Me too. I worked up quite a sweat during our little golf game. People don't think golf is physically demanding, but it is. I really burned a lot of calories," Joanne explained as Mike carefully eased the car into the stream of traffic.

"I can think of another way for you to burn off a few more," Mike chuckled seductively.

"Not if we're to keep our reservation at Dante's. It's pushing five already," Joanne replied with a shrug.

"Oh, well," Mike sighed. "I can wait until tonight, but just barely."

"Before graduation, you waited longer than just a few hours," Joanne added.

"Yeah, but that was different. We didn't have much control over that. Now that we're no longer students, we're filling our time with everything we've missed. I guess, in a way, we still don't have much free time," Mike said glibly.

"We'd better enjoy these days as much as we can.

You'll be in a different kind of training in less than thirty days," Joanne reminded him as Mike pulled into the parking lot of his apartment building.

"Even more reason to enjoy ourselves completely during the time we have. We don't know when we'll be together again," Mike said sadly.

"I know, but I try not to think about the long haul that's ahead of us. Between your nuclear and submarine training and my flight training, we'll be in school forever," Joanne replied as she linked her arm through his.

They rode the elevator to the fifth floor in silence. The reality of being miles apart and burdened with studies again weighed heavily on both of them. With luck, they would have the long weekend holidays together. Life at the Academy had taught them the importance of perseverance and patience, lessons they had learned well.

Chapter Three

Thirty days of leave had passed in a whirlwind of activity. Joanne and Mike had spent as much time together as possible while still seeing family and friends. Not surprisingly, they had discarded their "to do" list in favor of enjoying a less regimented lifestyle that allowed flexibility and leisure. Originally, they had planned to rent a boat and cruise the bay. But they had quickly abandoned the idea in favor of playing golf, going to movies and the theater, and savoring long dinners together. They had gone to clubs, dined alfresco in the park, rented paddleboats on the tidal basin, and played tourist in DC and Baltimore. They had stayed up late and risen early, not wanting to miss spending time together. Waking up in Mike's apartment with their arms and legs interlocking had become their favorite time of the day.

Neither Joanne nor Mike had worn a uniform since graduation day. However, on their last day of military leave, they had donned their whites and returned to the Academy for a last look at the school that had brought them together. Although they easily remembered all that they disliked about the Academy, they also relished sweet memories.

Standing in the shade of the chapel dome, they

watched the newest batch of midshipmen march toward the parade field in the hot summer sun as the band played "Anchors Aweigh." Harried upperclassmen, who had spent their summer training the new freshmen in military basics, snapped quick salutes as they rushed past. Memories, both good and bad, filled them with joy and sadness as they breathed the familiar aroma of sweat, salty water, and King Hall chow.

"It'll be a long time before we see this place again," Joanne sighed, discreetly slipping her hand into Mike's.

"I was thinking the same thing," Mike replied, giving her a little smile. "For better or worse, the Academy gave us a firm grounding—a 'port in the storm,' if you will. We always knew what they expected of us and how to produce it. Not anymore. We're on our own now. We have to learn new rules and how to play by them."

"I'm scared," Joanne confessed softly.

Studying her face intently, Mike replied, "So am I."

"I'll call you every night," Joanne promised fervently.

"If you don't, I'll call you," Mike chuckled.

"We'll tell each other everything. Having someone to share things with will make the experience easier," Joanne said, holding tightly to Mike's hand.

"We'll spend all holidays together and as many weekends as possible," Mike promised, pulling Joanne against him despite the glances of the passing midshipmen.

"I guess that'll have to be enough," Joanne sighed softly.

Looking up at the chapel that had been the site of comforting worship services and entertaining concerts, Mike said, "We'll make it work, you know. The odds are against us, but we'll survive the distance. You'll see. We love each other. Nothing, not even the navy, can keep us apart."

Smiling bravely, Joanne replied, "It'll be tough."

"I know. And one day, we'll return and have our wedding right here in the chapel," Mike said.

"Don't take anything for granted, Mike Shepherd. You haven't asked me yet," Joanne teased lightly.

"It's a foregone conclusion," Mike replied, kissing her gently.

"A woman still likes for her man to pop the question. Besides, I might not accept your proposal," Joanne responded, resting her head on his shoulder.

"Not to sound too conceited, but I'll worry about that when the time comes. For now, it seems like a fitting end to one life and a great beginning to another. Let's make a promise. No matter what happens, we'll return here every year on this date as a way of renewing our promise and keeping our sights set on the future," Mike suggested hopefully.

"That might be hard if you're underwater," Joanne chuckled.

"I'll find a way. You're probably right. We might not be able to meet on same date, but we'll get here during the month," Mike promised.

"It's a deal," Joanne replied, chuckling through the tears at the idea of their future together.

At that moment, the rain from one of those quirky summer storms began to fall. Dashing to Mike's car, they paused for one last look. Life at the Academy had been hard, but at least they had been together and surrounded by friends. Now they did not know what to expect.

As the raindrops wet their uniforms, Mike pulled

Joanne into this arms and kissed her soundly. Public displays of affection while in uniform were against Academy rules. However, they were no longer midshipmen. As junior officers, they were allowed that right. As lovers on the eve of separation, they saw no reason to hesitate.

"Oh, darn!" Joanne exclaimed as she clung to Mike's muscular arms. "I promised myself that I wouldn't cry."

"Don't be too hard on yourself. Tears are understandable. We're navy, but we're human," Mike said, his own eyes damp.

"If I start crying now, I'll be a soggy mess on the plane," Joanne said, wiping tears and raindrops from her face with trembling fingers.

"We'd better hurry or you'll miss your flight and really have something to cry about. You don't want to be late on your first day on the job," Mike advised, helping her into the car.

"The time passed too quickly," Joanne commented. "It seems like only yesterday that we graduated. I can't believe that our leave is over."

"It's been the quickest thirty days of my life . . . and the best," Mike said.

"Mine too," Joanne sniffed.

"Crying again?" Mike asked as he steered a course to Baltimore Washington International Airport.

"No. Well, maybe a little," Joanne confessed softly.

"Me too," Mike replied though a throat tight with unshed tears.

Joanne and Mike arrived at the airport in record time. Even the usually heavy traffic seemed to part as if to accommodate Joanne's flight. Fate, too, seemed to be working both with and against them, helping them easily flow through traffic despite the rain. Joanne and Mike hated the reality of their imminent separation, but could no longer deny its inevitability.

After checking her bags, Joanne and Mike sat in front of the large window watching the cabs pull up and discharge passengers. Mike would have liked to stay with her in the boarding area where they might have been able to find a quiet spot, but security measures would not allow him to go past the gate. They had to be content holding hands in front of strangers who smiled with sad eyes at the young officers who would soon be separated.

"That's my flight," Joanne said as the announcement ended.

"I know," Mike muttered, unwilling to release his hold on her thin shoulders.

"I have to go. It'll take a while to clear security," Joanne said, rising slowly.

"I'll go with you as far as I can," Mike stated, holding tightly to her hand.

"I'll phone from the airport as soon as the plane lands," Joanne promised, fighting futilely against a new wave of tears.

Mike could only nod in understanding. His throat was now too constricted to allow him to speak. The sight of her wet cheeks almost reduced him to tears, too.

Wiping the tears, Joanne stated, "This is it. I'm really leaving for flight school. I've wanted this so badly, but now I hate to go. Florida's so far away. I hadn't counted on loving you so much. We have to promise that we won't let anything come between us. Not ever. Promise?"

"I promise. We'll be together forever. I love you.

Fair winds and following seas until we're together again," Mike said, repeating a Navy credo.

"Fair winds," Joanne whispered, kissing him lingeringly before walking toward the crush of people and the metal detectors.

Mike watched her back disappear into the crowd as long as he could. As the mass of people converged, he jockeyed for a better position but still could not see Joanne. Knowing that the current had propelled her toward the waiting plane, he swallowed hard and walked away. Mike could feel people's eyes on him, and he did not try to hide his emotions. The woman he loved had just left for flight school and had taken his heart with her.

The ringing of Mike's cell phone interrupted the walk to his car in a distant parking lot. Rather than take the shuttle bus, he had decided that the exercise would lighten his mood or at least give him a chance to deal with the pain of Joanne's departure. The insistent telephone was an interruption that Mike did not relish.

"Yes?" Mike demanded impatiently without stopping his steady march toward the satellite parking lot.

"It's me. I just wanted to tell you one more time how much I love you," Joanne said above the noise in the terminal.

Stopping short, Mike replied, "I love you, too, and always will. We'll survive this separation. We love each other too much not to make it."

"I know we will. It's just so much distance and hard work with little time off," Joanne responded bravely.

"Five years' commitment for me and seven for you. It's hard to imagine it now, but the time will pass. We'll see each other as often as possible.

Phone calls will help, too. If you'll still have me, we'll get married in two years. The really tough part will be behind us by then. I'll have completed my certification, and you'll be a pilot. Staying focused on that will help some," Mike said, trying to sound optimistic as his heart was breaking.

"I know. Two years is still an eternity. It's a lifetime before our next long weekend. Oh, darn, I gotta go. They've just announced the last call for my flight. I'll call again tonight. I love you," Joanne said, rushing toward the flight attendant.

"Love you, Joanne," Mike shouted against the roar of planes overhead taking off and landing at the busy airport.

For a while, Mike could only stand and stare at the phone in his hand. He had never felt so completely alone. Hearing Joanne's voice so close and not being able to hold her had only made the loneliness deeper. The days would pass much too slowly until they could be together again. Immersing himself in the demands of training would help, but nothing but seeing her again would fill the emptiness.

Pulling out from the parking lot, Mike stopped and scanned the sky as a Boeing 747 roared overhead. He did not know if Joanne was on it, but, just in case, he offered a silent prayer for her safe journey and the survival of their love. Seeing an aircraft overhead had always stirred emotions of awe and respect for flying and those who piloted planes. Now, with Joanne on her way to flight school, Mike would forever see an aircraft and think of her. Wherever life and their careers took them, reminders would keep them fresh in each other's mind.

Mike knew that he would feel better as soon as he

had something worthwhile to do to take his mind off the pain of missing Joanne. As he unlocked his car, he decided to leave for Charleston and the year of nuclear training as soon as he threw the few remaining belongings into the trunk. The Navy had moved the rest of his things as it had Joanne's, leaving Mike with only one duffel bag and his computer to transport. Waking up in a new apartment with new roommates in a new city would help to ease the loneliness. If he stayed overnight in his current apartment, Mike would miss Joanne all the more every time he turned over and saw her empty side of the bed. He needed to sleep on sheets that did not hold the sweet smell of her perfume. He had to start living a life with her on the outskirts rather than as its center.

Mike would stop by his parents' house and make them understand his need to leave ahead of schedule. They knew that Joanne was the most important element in his life. They had seen the glances of adoration that passed between their son and the woman who had captured his heart. Mike would explain that he simply had to go.

Tossing his bag into the trunk, Mike felt relief about his decision to make the drive south that day rather than the next. He needed something to take his mind off the heavy ache in his chest. He had left a hastily scrawled note for his roommates, knowing that they would agree with his decision and would be glad not to have his sad expression and drooping shoulders moping around the apartment. They would find themselves in the same situation of leaving family, friends, and loved ones behind soon enough and would want to keep the mood light for as long as possible.

Stopping by his parents' house, Mike took one

last look at the home in which he had spent his youth. He would miss the columns by which he had measured his growth and the tree from which he had dangled. Most importantly, his heart ached for the people he would leave behind. His mother and father had guided and supported him through every event of his life. Now, he had to leave the nest.

"Mom, I've come to tell you guys goodbye," Mike shouted from the front door.

"You're leaving now? I thought we'd have another evening with you," his mother said as tears welled in her eyes.

"I've gotta go. There's no point in prolonging the inevitable. Joanne just left. Staying here longer would only make me feel worse. I'm heading for Charleston now," Mike said, hugging his mother tightly.

"Drive carefully, son," his dad advised, pulling his child into his arms.

"Call as soon as you arrive," his mom said, holding on to her son's arm as they walked to his waiting car.

"I will. I'll be okay," Mike replied bravely.

"I know you will. I'll miss you," his mom replied as the tears trickled down her face.

"I'll be home for Christmas. Make all of my favorite dishes," Mike called as he backed down the driveway. His parents waved until his car was out of sight.

Turning his attention to the open road, Mike switched on the radio. Instantly one of his and Joanne's favorite songs began to play. Instead of making him feel worse, the music helped to cheer him up. Singing loudly, Mike steered the car toward his new life, embraced by the warmth of his memories of Joanne.

Joanne sat in the aircraft, staring out at the expanse of ground below her. Somewhere in that ever-shrinking maze of farmland and highways was the man she loved and would not see for months. One day, they would build a life together, but not now. At this moment, they belonged to the United States Navy and had a commitment to honor. It was a hard price to pay for a top-rate education. However, they had made the promise long before they fell in love and would keep it despite the heartache and pain of separation. Life at the Academy had taught them that some principles were worth the hardships—honor, courage, fidelity, service. Joanne hoped that on the lonely nights in Florida, with only her books for company, she would remember the Academy's lessons.

Leaning back in her seat, Joanne closed her eyes and breathed deeply. One day in the not too distant future she would sit in the first chair and pilot a jet. It would not be one of these luxury liners on wings, but a combat aircraft serving her country. Joanne knew that she was ready for the challenge. She had graduated from the Academy at the top of her class and would do the same from flight school. Nothing, not even missing Mike, would stop her from achieving her dream and earning her wings. She knew that he felt that same way about his career as a submariner. Joanne would not have fallen in love with him if he had not been as dedicated and driven as she was.

"Something to drink, ma'am?" the flight attendant asked, interrupting Joanne's thoughts.

"No, nothing. Thanks," Joanne replied with a sad smile.

"I know it's tough leaving someone you love. My fiancé's in the army, stationed in Iraq. I think about him all the time. At first, you'll think that your heart'll break, but you'll get used to it. Time'll pass. Before you know it, you'll see him again," the sympathetic flight attendant said.

"And when our leave is up, the pain will start again," Joanne replied, accepting the soda the flight attendant pressed into her hands.

"Each time the pain is a little more manageable. You won't miss him any less, but the pain will become familiar and tolerable. I guess that's just survival," the flight attendant said with wisdom garnered from experience.

"I hope you're right, because this is dreadful. I don't ever want to feel this hollow again," Joanne added, sipping the soda absently.

"The first separation is the worst, I promise. Try to rest and enjoy the flight. I'll check on you again soon," the flight attendant stated with a warm smile.

"Thanks for the words of comfort. I really needed them . . . and the soda," Joanne said with a smile.

"Don't mention it. We're all in this together. If we don't help each other, what's it all for?" the flight attendant responded as she continued down the narrow aisle with the beverage cart.

Turning from the empty seat beside her, Joanne stared at the institutionally gray bulkhead wall. She was too far forward to be able to see the ceiling-mounted television, and her little monitor was not working. Joanne hardly ever watched television and preferred to read when alone anyway. Without bidding, she remembered that Mike had insisted that she reserve a bulkhead seat for the extra legroom. She was glad she had taken his advice for the opportunity to stretch her muscles. Although her heart was heavy, her body was comfortable in the spacious area.

Looking at her watch, Joanne calculated her arrival in Florida and at the apartment she would share with other student-pilots, all recent graduates of the Academy. She was airborne and on the way to a new adventure, leaving behind everything she loved and held dear. She missed her parents but knew that distance would not dim the love that existed between them. She missed the best friends who had seen her through every crisis of her life. For the first time, Joanne was basically alone. As a new college graduate, she had joined the tens of thousands who had taken their first steps from the familiar nest. She would survive and thrive.

Despite the rigors of the Academy that had precluded frequent visits home or trips to her friends' colleges, Joanne had still lived in her home state. Now, she was on her way to a foreign city in a distant state. Except for the familiar faces of people who had graduated from the Academy with her, all of whom she only knew in passing, Joanne faced her first test as an adult. She had to live on her own, pay the bills, and prioritize projects. Most importantly, she had to survive without Mike. It was a daunting task . . . and she was ready.

Chapter Four

The rest of summer passed into fall with Joanne and Mike so busy with their studies that they hardly noticed the change of seasons. They phoned as often as possible but seldom found the time for lengthy conversation and usually spoke while rushing from one activity to the other or just before falling asleep. The conversations were brief, but at least they kept connected through them. They discovered quickly that they could express their love in relatively few words.

Their training completely consumed all of their free time, leaving them only a few hours for sleep. Mike was so busy in his nuclear-power studies that he often fell asleep without eating dinner in the officers' mess, returning home too late to do more than fall into bed fully dressed. Joanne fared only slightly better, managing to find time for only the necessities of life, like eating and showering. She too usually grabbed meals on the run despite having a completely stocked kitchen at her disposal.

Study and duty even crammed weekends and holidays, making travel from their bases impossible. They spent long holiday weekends catching up on laundry and reading assignments for the weeks to come. Often military obligations limited their time

for even those activities, causing them to have to
study into the night and forgo much-needed sleep.
Even the e-mail between them soon trickled to a
minimum. Although they never stopped thinking
about each other, love would have to wait until
their training ended.

Joanne stopped in the middle of her stride as the
phone started to ring. She had been in the process
of packing her fishing gear in her car. The weather
was perfect. She and her new friends had planned
to take advantage of the free weekend. She knew
that Mike would love the water and her roommates.

"Where are you? I thought you were planning to
visit this weekend?" Joanne demanded as she tried
to hide her disappointment.

"I can't. I've got watch. Maybe next week'll be
better," Mike replied, leaning close to the window
for a better cell connection.

"It won't work for me. I'll be on duty," Joanne
sighed.

"I guess we'll have to wait. I miss you," Mike said.

"Not as much as I miss you. I'm in Florida where
the fishing is top-drawer, but you're not here.
There are golf courses all over the place, and I have
no one to beat," Joanne teased lightly to cover her
sadness.

"Same here," Mike commented. "I shot a sixty-
seven last weekend, but no one saw it. The best
round of my life, and you weren't here to take me
to dinner."

"We'll have to make up for lost time when we see
each other," Joanne suggested.

"That's not all we'll have to do," Mike chuckled.

"You have a one-track mind," Joanne laughed.

"Yeah, but you were on the same track," Mike
joked.

Sighing, Joanne said, "It's harder than I thought. I didn't expect to think of you all the time. I'd thought studies would push you from my mind once in a while, but nothing helps."

"I know. I feel the same way. We'll have to cram a lifetime into our vacation," Mike promised.

"A lifetime of loving you in one week just isn't enough," Joanne stated.

"We'll make enough. You'll be so tired of me by the time our vacation ends that you'll be anxious to return to Florida," Mike replied, chuckling.

"Not hardly!" Joanne laughed.

"Well, I gotta run. I'll call later," Mike stated, grabbing his cover and locking his apartment door.

"Okay. I'm going fishing this afternoon. I should have plenty to brag about when you call. I love you," Joanne replied, trying to sound upbeat.

"I can't wait! I love you, too."

Sighing, Joanne turned her attention to the packing. Although their plans changed often, Joanne had not learned to roll with the disappointment. She missed Mike and wanted to be with him. The weekend would have given them a chance to relax together. Now, she would have to wait for Christmas break. The Navy had managed to intrude into their lives once again.

However, even their studies took a break for a short Christmas vacation. The instructors and students looked forward to getting away from their obligations for a week. For the first time since leaving Maryland, Joanne and Mike would return home.

Joanne and Mike had promised to spend Christmas Day at their parents' but had reserved the rest of the week for themselves. They would return to Mike's apartment in Charleston on the day after

Christmas and spend the rest of their vacation together before Joanne had to fly back to Florida.
They would make every minute count before duty
called them away again.

Sitting in the plane on the morning of the
twenty-third, Joanne was surprised at the nervousness that consumed her. She had only seen Mike
once since the summer. So much had happened
during their separation. She had experienced a
new level of independence despite having two
roommates and countless study buddies. She had
grown and changed, perhaps not drastically but in
small ways. Joanne was sure that Mike had also become someone other than a newly commissioned
officer. From the little that he had time to share
with her, she knew his experiences in nuclear
school had been just as eye-opening.

As the flight landed, Joanne felt her stomach
lurch but not from motion sickness. She was home;
Mike was not far away. All of the doubts and fears
that she had managed to push from her mind while
studying for exams now flooded to the front. She
was scared and excited and so desperately in need
of seeing Mike again.

Mingling with the crush of holiday travelers,
Joanne breathed deeply and smiled. She was home
among the familiar smells of soft pretzels and mus-
tard, hot dogs and ketchup, and—in her memory
at least—Maryland blue crabs. She loved the hub-
bub of people making their way home, the laughter, and even the handmade signs welcoming the
excited and weary travelers home.

Joanne was so absorbed with the thrill of being
home again that the blaring voice of the public address system almost made her jump from her shoes.
Listening carefully, she heard, "Ensign Joanne

Crawford, please meet your mother at the ground-level car-rental station in the baggage-claim area."

Smiling, Joanne chuckled to herself. It was so like her mother to have her paged although they had made pickup arrangements before she left Florida. Although she had packed only one duffel bag, the baggage-claim area provided the most opportunity for finding each other in the throng of holiday travelers. Her mother was as excited about having her daughter at home again as Joanne was about being back in town. Knowing the heightened level of security in the airports, her mother had insisted on parking and waiting for her in the terminal rather than trying to circle the airport passenger-pickup area.

Rushing through the press of people, Joanne hurried toward the escalator. She had not seen her parents and neighborhood since the first of August, the longest that she had ever been away from her home, her family, and her state. Finding a line of people waiting to board the slow-moving conveyance, Joanne quickly shifted direction and headed toward the stairs.

Holding her duffel bag securely, Joanne squeezed through the crush at the baggage claims and trotted toward the car-rental area. A huge smile brightened her face and tears of happiness burned behind her eyes as she quickly surveyed the people trying to rent cars in the busy terminal. Her heart pounded loudly as she searched the faces for the familiar face that had once laughed at her antics, soothed her tears, tucked her in at night, read her bedtime stories, and banished childhood demons.

Not seeing her mother in the crowd, Joanne slowed her steps. Slowly, her smile began to fade. She knew that she was in the right place, but she could not find her mother. For an instant, Joanne had a flashback to the time that she had become separated from her mother while they shopped in the lingerie section of a large department store. She had been barely four and only knee-high. Everyone had looked so tall, and she had felt so afraid. She had rubbed her eyes and sobbed, too frightened to move. Now, at twenty-two, she felt like a lost little girl again. Despite the distinguished navy uniform, she wanted her mother and her home. She had been away on her own too long.

"Looking for someone?" a voice from somewhere behind her asked, but Joanne ignored it, thinking that the man was not speaking to her.

"Ensign Crawford, are you looking for someone?" the voice repeated.

Joanne's heart stopped and then started beating so hard that she thought it would surely break. Spinning around, she looked into the smiling face of the most handsome man she had ever seen in her life. Crossing the distance between them in one bound, Joanne dropped her bag and threw herself into Mike's open arms.

"Oh Mike! Oh Mike! It's you. It's really you," Joanne sobbed into his neck as she clung to his uniform-clad shoulders. He smelled of wool and soap.

"So long. So long," Mike whispered into her hair as he held her so close they breathed as one.

Slowly, a trickle of applause swelled into a thunderous roar as women brushed tears from their cheeks and men smiled shyly. The sight of two navy ensigns locked in a lovers' embrace in a busy airport was reminiscent of scenes of soldiers returning from war. These two had not experienced war, but the separation had been no less grueling.

Feeling her face burning, Joanne eased from

Mike's arms and said, "For people who aren't supposed to draw attention, we're certainly making a spectacle of ourselves."

"I don't care. I haven't held you in so long. You feel great," Mike replied, hugging her again.

"So do you. Let's find my mother and get out of here," Joanne suggested, taking Mike by the hand.

"She isn't here," Mike stated calmly.

"What? Why not? She had them page me," Joanne exclaimed.

"I know, but it really wasn't your mom. It was me. I wanted to surprise you," Mike replied with a huge grin.

Laughing, Joanne responded, "It's a good thing you didn't use your name. I bogarted my way through the crowd to get here as it was. If I had known it was you, I would have fought my way down here. I would have sprouted wings and flown."

"Not a bad idea for a pilot. In the days before 9/11, I would have been able to meet you at the gate . . . maybe even hold one of those signs with your name written in big, bold letters. This was the best alternative I could think of," Mike commented as they braved the crisp December evening for the walk to the short-term parking lot.

Hugging his arm, Joanne said, "I'm glad you didn't. It's always too crowded there. This was perfect. I'll remember it all my life and tell our children about the night you gave me the best Christmas present ever."

"Well, you're certainly easy to please. I guess I can return all the gifts I bought you," Mike chuckled. He felt warm and happy despite the stiff wind. In fact, he was happier than he had been since saying good-bye at the same airport months ago.

"Oh, no, you don't," Joanne replied, sliding into

the passenger side of Mike's familiar car. "I spent the little free time I had shopping for the gifts I bought for you. We deserve as much special treatment as we can get this Christmas. We've worked hard and slept little. I want it all."

"It will be special because we're together. What do you say we save some of the presents to open in Charleston when we're alone?" Mike suggested.

Placing her hand on his shoulder, Joanne commented, "I didn't know that you were such an old softy. You've become a romantic."

"Maybe," Mike smiled contentedly at the woman he loved. "All I know is that I want this to be the most spectacular Christmas vacation either of us has ever had."

"I think we can arrange that, although you'll have to go some lengths to outdo the ones we had while at the Academy. Being away from there was always a great gift. You know, I once thought that I lived in a goldfish bowl there. It's probably worse now," Joanne said with a shrug as she edged a little closer to Mike.

"I know what you mean. Everyone's watching us now. That's even more reason to do it up right this holiday. If everything goes the way I've planned, I can top any of those midshipman leaves," Mike replied with confidence.

"When did you have time to plan anything special?" Joanne queried, studying his handsome profile. "I thought you were too busy with your studies. I know I didn't have time to do anything other than make a quick trip to the store for gifts for everyone."

"I shopped on the Internet when I should have been studying for the last exam," Mike shrugged like a kid caught postponing his homework.

"Ah, I see. I hope you did okay on it," Joanne teased in a maternal tone of voice.

"Well enough," Mike said. "I earned all twenty-eight graduate credits and the right to spend the next six months in power school. I guess you did everything by the book, huh?"

Feigning a self-righteous pose, Joanne replied, "Of course! That's why I didn't have any free time until late last night. If the shops hadn't been vying for every dollar and staying open to obscene hours, I would have come home empty-handed and had to shop tonight."

"And no one would have minded one bit, especially not me. All I want for Christmas is you," Mike stated as he skillfully eased the car into the never-ending procession on the highway.

"You sound like a country-song lyric. They've been playing that song to death on the base," Joanne laughed happily.

"Maybe so, but it's true," Mike protested with mock offense in his voice.

"Me, too. I want to spend as much time burning your image into my memory as possible. That's all we'll have as soon as we return to training," Joanne said with a sigh.

"Let's not think about that. We have ten whole days to enjoy. School and the Navy don't exist," Mike instructed firmly.

"I can do that," Joanne replied as she leaned back in the seat and watched the traffic whiz past.

"By the way, my mom has planned a really big Christmas dinner," Mike said casually.

"Mine, too. I guess that means that we won't see each other tomorrow," Joanne replied, trying to keep disappointment from creeping into her voice.

"I don't think so!" Mike said emphatically. "There's

no way that I'm not seeing you every day of our leave and especially on Christmas Day. Mom wants you to come for breakfast. I'll pick you up at nine tomorrow morning. We'll spend the morning and early afternoon with them. I'll bring you back so that you can spend the rest of the day with your family while I eat dinner with my folks."

"That sounds like a winner to me," Joanne smiled happily. "I was wondering how you'd work that out. You possess stellar officer problem-solving abilities in sorting out that dilemma."

"And to think that I did it all by myself," Mike laughed and reached for Joanne's hand.

"What'll we do tonight?" Joanne asked, glancing at the skyline that she had missed so much while in Florida.

"If it's okay with you, one of my buddies from school is having a party tonight at his parents' house in Columbia, Maryland. I thought we'd go for a little while. I'd like for you to meet a few of my friends," Mike said, pulling into the driveway of Joanne's parents' house.

"Sure, but didn't they graduate from the Academy?" Joanne demanded, studying the familiar house and feeling her heart leap for joy at the sight of it.

"Yeah, but they weren't in our companies, and they weren't company officers, either. I only knew them because they were naval arch majors," Mike replied as he shut off the engine.

They walked in silence up the stairs of her parents' house. It seemed as if only yesterday she had left for Florida. So much had happened that she had not been able to share with them. She had lived a parallel existence that had caused her to miss the events of her family's life, and she hated not knowing more about the way they had spent their days.

Joanne was glad to be home although she felt a little like an outsider. Her parents had treated her like a third adult in the family unit, not as a child. She had missed the familiar dinnertime discussions and the quiet evenings at home. Although she wanted to spend every minute with Mike, she also wanted to visit leisurely with her parents. Joanne was not ready to cut the cord that connected them and saw no reason to do it. When she married Mike, her family would simply enfold him into its embrace.

Studying Mike's face in the glow of the front porch light, Joanne asked, "Do you think we could spend some time with my parents, too? It's been a long time since I've seen them."

"Sure. Your mom already invited me to dinner tonight," Mike smiled, pulling Joanne close for one last kiss before entering the house.

Melting against him as the night air chilled her cheeks, Joanne purred, "It feels so good being in your arms again. I hate being separated from you."

Looking deeply into her eyes, Mike replied, "It's harder than I thought it would be. Missing you is a dull ache that doesn't go away regardless of the amount of work they heap on me. I'll be glad when our training's over, and we can be together more."

"I wonder if we will have time together any time soon. The navy's pretty demanding of our time. You have power school ahead of you, and I have more in-depth flight training. The two years might have passed before we have any real leisure time," Joanne commented as she fumbled in her bag for the key.

"We'll find a way," Mike said with confidence.

"That's what we thought last summer," Joanne sniffed.

"It'll be different when I'm through with this sub training. Nine more months and I'll deploy to a sub base. I'll live a normal nine-to-five life then," Mike stated firmly.

"We'll see. I've heard that the demands of qualifying take up a lot of time," Joanne replied skeptically as she breathed deeply of the fragrances of home.

"Always the pessimist," Mike whispered into her ear.

"No, a realist. I've heard about the rigors of sub duty . . . six months under way at a time. This might be as good as it gets. We'll wind up marrying strangers," Joanne replied, tossing her duffel bag onto the steps just as she had done with her backpack as a kid.

"But the getting to know you part will be a lot of fun," Mike joked, kissing her lightly on the tip of her nose.

"Is that you, Joanne?" Angela Crawford called from the kitchen.

"Hi, Mom!" Joanne shouted in response. "Boy, it smells good in here."

"I've fixed your favorite foods. I'm so glad you're home," her mother said, as she rushed down the hall and pulled her daughter into her arms.

"You're crushing me! But don't stop," Joanne whined playfully.

"My baby! I've really missed you. I've been alone in this big house with only your father for company," she cried, wiping tears of joy from her lashes.

"At least you weren't in the company of strangers. I'll trade places with you," Joanne offered.

"Not on your life. This is where I belong," her

mother replied. Turning to Mike, she added, "You do look good in that uniform, ensign. Give me a hug!"

At that moment, Mr. Crawford appeared from the direction of the family room and joined them. Studying the faces of Joanne and Mike, he quickly assessed the lack of sleep that had created the deep circles under their eyes and the slight slump to their young shoulders. He knew that, as they were young people in love, rest would not be the first thought on their minds. However, he hoped that they would catch up on the sleep of which their studies had deprived them.

"Dinner's ready. I know both of you must be starving," Angela Crawford said, dabbing at tears of happiness that were tinged with the sad knowledge that the visit would be much too short.

"Just point me in the direction of the kitchen," Mike laughed as he tossed his uniform jacket onto the banister beside Joanne's.

"Children are always hungry regardless of their age and rank," Craig Crawford commented, following his family to the table.

"Good! Now I have someone who'll eat everything I prepare. You're too picky," Mrs. Crawford said, pecking her husband on the cheek.

"I'm not picky. I'm simply watching my boyish physique," Craig Crawford added sheepishly.

"Okay, you two. Boy, have I missed this!" Joanne cried, looking at her happy parents.

Joanne and Mike barely looked up from their plates as they devoured the pecan-encrusted chicken, fresh beets in orange sauce, collard greens with pearl onions, homemade rolls, and mashed potatoes with blue cheese and sour cream. They had enjoyed so few leisure hours while in training that eating had become a matter of supporting life rather than feeding the soul. Mrs. Crawford's cooking revitalized both their minds and spirits.

Adding another spoonful of potatoes to his plate, Mike commented, "This is the best meal I've ever eaten, and it's not just because I'm hungry. I sure hope Joanne can cook as well as you, Mrs. Crawford."

"Wishful thinking," Joanne countered with a snicker.

"You're a good cook, Joanne. With practice you'll become even better. You just need to work on it a bit," Angela Crawford said, defending her daughter loyally.

Adding realism, Craig Crawford said with a laugh, "If you call making BLTs being a good cook, then Joanne's got it licked."

"Hey, I don't remember hearing you complain when you were eating them," Joanne rebutted, laughing.

"A BLT beats tuna straight from the can any day," Mr. Crawford said, smiling warmly at his beloved daughter.

Rising to her defense, Mike offered, "I like BLTs. I could eat them every day."

Mrs. Crawford quipped as she cleared the plates for dessert, "If you marry Joanne, you'll have to eat them three times a day."

"I won't mind," Mike replied with a loving smile. "Besides, I can cook a little . . . baked chicken, steak. We'll survive."

Looking over his water glass, Craig Crawford asked, "Do I hear wedding bells?"

Patting Mike's hand, Joanne replied, "Not until we've both finished our training. I've seen the effects of military life on marriages, and I don't like what I've seen. We're in two different divisions with conflicting requirements. I'll be in the air. Mike will be under the sea. That's not the way to be married."

Bringing the apple pie to the table, Mrs. Crawford said, "Then how many more years do we have to save money for this extravaganza?"

"We haven't reached that point in the discussion yet, Mom," Joanne replied and added, "Besides, it won't be a big blowout. Mike and I want everything to be low-key . . . service in the Academy chapel with his father presiding and the reception in Bancroft. Simple."

Looking a bit surprised by the depth of Joanne's preliminary preparation, Mike asked, "When did you have time to plan the wedding? I thought you were as busy as I was."

"I was. I worked this out during our last trip to the Academy while standing on the chapel steps and on the Bancroft terrace overlooking the field. It was a piece of cake! Considering that we lived on the Yard for four years, we know exactly which buildings we want to use," Joanne replied with a snap of her fingers.

"Or maybe you'd rather have a piece of pie?" Mrs. Crawford joked, offering Mike the first slice.

Everyone laughed comfortably at the ease of their discussion. Any nervousness Mike felt at being included in family discussions had faded with the opening foray. The good-natured teasing had made him feel right at home. He hoped that Joanne would feel as comfortable with his parents at breakfast the next day.

After helping to clear the dishes, Joanne and Mike left for the party in Columbia, a suburb halfway between DC and Baltimore. The evening with her parents had been too brief, but they had another obligation and could stay no longer. Hugging her parents, Joanne promised to make it an early evening; she was too tired to do anything else.

As Joanne and Mike made the short drive, they chatted happily. They could feel the tension of their studies lifting from their shoulders. They were home. They were together. They were in love.

Chapter Five

Joanne woke early on Christmas morning, just as she had as a little girl. Stretching languidly, she forced herself from the warm, comfortable bed. The house was silent except for the familiar sounds from the kitchen. Although it was only seven-thirty, her mother had already begun the dinner preparations, filling the house with fragrances that brought back comforting memories of childhood Christmases when life was much simpler.

Although Joanne had already met Mike's parents, she wanted to make an especially good impression that morning. Christmas was such a special time for everyone, and she felt honored to have been invited to take breakfast with his family. Scrubbing herself briskly, she decided to wear the navy blue wool dress with the blue-and-red-checked bolero jacket. It would make just the right statement of chic yet conservative good taste. The outfit flattered her figure and appeared businesslike while not being too formal or tailored.

Fighting her way into the unfamiliar pantyhose, Joanne chuckled to herself. She would only put herself to this much trouble for Mike. Having worn a flight jumpsuit while in training, she had forgotten the ordeal of pulling pantyhose over her shapely legs to which she had liberally applied perfumed body lotion. Popping her finger through the leg of one pair, she hastily reached for another and succeeded in encasing her legs and hips in sheer navy blue nylon.

Slithering into the dress and jacket, Joanne looked at herself in the full-length mirror that hung on her closet door. Giving the skirt an extra little tug, she vanished into the bathroom for a quick application of blush and lip gloss. Rather than wearing her hair in a French braid as she usually did when in uniform, Joanne decided to let the curls brush her neck. Satisfied with the completed package, she trotted down the stairs and into the kitchen.

"Merry Christmas!" Joanne called from the door.

"Merry Christmas to you, too. Don't come too close," Mrs. Crawford warned. "You don't want to get food splats on your clothes."

"Gee, it's good to be home," Joanne smiled at the familiar greeting.

"You're in a good mood for so early in the morning. I thought you were the sleep-late girl, but you're up before noon," Mrs. Crawford commented, offering her cheek for the first kiss of the day.

"Sleeping late's a luxury these days. Besides, I miscalculated and thought I'd need longer to dress. Mike's not due here until nine. I'm having breakfast with his family and then coming home for dinner," Joanne replied as she poured a glass of orange juice and popped her vitamins.

"You look lovely. Make sure your father sees his grown-up little girl," Mrs. Crawford advised, smiling at the beautiful woman her child had become.

"Where is Daddy? Sunroom?" Joanne asked, looking around the kitchen.

"Of course. He decided that he'd stay away from me while I'm in the cooking mode. Years of experience, I guess," Mrs. Crawford laughed warmly.

"I'll set the table and then pop in on him," Joanne said, falling into the usual Christmas-Day pattern.

Mrs. Crawford smiled. She loved having Joanne at home again. The house was much too quiet without the sound of her daughter's laughter and footsteps. Christmas would not be as festive without having Joanne in the house. She hoped that Joanne's military obligations would never take her far from home at holiday time, although Mrs. Crawford knew that Joanne would have to go wherever duty sent her.

The rapid clicking of silver and tinkling of crystal echoed through the house as Joanne set the table for the family's feast. Her aunts, uncles, grandmothers, and cousins would swell their usual trio to a huge gathering. Extra leaves in the table and chairs from the kitchen would lengthen the dining room to accommodate the happy revelers.

Setting the last place, Joanne checked her watch. She would spend the next twenty minutes chatting with her father before leaving with Mike. Although she looked forward to spending time with the man she loved, she would miss the leisurely pace that usually began their family Christmas activities. To maintain as many of their old traditions as possible, the family had gone to service the previous night. Singing Christmas carols was as much a part of the family celebration as eating turkey and exchanging gifts.

As was his custom, Joanne's father had sequestered himself in the sunroom away from his busy and, sometimes, short-tempered wife. The radio at his side played Christmas tunes from days gone by. He smiled as Joanne entered, rising to give his daughter a big hug and kiss.

"Merry Christmas. You look terrific. I hope Mike appreciates the special gift that is my daughter," Mr. Crawford commented with misty eyes.

"Merry Christmas, Daddy. I'm sure he does as much as I appreciate him," Joanne replied, slipping into the seat next to her father.

"It's a hard thing watching my little girl grow up and fall in love. Having you go to college and then move away was difficult, but this love stuff is even harder. I'm used to being the most important man in your life," Mr. Crawford commented as the music played in the background.

"You're still the standard by which I judge all men. Mike has done an admirable job of living up to your level of perfection," Joanne responded gently.

"He's a nice guy. I approve. I can tell that you love each other very much," Mr. Crawford said, patting Joanne's hand.

"We do. That's what makes the separation so awful. We're both so busy that we have almost no time for each other. Phone calls last only minutes. It's tough," Joanne lamented.

"Once you've finished training and joined the fleet, things should get better. You'll find that the weekdays will pass quickly. Your salary will increase and so will your free time. You'll be able to spend more time together," Mr. Crawford stated.

Smiling, Joanne replied, "True, but the distance will probably be even greater by then. I'll be on a carrier somewhere and he'll be under the sea. We'll have to work even harder to keep our relationship together."

"I know I sound corny saying this, but if it's meant to survive, it will," Mr. Crawford said. "In fact, your relationship will grow even stronger because of having endured the hardship of distance. You'll see."

"I know, but knowing that doesn't make the loneliness any less deep," Joanne replied, rising as the grandfather clock in the hall struck nine o'clock.

"Being together has its pitfalls, too, you know," Mr. Crawford added with a grin. "Sometimes a little distance is a good thing. That's why I'm in here, and your mother's in the kitchen. When she's under stress, I put as much distance between us as I can while still remaining supportive."

Laughing, Joanne kissed her father and said, "I'll have to remember to buy a house with a sunroom."

The doorbell sounded as Joanne closed the sunroom door. She did not know if Mike was always punctual due to his Academy training or his father's need to start services on time. Whatever the reason, Joanne never had to wait for Mike.

"Merry Christmas!" Mike grinned as he entered the warm house, leaving the winter outside.

"Merry Christmas, Mike," Joanne replied, giving him a chance to enter.

Carrying an armload of gifts for her parents, Mike staggered toward the Christmas tree in the living room. As soon as he unloaded his burden, he pulled Joanne into his arms and kissed her firmly without looking for mistletoe or waiting for an invitation. He had been thinking about her all morning. In fact, he had arrived at her parents' home ten minutes early and had driven around the block to stay warm, not wanting to interfere with their family time.

"Wow! You look great! Very grown-up," Mike

commented as he studied Joanne's trim figure in the navy blue ensemble.

"I hope your parents will like it," Joanne said, kissing him again on his sweet lips.

"Of course they'll like it . . . they already like you. The way you look will only be an extra bonus," Mike explained, holding her tight.

"You look pretty good yourself. That sweater looks great on you," Joanne observed with a wink.

"It should; you bought it for me in Annapolis last summer. The shirt and tie are a little tight. I haven't worn civilian clothes in a while," Mike commented as he followed Joanne to the kitchen.

"You look as if you were born to be a civilian," Joanne quipped.

"That dress fits you better than any of your uniforms. I'd say that you make good civilian material, too. We'll have to find out one day," Mike said playfully.

"But no time soon. Twenty or thirty years from now will be soon enough," Joanne replied, stepping into the delicious-smelling kitchen.

"Well, Mike, don't you look dashing? Merry Christmas," Angela Crawford said, looking up from the cake batter that she was ladling into the pan.

"That's what I was just saying. Civilian clothes look great on him," Joanne said with a big smile of ownership.

"Not so fast, you two. This just happens to be the uniform of the day today. After this week of leisure, it's navy blue or khaki for me for a long, long time," Mike replied, kissing Mrs. Crawford lightly on the cheek.

"Then I'd better drink in the sight of my children in civvies while I can," said Angela Crawford, lightly touching both of them on the cheek.

"Who's a sight?" Mr. Crawford demanded.

Sighing, his wife explained, "No one's a sight in a bad way. I was just saying that Joanne and Mike make a handsome couple in their civvies."

"They certainly do. Merry Christmas, my boy," Craig Crawford responded absently as he reached for another cup of coffee, surveyed the many projects in progress, and quickly left.

Laughing, Joanne said, "We'd better get on the road, too, Mom. I'll be home in time for dinner."

"Enjoy your breakfast. Give my best to your parents. Their gifts are on the table at the front door," Mrs. Crawford said, returning to the cake batter.

Gathering the packages, Joanne and Mike moved swiftly to make the short drive from the Washington, DC, suburbs to the Shepherds' home in Baltimore. Neither of them wanted to keep his parents waiting. Mike had said that his mother's breakfasts were a special holiday treat that deserved to be savored leisurely while at the peak of flavor.

The drive along the interstate was usually a very boring one with only truck weighing stations and rest areas as diversions. However, as Joanne and Mike traveled together, they discovered that they covered the forty-five-minute drive in record time and hardly felt the minutes. They chatted constantly about nothing in particular but enjoyed each other's company considerably.

"What'll we do tomorrow after we reach Charleston?" Joanne asked, wanting to fill their days with memories to last through the long months of separation.

"It'll take us almost eight hours to get there, considering we'll make at least two pit stops and a couple of food breaks," Mike explained. "If we leave at nine in the morning, we'll arrive in time to drive around the city a little before it gets too late. We'll have to save the bulk of our sightseeing for the next day."

"Can we still go to Savannah and Hilton Head?" Joanne asked. "I'd really like to see both of those cities."

"Sure, I don't see why not," Mike commented. "It's a short drive to both of them. We'll go to Fort Sumter, too. It's a short ferry ride down the Ashley to the mouth of the river. It'll be a little cold this time of year, but I think you'll like it."

"The next time we have a break, maybe you can come down to Florida. We could act like kids and see Disney World, or maybe drive to New Orleans," Joanne suggested with a big smile.

Slowly, Mike replied, "That sounds like a good idea, but I don't think I'll have any real leave for a while. It'll be the summer before I'm free again, and then only for a week or two for relocation. Maybe we'll be able to take a few weekend trips if we can steal away."

For a moment, Joanne felt a heavy sadness. She had been so happy planning their lives together that she had forgotten that the Navy controlled their actions, not themselves. Mike had reminded her that their liberty was as precious as the freedom that they protected as members of the armed forces. As always, they would have to put their future on hold.

Forcing herself to brighten, Joanne, said, "Well, that's what we'll have to do. We'll have to spend a little money to do it . . . fly to the various places . . . but it'll work out. If our schedules aren't too tight, we should have a few long weekends soon . . . Martin Luther King Day and Presidents' Day. We can meet in Orlando one time and in New Orleans another."

Holding her hand firmly, Mike replied, "That's my girl. I knew you'd work it out."

Joanne's throat constricted tightly with unbidden emotion, forcing her to turn toward the window so that Mike would not see the tears that rimmed her eyes. She had promised herself that nothing would interfere with the few precious days they would have together. Not even the reality of their military commitment would mar the time. Now, reality burst into their short time together, forcing them to plan their lives to the minute.

Forcing cheer into her voice, Joanne responded, "I'm a very organized person. There's no scheduling problem that I can't overcome."

As the brave winter sun streamed through the window, they rode in silence for a few minutes, allowing the happiness of being together again to push away any lingering sadness. They had learned since graduating from the Academy as the first class of ensigns commissioned in wartime in decades that every minute of life counts. For two people in love, that lesson was even more important.

"I hope you're hungry," Mike said as he parked the car in front of his parents' house. The driveway was already packed. "My mom will expect you to eat like one of the boys."

"One of the boys! You're an only child, too," Joanne quipped.

"That doesn't matter to my mom. She expects everyone who sits at her table to have the appetite of a man working on a construction site. Besides, I only have male cousins, and they're already here," Mike laughed, easing his long legs from the car.

"I'll do my best. Thank goodness we don't have a

physical-readiness test to pass as soon as we report back," Joanne added with a chuckle.

"Don't remind me! I remember last Christmas. I ate like a pig and then had to work my butt off to get in shape for the physical-readiness test. At least that's behind us," Mike commented gaily.

Before Joanne could continue reminiscing about life at the Academy, Mrs. Shepherd opened the front door and swept her into her arms. Mrs. Shepherd was a tall, thin woman with short, gray-flecked hair. As an attorney from the "dress-for-success" generation, she had taken to wearing tailored clothing to prove that she belonged in a man's world and had found that she preferred the freedom of slacks to skirts and dresses. As a result, she lived in jeans and trousers all the time. On Christmas morning, behind her merry red apron, she wore green silk shantung slacks and a matching blouse that accentuated her height.

"Merry Christmas, Joanne! It's been so long since we've seen you. Come in," Mrs. Shepherd insisted.

"Merry Christmas. It's so nice to see you again," Joanne managed to gasp.

"Mike, go help your father take the food to the table while I chat with Joanne for a few minutes," Ann Shepherd directed, leading Joanne into the spacious living room tastefully furnished in antiques and art. In the corner beside the fireplace stood a huge tree decorated in a collection of family-heirloom ornaments, ones purchased on vacation trips, and items fashioned by Mike as a child. The eclectic mix worked perfectly to create a tree that captured the warmth and spirit of the season.

"Tell me all about your training. Has the experience been as all-consuming for you as it has for Mike? He hardly has any time for himself anymore," Ann Shepherd said, joining Joanne on the sofa.

"It's probably more demanding for him since he was taking the equivalent of twenty-eight credits towards a master's degree in four short months. My training's a little different. I have a combination of classroom, simulation, and flight experience. It's demanding but not as restrictive as his," Joanne explained reluctantly, not really wanting to discuss that part of her life.

"Well, it certainly doesn't seem fair to me. You're spending all of your youth in a classroom," Mrs. Shepherd lamented.

"True, but you went to law school," Joanne offered gently.

"I know, but that was different. Despite the hours of memory work and the tedium associated with some of the courses, it was an extension of the regular university life. I studied, but I had time to party, too," Mrs. Shepherd replied.

"Mike should gain more freedom once he enters the fleet," Joanne commented. "As for me, even now I have more flexibility in my day than he does in his. Besides, I'd rather take it slow and learn all the details of flight rather than whizzing through the information and missing something."

"I hope you're right," Mrs. Shepherd sighed. "Both of you made considerable sacrifice in attending the Academy; you certainly didn't have a normal university life. Let's face it; that wasn't a normal college environment. Kids in civilian colleges don't have to wear uniforms, live by a curfew, and take sports every day. Now, you're making even more. Other young people your age are working reasonable hours with weekends free. I realize that the compensation of a 'free' education with a military commitment price tag and invaluable training means something in itself, but you've given up a lot."

Speaking from a strong sense of duty, Joanne replied, "We knew this when we chose the Academy and the military. It's tough, but we wanted to serve, to contribute to an organization that's larger than ourselves. We'll survive."

Studying her closely, Ann Shepherd commented, "A long-distance romance must be very difficult to sustain."

Smiling briefly, Joanne replied, "It is. It definitely takes some work. However, the reward is worth the struggle. We've learned to prioritize and live every minute. Most people don't do that. They fritter away their time. They argue about silly things that don't really matter. We cram in all the memories we can when we're together."

Rising, Mrs. Shepherd said, "I think you're both wonderful people."

"Thank you. Knowing that we have support like yours and my family's means a lot to us," Joanne replied, accepting the hug that the older woman offered.

"What are you two doing in here?" Reverend Shepherd demanded. "I'm starving. Everyone's waiting. Merry Christmas, Joanne."

"We're on our way," Mike's mother replied, ignoring the impatience in her husband's voice.

As Ann Shepherd took her place opposite her husband at the table, Joanne slipped into a seat next to Mike. During their friendship at the Academy, Joanne had met all of the members of Mike's family and felt completely at home with them. Over a sumptuous breakfast introduced by a lengthy grace, they shared anecdotes about their careers, loves, and of course, leisure activities.

Exchanging quick glances, Joanne and Mike acknowledged that they were the only ones who had not seen the latest movies, attended the popular clubs, and played or watched the current sporting favorite. Yet, they did not feel sorry for themselves. Their reality was different and, in many ways, far richer. Besides, none of the others could say that they could manage a nuclear power plant or land a jet on a carrier's deck. They could not either yet, but the opportunity lay in their near future. In a matter of months, both would be proficient in those skills and more.

After disposing of the breakfast dishes and sending the cousins home with heaping plates of food, the Shepherd family assembled in the living room to exchange gifts. Although Joanne's family always waited until after dinner, wanting to extend the excitement of the day as long as possible, she enjoyed the hospitality of an early present exchange. Sitting in that wonderful living room with the flickering fire and Mike at her side, Joanne felt completely content and loved.

They all took turns opening their gifts, with Reverend and Mrs. Shepherd doing first honors. The Shepherds, without coordinating their efforts, had bought each other a robe and slippers, reducing the occupants of the room to gales of laughter. Mike had purchased a history of the South for his parents and a welcome sign for the front hall. Joanne's parents had sent them a lead-crystal bird in flight for their mantel. Joanne had given them a brass bell-shaped music box that played the title song from *An Officer and a Gentleman*, a fitting gift for the parents of a recent Academy graduate.

Their gift to Mike was a stack of DVDs with a portable player and CDs along with the player on which to listen to them. The Shepherds had bought Joanne an Amelia Earhart replica leather flight cap and scarf as well as a book on the history of non-military flight.

With their gifts piled around them, the Shepherds watched as Mike and Joanne exchanged their presents. Mike's gift to Joanne was a cashmere sweater set in a rich teal. Joanne had purchased a book on fly-fishing that Mike had wanted but not bought for himself while they were out shopping that past summer. She had added a burgundy sweater with gold trim at the neck as a little something extra. Everyone loved their gifts and vowed that this was the best Christmas ever. For Joanne and Mike, being together was the best gift they could have received.

The day had indeed started perfectly for them. The sun streaming in the front window sparkled off the Shepherds' collection of crystal animals and gave the room a storybook appearance. The flickering fire and the full stomachs combined to lull them into blissful euphoria. For a few hours, the reality of their fleeting leave seemed far away.

Amid hugs and promises of not allowing another six months to pass without a visit or call, Joanne and Mike started back to DC. Stretched out lazily as Mike drove, Joanne sighed contentedly. She had eaten so much at breakfast that she would not need to eat again soon, but, of course, she would since her mother would have labored lovingly over the preparation of the meal. Knowing that she would be the one doing the cooking as soon as they reached Charleston, Joanne enjoyed the feeling of having been pampered. Considering Joanne's culinary abilities, the memory of great meals would have to tide them over as they munched her BLT specials.

Parking the car in her parent's driveway, Mike turned to Joanne and said, "It's been a great day, hasn't it?"

"Wonderful," Joanne sighed, stretching languidly like a cat.

"There's more," Mike promised, reaching over her to open the door.

"Like what?" Joanne squinted against the sun.

"You'll see," Mike answered mysteriously.

"Tell me!"

"Nope."

"Show me!"

"Not yet."

"Please!"

"When we get inside. Unlock the door," Mike instructed with a mischievous grin.

Giving him a sideways glance of feigned annoyance, Joanne followed his instructions and opened the door.

"Is that you, Joanne?" her mother's voice called from the back of the house.

"Yes, Mom. Mike and I have returned," Joanne replied happily.

"Mike, have you changed your mind about joining us for dinner tonight?" Mrs. Crawford asked, stepping into the hall.

"No, thanks. My folks are expecting me," Mike responded, giving her the gift from his parents.

"Daddy and I will open this tonight with our other gifts. I'll phone them in the morning," Mrs. Crawford said as she vanished into the kitchen again.

Placing her gifts under the tree in her family's living room, Joanne smiled softly. The house was not as showy as the Shepherds', but Joanne loved it more than any place in the world. The tree in front of the living room window was not as ornate as the Shepherds', but it filled the room with the smell of the holidays just the same and swelled her heart with loving memories. Their ornaments were also family heirlooms, consisting of glass and porcelain figurines from her grandparents, lace tatted by her mother as a young girl, and little delicate pieces that Joanne had fashioned one year between swim meets. The sounds and fragrances in her parents' house would always make Joanne feel loved and safe.

Sitting on the sofa in the living room, Joanne demanded, "Now, where's that other gift?"

Without hesitation, Mike dropped to the floor at her feet. Taking her hands in his, he asked, "Will you marry me? I know we won't make it official for some time, but I'd be the happiest man in the world just knowing that you'll be my girl forever. I love you, Joanne, with my life."

At first, Joanne could only stare into Mike's dear, serious face. The love he felt for her showed so clearly in his eyes. Slowly, her eyes filled with tears. The day had been perfect. She should have been happy, but Joanne could only think about the long years of separation that lay ahead of them.

"Oh, Mike. I love you so much, but I don't think we should do this right now. We don't even know when we'll see each other again. It might be next month or it might be in six months," Joanne said softly as the tears of futility trickled down her cheeks.

Kissing her hands tenderly, Mike replied, "I know all that, but I need to take this step . . . to know that we're moving toward something permanent and lasting. I need to know that the military service can't come between us . . . that our love is stronger than our sense of duty and our commitment to serve others. I need this for the long, lonely days and nights ahead. It'll make the time seem shorter. I'm asking again, Joanne. Will you marry me?"

Kissing him gently, Joanne responded, "I need those things, too, but I think we'll only feel the pain of separation more and the futility of looking forward if we become engaged now. Neither of us wants to date anyone else, so that's not the issue. It's just that it'll be another two and a half years before you finish your sea tour. After that, you'll have a land tour somewhere that might not be near an airbase. Unless I mess up, I won't finish my training for three years. How can we plan for a future when our present is already committed to Uncle Sam?"

"You're not the only one who's good at long-range planning. I was thinking that we'd get married as soon as my sea tour's over," Mike explained. "I'll arrange my land tour around your duty location. There are plenty of Navy ROTC locations in this country. I'll get myself stationed to one of them. In the meantime, we'll have to work harder to find the time to see each other. I'll study more during the week. This next six months is application rather than instruction. I'll have more free weekends. It'll work. You'll see. Besides, you say you don't want a big wedding, but, from what I hear, any wedding takes time to plan . . . at least a year. We need to get on the list for the chapel well in advance of the date. We might just make the cut if we sign up now."

Looking into his hopeful face, Joanne could almost believe that the dream could become reality. Maybe they could plan a future while living under the constraints of the military life. They had attended the weddings of several classmates the week following graduation. The ones who had married Naval Academy graduates were not stationed in the same location and managed to make marriage work. Success required a lot of juggling, but six months later they were making it work.

Seeing objection change to uncertainty on Joanne's face, Mike said, "Our engagement won't be a traditional one; we can't expect that. However, we'll be working toward the life together that means so much to both of us."

"But, I . . ."

"People in high corporate ranks have commuting marriages all the time. We'll have a commuting engagement. After we get married and work out our billets, you'll see so much of me that you'll get tired of seeing my face," Mike added as he continued to break down Joanne's objections.

"Never! I love that face. Besides, wherever we live will have space for a sunroom," Joanne cried happily.

"Then say you'll marry me. You'll love the ring," Mike teased with a grin.

"I suppose since I'm not seeing anyone else and want only you in my life, we might as well get engaged," Joanne responded playfully. Immediately, she added with a serious tone, "Yes, Mike, I love you and would be honored to marry you."

Standing and pulling her into his arms, Mike kissed Joanne deeply. His hands caressed her back and shoulders until her legs weakened, and she leaned against him. Now that they had made the decision and taken the step, Joanne felt as if a degree of light-hearted happiness and a joy in thinking about the future had replaced the weight of the present. Although she had planned the wedding in her mind, Joanne had not really thought that the dream would become a reality so soon.

"You might want to slip this on the third finger of your left hand," Mike said as he flipped the lid on the little red velvet box.

"Oh my! It's gorgeous! Mike . . . I . . . wow!"

"I can't believe it. You're speechless. I didn't think that could really happen," Mike quipped with delight.

Joanne looked from Mike's beaming face to the ring that fit her finger perfectly. A halo of sparkling white diamonds surrounded the impeccable one-karat center stone and trailed around the band. She was stunned . . . speechless . . . and very happy.

Finding her voice, Joanne said, "This must have cost you a fortune. A smaller ring would have been just fine. We can return this as soon as we reach Charleston."

"No way!" Mike exclaimed. "I want you to have the best my sub bonus can buy. Besides, you'll wear it for a long, long time . . . at least fifty years."

"Only fifty?" Joanne teased, as she kissed his lips and cheeks.

"Don't push your luck," Mike replied, hugging her close. "That's long enough for any man to wake up next to the same woman, to share meals with the same woman, to raise children with the same woman. On second thought, I might like to try for seventy."

Kissing him playfully, Joanne said, "I'm so happy, Mike. You were right. Being engaged does make the wait have a purpose. We'll have to phone the chaplain immediately and get on the list. I'll need to make tentative arrangements with a caterer and start looking for a wedding gown. I'm not getting married in my uniform. There's so much to do, and I'll be in training with little time in which to do it."

Hearing her father emerging from his protective cocoon of the sunroom, Joanne whispered, "You'll have to ask my father's permission. It's only a formality. I know he'll say yes, but it's expected."

"I already did. I phoned him last week," Mike smiled. "He was only too happy to give you away. My folks are delighted, too. I was afraid my mom would say something this morning, but she didn't."

Looking incredulously at Mike, Joanne said, "How did you pull this off without one of them saying something? My parents can never keep secrets from me."

"Well, they did this time," Mike chuckled.

"We did what?" Mr. Crawford asked, fighting a grin as he entered the living room.

"Didn't tell me that you knew that Mike would propose to me," Joanne scolded lightly.

"Oh, that. Despite what your mother thinks, I do have some self-control," Mr. Crawford replied, hugging his daughter and shaking the hand of his future son-in-law.

"Self-control in what?" Mrs. Crawford demanded, coming around the corner with a huge smile on her face and tears of happiness glistening in her eyes.

"You knew, too, and didn't tell me!" Joanne cried and added, "Oh, Mommy, I'm so happy."

"Some things you just have to discover for yourself," Mrs. Crawford replied, hugging her daughter and smiling at Mike.

The happiness in the room seemed to bounce off the walls and enfold them. Joanne and Mike beamed constantly at each other and infected the long-married couple with their radiance. Soon all four were sharing the reaction to new love and a fresh engagement with the new couple exchanging quick kisses and the parents holding hands and looking shyly at each other.

When the clock struck five o'clock, Mike had to pull himself away from Joanne. He hated to leave her, but he had an obligation at home. They would be together again the next day, but it seemed as if so many hours would pass before he could hold her in his arms again. She walked him to the car, kissed him good-bye, and returned to her waiting parents, knowing that their life would one day consist of not minutes and hours but years.

Chapter Six

Charleston, a city of old-world charm and sophistication, welcomed the lovers with a week of perfect weather. While Washington and Baltimore shivered under a blanket of light snow, Charleston sparkled. The sun shone brightly, producing temperatures in the mid-fifties every day of their leave. Not that the weather really mattered. Joanne and Mike would have been happy anywhere as long as they were together.

Joanne and Mike had talked constantly during the eight-hour drive. She had dashed to the store before he arrived and purchased an armload of bridal magazines. Flipping through them, she shared the discussion of flowers, meals, and honeymoon locations.

"I didn't think I'd like this wedding-planning thing, but it's growing on me," Joanne stated as she turned yet another glossy page.

"Yeah, like a wart or a fungus," Mike laughed, steering the car down the interstate.

"No, silly!" Joanne chuckled. "It's fun. I get to look at all these gorgeous photos of incredibly beautiful people dressed in wedding finery. It's like playing with dolls again, only this time, I'm the doll."

"You're certainly prettier than any of those women," Mike said, taking a quick glance at the open page.

"You're far from impartial," Joanne cooed contentedly.

"Darn right! You don't think I'd fall for an ugly woman, do you?" Mike replied, laughing heartily.

"Beauty's a surface quality. It's what's inside the person that counts," Joanne sniffed.

"I know that, but it helps if the inside's enclosed in an attractive outside," Mike rebutted.

"You mean that you wouldn't have fallen in love with me if my appearance hadn't been up to your specifications?" Joanne asked, studying his handsome profile.

"I didn't say that at all," Mike said in self-defense. "As a matter of fact, my first memory of you is not of a beautiful woman wearing an expensive evening gown like one of those models."

"I was probably wearing the white works uniform. That thing never did much for my figure," Joanne commented with a huff.

"No, that's not my first real memory," Mike replied. "You were decidedly unattractive the first time I noticed you during that hot summer of training. As I recall, one of the worst thunderstorms in history had dumped gallons of rain on the Academy the night before our exercises. The ground was soggy and oozing water. The air was thick with humidity. I had just finished the rope climb and was heading toward the wall when I heard this loud shout and an equally loud splat. I looked around to see this brown slime-covered person rising from an oozy puddle of bubbling muck. At first I thought it was one of my roommates, but as I got closer to the smelly, cursing mess, I recognized the dripping mass of humanity. I couldn't really see your face since you were completely covered in mud, but I recognized your voice. You were a mess, but you didn't cry or ask to change clothes. You slogged along in your wet clothes, completing the course ahead of the rest of us. Good thing, too, because you really smelled."

"That's your first real memory of me? That's awful!" Joanne groaned and laughed simultaneously.

"That's when I fell in love with you," Mike stated with a smile. "Any woman who could look like that and smell like a prehistoric swamp critter and still persevere as the muck dried to concrete was the girl for me. You never asked for mercy, leniency, or any special treatment. When you found a hose lying on the field, you washed your hands and face and kept going. You were great."

"I certainly have a lot to live up to," Joanne commented. "If that's the woman you first loved, I don't know how I'll outpace that. And here I sit trying to pick out a wedding dress. What I really need to do is to find a good swamp to roll in for a while."

"To live up to your standards, you'll have to give birth to our kids, command a battalion, fly a bomber, drop a few on the enemy, and come home in time to cook dinner," Mike joked.

"You don't expect much," Joanne laughed.

"Only that you'll love me for the rest of our lives," Mike replied softly.

Taking his hand, Joanne responded, "That I can do."

They rode in silence for a while until Joanne blurted, "Flowers! What kind of flowers do you want on the altar?"

"Aren't you rushing things a little bit? We don't even have a church," Mike commented.

"Oops!" Joanne said. "I forgot to tell you that I put our names on the chapel list. Did you know that there's a four-year wait for Commissioning Week? Good thing we don't want that one. Anyway, we're tentatively scheduled to get married on June twenty-fourth. We'll know the exact date a year in advance so that we can order the invitations and arrange for the caterer. I signed up to use Bancroft for the reception, too."

"Just think, by the time we get married, I'll have finished my first sea tour and you'll be a pilot," Mike reminded her.

"Yeah. Time sure flies, doesn't it? Back to the flowers—what kind do you like?" Joanne asked again.

"White roses."

"Me, too!"

"Good. That's settled," Mike said.

"With calla lilies for contrast," Joanne continued. "That's what we'll have. I love doing this! I feel like a real woman, not like a military officer. It's been a long time since I've been able to focus on real girly stuff. I was almost afraid that the Academy had trained femininity out of me."

Reaching for her hand, Mike said, "Take it from me—you're all woman. The Academy life didn't rob you of that."

"You're sweet but not impartial," Joanne replied. "Thank goodness we have leave. It gives me a chance to stash my uniform and become a woman again. It's different for a man. Being an officer doesn't unsex you, but it neutralizes me."

"Do other women feel that way?" Mike asked, negotiating the traffic in the thickening twilight.

"I don't know. I don't have time to chat with the other female pilots. The other mids at the Academy shared my opinion. I doubt that being in the fleet has changed their minds much," Joanne replied, flipping magazine pages.

Showing his support, Mike said, "We'll have to make sure that you're the most feminine woman ever to get married in the Academy chapel. No uniform for you. No bridesmaids in uniform either. Flowers, lace, perfume, satin . . . all that girly stuff you've found in those magazines. It'll really be your day to shine."

"It's your day, too. You'll look handsome in your tux," Joanne commented.

"According to the rules, one of us will have to be in uniform. Besides, I want sword bearers to line the steps as we leave," Mike suggested.

"Sword bearers! I completely forgot about them. They're the best part of a military wedding. But I still don't want a big show. I don't want my parents to have to mortgage their home to pay for our wedding. We'll do something simple and tasteful," Joanne insisted.

"And feminine," Mike added, pulling into his apartment parking lot.

"We're here? That didn't take long at all," Joanne said as she stared into the glow of the streetlights.

"Good company made the trip seem shorter. Don't expect too much. This is a bachelor pad, remember," Mike replied, unlocking the front door and ushering her inside.

Standing in the apartment's small foyer, Joanne surveyed the interior. Mike's parents had given him living-room and dining-room furniture as well as his bedroom suite. His roommate had added the kitchen bistro set and the entertainment center.

Despite the lack of a feminine presence, the apartment had warmth and a sense of home.

"It's really nice! I'd expected to see shades of brown and gray," Joanne commented as she followed Mike through the apartment.

"It'll do until the next move and the one after that. Once we get married and settle down, the decorating task is all yours," Mike said, making space in his dresser and closet for Joanne's things.

"Take me out on the town. I can unpack later," Joanne suggested, throwing her arms around his waist.

"All right. Let's go for a walk. That's the best way to see the old section," Mike replied, taking Joanne's hand and leading her outside.

Strolling past historic homes with short front yards on deep lots, Joanne was taken by the beauty of Charleston. Lights twinkled behind sheer curtains flanked by heavy drapes. Unlike home, where snow covered everything, pots of begonias and geraniums graced the elegant porches and the grass still showed green. Even in late December, people strolled the quiet streets.

"I could live here," Joanne announced, surveying the area.

"I thought you'd like it. We'll have to put it on our short list," Mike said with a smile.

"Not unless I can transfer from the flight community. There's no real career base for me here. But it's lovely just the same," Joanne replied with a touch of sadness in her voice.

"Maybe you will have changed your mind about being a pilot by the time we're ready to buy a house," Mike suggested.

Looking at him in the light of a streetlamp, Joanne said, "Not hardly. It's what I've wanted to do all my life. Flying is my passion. I won't ever give it up."

"But it'll take you away from me," Mike protested.

"So will your life in a submarine," Joanne retorted. "I don't see why I have to sacrifice my dreams for domesticity."

"I didn't ask you to make a sacrifice. I only said that flying would interfere with our married life. Our bases aren't the same," Mike replied gently.

"Then one of us needs to request reassignment once our first tour ends . . . and it doesn't have to be me," Joanne responded heatedly.

"We can't follow different paths and be married. It just not feasible. It'll be easier for you to request a land assignment that it would be for me. Women do it all the time when they become pregnant," Mike insisted.

"When I become pregnant, I'll do whatever I need to do to protect the baby, but right now I don't want to change my plans and abandon my dreams," Joanne replied angrily and added, "I told you this engagement business wouldn't work as long as we both have our hearts set on a military career."

Taking Joanne into his arms, Mike said, "I'm sorry. I didn't mean it to sound as if I were belittling your dreams. I know that being a pilot is as important to you as being a submariner is to me. Please don't give up on us yet, we have almost three years to work this out. I'll start putting out feelers to see what other options are open to me. I know someone who changed to meteorology and had a great land-based career. I'll start checking it out immediately. Who knows? I might not like being confined to a sub for six months at a time."

Sighing, Joanne replied, "I'll look into my options, too. Encryption isn't a bad choice once my training's over and I've flown for a while. Intelligence is a good deal, too, especially an assignment at the Pentagon. When we start having our family, it would be the perfect spot for me."

Breathing deeply, Mike relaxed a little. He had come so close to upsetting their relationship. He made a mental note to be more careful with his wording. He knew that Joanne would not abandon her dreams any more than he would give up his childhood desire to be a submariner. As a military couple, they would have to become accustomed to long separations and the difficulty of coordinating careers.

Joanne and Mike strolled hand-in-hand for the rest of the evening, stopping at a neighborhood restaurant for a late snack before returning to his apartment. Neither mentioned their careers again, although they were both aware that the military occupied a prominent role in their relationship. For the rest of their leave, they agreed to focus on their love and let the rest take care of itself.

That night, they slept in each other's arms. The quiet of the apartment and the dark street quickly lulled them to sleep. The long drive, the argument, and the lovemaking had tired them out. As they lay curled into each other's arms, nothing mattered except making memories to live on while separated.

The next morning, Joanne woke early, showered, and started breakfast. Padding around the apartment in her fuzzy slippers, she felt strangely domestic and relieved that Mike's roommate had not returned. They had the apartment completely to themselves.

By the time Mike appeared, Joanne had made

pancakes, scrambled eggs, and fried bacon. She had even set the dining room table with Mike's blue-rimmed dishes rather than simply arranging their plates at the breakfast bar. He smiled broadly as she tossed the towel that had served as an apron onto the counter.

"Hey, you lied! I thought you couldn't cook. Maybe I should sleep late every morning," Mike cooed, pulling Joanne into his arms.

"Not if you want breakfast. Tomorrow's your day. Besides, I can handle this. Bacon is my staple. Scrambled eggs are easy in a nonstick pan. The instructions for the pancakes are on the box. I can do this," Joanne replied, kissing him lightly on his stubbly chin. "Cactus face!"

"I thought I'd take a holiday from shaving," Mike beamed, pleased with his day-old beard.

"That'll be a facet of you I've never seen. From clean shaven to scruffy in how long?" Joanne asked, slipping into her seat.

"About three days, I think. I'll shave if you don't like it," Mike offered, munching a piece of crispy bacon.

"It might look nice," Joanne replied, pouring syrup on a heaping stack of pancakes. "What's on tap for today?"

"I want to show you Fort Sumter and maybe even drive to Savannah. We can eat dinner there," Mike responded. "Great eggs! You're almost as good a cook as our mothers."

"I'm wise to your tactics, Ensign. You think that if you lay on the compliments, I'll decide to handle all of the cooking. Wrong!"

"I tried," Mike conceded happily.

"Let's hit the road as soon as you clean up the mess I made in the kitchen," Joanne said. "I don't want to miss a thing. There's much to see and little time."

Mike finished his meal and helped Joanne clear the dishes. Straightening the kitchen in record time, they stepped into a surprisingly warm winter day. Heading the car into town, Mike gave Joanne a tour of Charleston, the naval station, old slave plantations and finally, the Ashley River, on which some of the most beautiful and elegant mansions of Charleston's distinguished past still resided.

Joining a few other tourists, they boarded the ferry that would take them to Fort Sumter. Joanne gazed in disbelief at the homes that had stood on the banks of the Ashley since before the Civil War and had survived the bombardment of the city as the South fought for possession of the atoll on which the fort stood. The structures with their elegant columns and intricate carvings were more breathtaking than any she had ever seen.

Stepping onto the barren island at the confluence of the Ashley and the Atlantic, Joanne tried to imagine soldiers living in such meager conditions within a short boat ride from the glory of the South. The fort was dull and drab and mostly gray and a deep, dark mossy brown. Although the exhibits were well presented, the fort itself was depressing in its starkness. The blue of the water and the sky did little to enhance what must have been an incredibly lonely place to live.

Pulling her jacket closer, Joanne said, "It must be at least ten degrees cooler out here."

"It's not like this in the summer," Mike replied, throwing his arm over her shoulder for warmth. "When I came here in September, the heat was unbearable. There aren't any trees to block the sun."

"I can't imagine living here," Joanne said as she

peered into the living history rooms. "The quarters are tiny, and this mound of rocks is definitely not hospitable. We think some of our bases need work. They look like paradise compared to this place."

"Military people were definitely treated like third-class citizens then. This is a dismal place," Mike agreed, as he led Joanne to yet another room.

"They were completely dependant on supply boats, too, for all provisions except for fish. Their meals must have been boring," Joanne said, studying the small galley.

"It's a no-frills place," Mike nodded in agreement.

"I've seen enough. I'm not dressed for the wind that whips around this place," Joanne announced, leading the way to the ferry landing.

Arriving only a few minutes before the ferry's scheduled departure, Mike and Joanne purchased cups of hot chocolate and boarded. Since few people had made the little journey into the past, they had their pick of seats. The warmth inside the cabin did much to chase away the chill of the fort.

"Where's your spirit of discovery . . . your desire to experience the old way of military life?" Mike quipped, handing her a hot chocolate.

"In the library," Joanne said, warming her hands on the cup.

"You'll like Savannah much better. It's warm, beautiful, and full of shops and museums," Mike commented, watching the sun kiss Joanne's rosy cheeks.

"I can do that," Joanne replied, sipping gratefully as the ferry returned them to Charleston and the beauty of the South.

By the time they reached the car, Joanne's fingers and toes had defrosted and her spirits had risen. The warmth of the car quickly lulled her to sleep despite her desire to continue reading the many magazines that littered the floor around her. Mike only looked at the woman beside him and smiled. He loved the feeling of familiarity that had so quickly settled into their lives.

"It's about time you woke up. I didn't have anyone to talk with the entire trip," Mike complained gently.

"I'm so sorry. I guess I'm still sleep-deprived from the long study hours." Joanne yawned and stretched. Pointing to a familiar sight, she added, "Look! There's the park from *Midnight in the Garden of Good and Evil.*"

Joanne was the first one out of the car and ready to explore. Her hardly used camera clicked overtime as she turned from one sight to the other. First, she snapped photos of the fountain in the park and then the Mercer House. Famous churches, park benches used in the film, and university shops found their way into her compositions. Nothing escaped her quickly snapping fingers.

"I knew you'd like it here," Mike smiled as he followed Joanne from one photo opportunity to the other.

"Savannah's even more beautiful than Charleston. I could live here, too. This is great!" Joanne commented, rushing to snap a picture of the fountain from another angle.

"Wait until you see Hilton Head and some of the islands. It's a great place, but it's hot and humid in the summer," Mike said happily.

"I feel as if I've stepped into a time of civility and charm. Only for us, it would have meant hard labor and ratty clothing," Joanne said, remembering the reality of southern living for blacks.

"The local black people of this area brag about their long-held freedom. They managed to escape slavery by living in their own little islands. That's why

I want you to see them. A lot of the people still sell the wares that their families have been making for generations," Mike said, sounding like a tour guide.

"Let's go. I'm ready!" Joanne urged, heading back to the car.

With Joanne practically dragging Mike around town, they stopped only long enough to purchase two sweatshirts as mementos of the trip, and sandwiches and sodas for the drive. Although a wealth of elegant restaurants lined the waterside malls in Savannah and dotted the islands, Joanne wanted to see as much as possible before the winter sun began to set. A leisurely meal would have interfered with her plans.

Joanne and Mike had barely driven past the city limits when Mike stopped the car at a roadside display. Dozens of intricately woven baskets covered the table and overflowed onto the blanket on the ground. They were stunning examples of the local Gullah handicraft.

"Let's buy one each for our mothers," Joanne insisted, studying the baskets closely.

"Don't you want one?" Mike asked.

"I sure do, but I don't think it would survive the moving. You'll have to bring me here on our honeymoon. We'll buy several for our home," Joanne smiled as she carried her purchase to the car.

"A honeymoon in Hilton Head sounds like a winner to me," Mike agreed as they started toward the island. "But I thought you said you always wanted to go to Hawaii."

"I do!" Joanne exclaimed. "I guess we'll just have to come here for our first anniversary."

This time, Joanne did not fall asleep. Instead, she scanned the marshes for egrets and other waterbirds about which she had only read but had never seen. Although she did not spot any, she searched for alligators, too. The marshes were the home to a large variety of animals of all species. Some of them were especially pesky.

"Oh! Something bit me!" Joanne cried as they stood at the side of the road snapping photos.

"It must have been a no-see-um," Mike said knowledgeably.

"A what? Oh!"

"It's a tiny mosquito. Look at your arms. You can barely see one right there," Mike said, pointing to the pest that had perched in preparation of making Joanne its dinner.

"Not this one," Joanne responded as she squashed the bug. "That's one no-see-um that won't have a snack."

"They're a lot worse than this in the summer," Mike said, laughing at her momentary triumph.

"Let's go. They're massing in force," Joanne said, running to the car.

Laughing, Mike joined her, waving his arms to keep the bugs from his face and ears. Even an encounter with the pesky little bloodsuckers would one day turn into a memory to hold dear as he sat alone in his apartment or on his berth in the sub. He would remember the expression on her face and the sight of her sprinting to the car.

Joanne, too, would remember their trip through the marshlands and the no-see-ums. The elegant Charleston and Savannah homes would remind her of the past and a future that might one day be within their grasp. The memories would carry her through the long, lonely nights that lay ahead until they would be together again.

Chapter Seven

All too soon, their leave ended and the holiday season was over. Joanne and Mike returned to the routine of their lives with quickly snatched phone calls being their main form of communication. Mike's study and work schedule was so rigid that he was unable to visit Joanne in Florida in January or February. As one month grew into another and winter turned to spring, the opportunity for long weekend breaks dwindled.

As the bugs, heat, and tourists of summer flowed into Florida, Joanne sat cross-legged on her bed. Piles of clean clothing littered the room. The silent phone beside her reminded Joanne that Mike had still not returned her call. The sparkling diamond on her left hand was her only connection to the man she loved and missed.

"Got a minute?" Sandy, her roommate, asked, popping her head into the room.

"Nothing but," Joanne replied with a sad smile.

"Mike hasn't called? He will, don't worry," Sandy commented as she flopped into the chair by the bed.

"I know. He always does. It just that the conversations have been brief and sparse lately. I miss him.

His sub's under way. It'll be a while before he'll be able to call," Joanne explained with a sigh.

"You'll feel better once you can share the news with him," Sandy stated, flicking at the lint on her shorts.

"At the rate we're going, I'll be in Washington by then," Joanne quipped dryly.

"At least the weather's good for the drive," Sandy commented, already missing her buddy.

"Yeah, but Mike won't know where to find me, not that I ever see him anyway. This long-range relationship is difficult at best," Joanne sighed.

"He'll call. This isn't the first time that you've been out of contact for a few days," Sandy reminded Joanne.

"I know, but I haven't been able to tell him about the change in orders. He doesn't know that I . . . I won't be flying anymore," Joanne sniffed, reaching for a tissue.

Putting her arm around her roommate's shoulders, Sandy replied, "I know you can't see it now, but everything works out for the best. It's a cliché, but it's true. You'll see."

"Like everything else horrible in life, one day I'll look back on this and not think it was so awful. But right now, I can't think of much that's worse than this," Joanne cried, dabbing at her eyes.

"What did your parents say when you told them?" Sandy asked gently.

"They were relieved," Joanne sniffed loudly. "They never really wanted me to be a pilot. You know, scared of crashes. They're thrilled that I've been reassigned to Intel."

"Already something good's come of it. Your parents won't have to worry anymore. Mine still live with the fear that someone will phone with the news that my plane crashed," Sandy commented about the reality of flight.

Studying her roommate's face, Joanne said, "I guess I didn't know how frightened they were until I told them about this. I could hear the relief in their voices over the phone. Mom even cried. I guess I'm the only one who's disappointed."

"You can't help the way you feel or the chain of events that led to this. You've been very brave through the whole thing. I don't think I could have endured what you have," Sandy said.

"I certainly didn't know about it. I wouldn't have nourished this dream if I had known that I'd have this problem," Joanne said.

"You couldn't have known until you entered flight training. Not many of us get this. Besides, they can usually condition us out of it," Sandy reminded her.

"I'm one of the lucky ones with air sickness that so severe that the military can't even put a stop to it. Some consolation," Joanne whined into her tissue.

"You tried everything. All the tests, the training . . . nothing worked."

"I know. If anything, it got worse. I'm afraid to fly in any kind of plane now. I guess I'll have to stick to the highways for a while," Joanne stated flatly.

"I think you should look at the bright side. You'll have a regular life without endless hours of flight training. You'll have a more permanent home rather than this transient one we live now. You'll be free to live with the man you love," Sandy said, counting the reasons for happiness.

"If he's ever in port again. But I won't have my dream of becoming a pilot. That hurts. I've wanted it for so long," Joanne sighed as she tossed a pile of tee shirts into her duffel bag.

"But you'll have changing seasons and a chance to see your parents. You've missed having both," Sandy replied comfortingly.

"You're right, but it'll take time for me to accept the loss of a dream," Joanne commented, searching for the other jogging shoe.

"Do you think you'll stay in the navy?" Sandy asked as she helped Joanne finish packing the trunk that the movers would haul away the next day.

"Sure! I love this life. I won't be able to fly, but I'll still be able to serve. Our paths will cross again one day. Who knows, you might decide to change to Intel after you finish your flight obligation," Joanne replied, smiling for the first time in days.

"That's not a bad idea. In fact, the more my boyfriend talks about marriage and kids, the more I think that I might want to request a change. We'll see. That's years down the road," Sandy responded.

"I'll send you all the Intel propaganda I can find to whet your appetite," Joanne chuckled, trying to lighten the gloomy atmosphere in her room.

"See, you're feeling better already," Sandy commented with a smile.

"Maybe a little. Dreams come and go. I'll just have to get used to not having this one," Joanne replied.

Smiling, a touch of wisdom creeping into her voice, Sandy said, "We all have dreams that fade in the light of day. Remember that Marine I thought I loved and wanted to marry? I saw him last night at our usual bar, and I'm glad that relationship didn't work out. He was so arrogant and so full of himself

as a Marine. Marriage to him never would have
lasted."

"At least you found out before you had invested
too much of your time. I guess in that way, I'm
lucky, too. I could have endured all the training
and then discovered this medical problem after I
had been assigned to a base or carrier. That really
would have been a bummer," Joanne commented,
zipping the stuffed duffel bag.

"What time will the movers arrive tomorrow?"
Sandy asked, looking at the messy room.

"Early tomorrow morning. I'll leave right behind
them. This is my last night in Florida. I just can't believe it," Joanne sighed.

"You know that I keep an air mattress in the
closet. You can visit any time you're in need of a
little sun and surf," Sandy said.

"Thanks. After a Washington winter, I might just
take you up on it," Joanne replied, chuckling.

"I'm hungry. Let's go out to dinner tonight,"
Sandy suggested. "It's your last evening here.
You've finished your share of the packing. The rest
belongs to the movers."

"You're right. Let's do something memorable,"
Joanne quipped, tossing the last item into the duffel bag and zipping it shut.

The roommates wandered down the street for
their last meal together. Sandy would continue her
flight training as Joanne moved into the unknown
of Intel. With luck, their paths would cross again
one day.

The Italian restaurant around the corner was
their favorite hangout and an appropriate place for
a last dinner together. As Joanne and Sandy entered, a sea of familiar faces greeted them. Rising,

the men and women of Joanne's flight squadron lifted their glasses in tribute.

"Fair winds, Joanne!" they shouted.

"Let's give three cheers for one who goes before us!" someone instructed from a table by the window.

"Hip, hip, hooray!" came the response.

Fighting back tears, Joanne said, "Three cheers for those we leave behind. Hip, hip, hooray! You guys are too much."

"We couldn't let you get away without a proper send-off," one of her fellow student pilots replied, slapping her on the back.

"You're the lucky one. We're stuck here with the lovebugs!" another called.

"I'll miss you guys," Joanne said, slipping into the seat of honor they had reserved for her.

"Not as much as we'll miss you. Who'll bring us brownies every day?" one of her classmates asked.

"You should be happy not to have to eat those burned-up things," Joanne laughed.

"They've been pretty good lately. You finally got it right," another classmate commented.

"I guess I had to learn to cook something other than BLTs," Joanne quipped with a touch of sadness in her voice at the memory of that last family dinner with Mike.

The good-natured banter continued as they devoured pizzas washed down with pitchers of beer and soda. By the time the evening ended, Joanne felt much better, having heard stories of other pilots who had washed out due to illness and worse. She was tough, and she would survive.

The next morning, Joanne watched as the movers loaded her furniture and cardboard wardrobes into the truck and headed toward the interstate. Hugging her roommate, Joanne pulled from the parking lot, saying farewell to the dream of flying and Florida. She was heading toward a new career in an old familiar town.

By the time Joanne reached Charleston, she was looking forward to the new direction in her life. She missed Mike terribly, especially as she walked the streets that they had once toured together. This time, she was on her own. He had not phoned, and she had given up hope. Loving a man assigned to a submarine meant weeks and months of waiting. Reluctantly, she had come to the conclusion that this was her time to wait.

Before falling asleep in the bachelor officer's quarters, Joanne phoned her parents, who did not like the idea that she was traveling the interstate alone and were relieved to hear that she would spend the night on base. However, driving her car to Washington herself rather than shipping it and flying up was the least expensive route. Besides, Joanne did not mind the solitude of the open road and was not ready to board a plane. She needed time to adjust her thoughts and attitude before reporting to work. Having to socialize with a new roommate, unpack, and visit her parents would not give her sufficient time to complete the grieving process.

Joanne had decided not to return to her parents' home although she knew the door was open for her. She had found an apartment in DC. She wanted to remain independent. Living with her parents, although comfortable and comforting, would have reduced her status to that of a child again. Instead, she had arranged to share an apartment with another Academy graduate also assigned to Intel. They had known each other slightly while

undergraduates and looked forward to living together.

"Mom, I'm in Charleston. Of course I've eaten.
You know I never skip meals. The bachelor quarters
is fine for a night. I'll leave early in the morning
and should arrive in DC no later than eight,"
Joanne explained.

"Be sure to lock your hotel door," Mrs. Crawford
advised.

"I will. I'll even put a chair under the knob,"
Joanne replied, feeling the warmth of the familiar
admonitions spreading through her.

"Does Mike know yet?" Mrs. Crawford asked
slowly.

"No, he's hasn't returned my call. He'll find out
soon enough," Joanne responded with a sigh as a
pang of loneliness coursed through her.

"At least DC is closer to Norfolk. Maybe you'll
be able to see more of each other," Mrs. Crawford
suggested, knowing that Joanne still struggled with
the disappointment of the change.

"We'll see. I'd have to turn into a mermaid to
catch up with him," Joanne chuckled.

"I'm glad you're feeling better, dear."

"Not better, just resigned. There's nothing I can
do about any of this except accept it. Intel might be
fun," Joanne said, and added, "Not like flying, but
stimulating just the same."

"That's my girl. I knew you wouldn't stay down
long," Mrs. Crawford said cheerily, always one of
Joanne's best supporters.

"Night, Mom. I'll talk to you tomorrow. Kiss
Daddy for me," Joanne said as she stretched and
yawned. The fatigue of travel had finally caught up
with her.

"Drive carefully, dear, and call as soon as you get here," Mrs. Crawford replied.

Reluctantly rising from the bed, Joanne padded across the carpet in her sock feet and checked the door. Smiling, she again felt the warmth of love. As soon as her head hit the pillow, Joanne put thoughts of Mike and flight school from her mind. She had a long drive ahead of her and needed the rest.

The chirping of her cell phone startled Joanne from the first sweet moments of slumber. Her first thought was that her mother was calling with additional advice. Reaching sleepily for the noisy phone, Joanne pressed the talk button without opening her eyes.

"Yes, Mom."

"Hi, babe. It's me," Mike's voice said, jolting her into wakefulness.

"Wow! You called," Joanne laughed happily.

"I only have a minute. I'm standing only inches from the water. You sounded down. What's your news?" Mike asked.

"I've been reassigned to Intel," Joanne replied without preamble.

"Why?"

"I've this really bad altitude sickness problem. Since you went under way, I've had all kinds of training and tests, but nothing worked. I'm on my way to DC now. As a matter of fact, I'm in the bachelor officer's quarters in Charleston," Joanne said, keeping emotion from her voice.

"Sorry, kid. I love you and wish I could be there with you. I know how much you wanted to fly," Mike said sadly.

Sighing, Joanne explained, "It's just as well that you're not here. I need to toughen up a bit and grow up, too. I can't expect you to be by my side all the time. Chances are you'll be under way for a lot of the events of our life together. I'm doing okay. When will I see you again?"

"I don't know yet. Maybe in two weeks . . . maybe more. At least the drive's shorter now," Mike commented.

"Where exactly are you?" Joanne demanded. "The transmission's awful."

"We're lucky to be having this conversation at all. Let's just say that if I don't end this call right now, I'll be in Davy Jones' locker," Mike shouted over the crashing of waves.

"Okay. Call again soon. I love you," Joanne shouted into empty airtime and added, "Mike!"

Tossing the phone onto the night table, Joanne once again settled down to sleep. Adjusting the pillow, she sighed and fell into a peaceful slumber. Mike's call had removed a heavy load from her shoulders. This time, no one disturbed her, and the night passed peacefully.

Joanne hit the road early the next morning in an effort to miss the local rush hour and reach Washington as early as possible. She listened to music and sang along to combat boredom, and munched cheese crackers and fruit to keep her energy up. By evening, she had reached the city limits and was on the way to her new home.

Unlike Florida, DC was not new to Joanne. Having grown up with the sights of the city around her, she felt at home as soon as she saw the monuments. Despite the disappointment of leaving the flight community, she would enjoy being back in familiar territory. Even without Mike at her side, Joanne would have comforting surroundings and loving family in her life again.

Arriving after dark, Joanne discovered that Gail, her new roommate, had left a note that read, "Sorry I can't be here to greet you, but my boyfriend arrived unexpectedly. Your furniture came before I left. I'll see you later."

"At least one of us will see her boyfriend," Joanne muttered as she unpacked her stuff and rearranged the furniture in her bedroom. Her living-room furniture blended well with Gail's. The apartment was definitely well furnished.

Looking around in the refrigerator she found leftover pizza with another note from Gail. Joanne devoured the treat, then put the finishing touches on her room and phoned her parents. She would live here at least six months and maybe more, depending on her training schedule.

"Who are you?" Joanne asked of the big black cat that appeared from the darkness of Gail's room. "Too bad you can't talk. I could use a little companionship right now."

The cat meowed, rubbed against her shins, and perched on Joanne's bed. Smiling, she scratched the animal's ears and muttered, "I see I have a new friend. Nice to meet you."

The hour was late, and Joanne was very tired. After securing the locks, Joanne slipped into her bed and quickly fell asleep with the cat snuggled against her. She missed Mike, but being here felt just right. Her future in Intel would begin the next day.

Chapter Eight

With each passing month, Joanne discovered that she enjoyed her new Intel assignment more than she had expected. To her surprise, she found living in her hometown near her parents to be comforting and not at all constricting. She and Gail had quickly become good friends and discovered that they shared many of the same interests. The slower pace of the Intel assignment allowed them to explore the city and take an occasional day trip to the historic areas surrounding DC. Joanne liked having someone with whom to share her favorite childhood haunts. She was far happier than she had imagined that she would be away from the flight community. Although she hardly ever heard from Mike, the ring on her left hand constantly reminded her of their love and their plans for a life together.

One bright, sunny fall morning, Joanne walked across the parking lot to her car, carrying a basket of apples that she had picked herself. Her mom had promised that she would bake Joanne a pie if Joanne would provide the apples. Since the fall weather was so beautiful, Joanne and Gail had done exactly that. Now, it was time to deliver them to her mother and collect on the promise.

Armed with the overflowing basket, Joanne intended to spend the afternoon doing chores for her parents while her mom turned the healthy treats into a rich, sinfully delicious dessert that she and Gail would savor slowly. She had just closed the trunk when she heard someone approaching. Squinting into the sunshine, she stared at the approaching figure, but she could not make out his face. The man walked with a strangely familiar list and sway. Even the baseball cap that further obscured his face tilted in a familiar way.

"Hi, babe," the man greeted her.

"Mike!" Joanne shouted, throwing herself into his outstretched arms. "What are you doing here? How long will you stay?"

"Later. I'll answer all of your questions later," Mike replied, silencing her with a long, sweet kiss.

Joanne could think of no reason to argue as Mike took the keys from her fingers and led her into the apartment building. All thought of the apples, the pie, and her mother's long list of chores vanished from her mind as Mike gently allowed his lips to trail along her ears and neck, causing the elevator ride to take on an unfamiliar titillating character. His hands explored her back and shoulders in ways that made her feel warmer than the sun ever could and turned her knees and fingers to jelly. As she unlocked the door to her apartment, Joanne wanted answers to her questions, but she wanted Mike more.

Pushing the cat from her room and locking the door, Joanne quickly pulled back the covers. Mike wasted no time in tossing their clothes into a heap on the floor. The cool sheet covered their hot bodies as they rediscovered each other's pleasure spots. Their arms and legs intertwined as memory led them to old familiar places and new heights. Later that afternoon, several empty condom packages lay crumbled on the night table, reminders of a joyous reunion.

"Now will you answer my questions?" Joanne asked as she nestled against Mike's chest.

"Which one?" Mike responded, pulling her still closer.

"All of them," Joanne sighed, happier than she had been in months.

"I drove up this morning. I'm on leave for a week. After that, I'll get under way again," Mike answered slowly.

Studying his face, Joanne asked, "What aren't you telling me?"

"Nothing," Mike replied and looked toward the window through which the sun still streamed.

"Mike, I know you're holding something back. You'll have to tell me eventually. You might as well do it now," Joanne insisted, turning his face toward hers.

"I'll be under way for at least six months this time. We're going to the Mediterranean," Mike responded, studying her face.

"Six months of little or no contact. That's a long time," Joanne sighed. "That'll make this last underway look like a weekend."

"That's why I didn't want to tell you now. I wanted us to enjoy our week together," Mike stated, pulling her into his arms.

"I'm glad I know. Every minute will be even more precious, knowing that there's no chance of seeing you again for a very long time," Joanne said, kissing his lips and nestling against his chest.

"You're the darnedest woman," Mike exclaimed proudly. "All the junior officers advised me not to tell you until the end of my leave. They said that their wives and girlfriends fall apart with the news. You're a wonder."

"Don't forget that I'm Navy, too. We go and do what we have to. Orders come before personal preference," Joanne replied, giving him the party line to make both of them feel better. She would cry and feel miserable after he left. Now was time to be brave and make memories to live on until his return.

"I should have known you'd take the news like this. It really makes the separation easier knowing that you understand. I don't envy the other guys who'll leave to tears," Mike said, kissing Joanne gently.

Joanne allowed her silence to speak the words that she did not feel. In reality, she was no braver than the other women; she was simply better at hiding her pain. She knew that Mike was upset about getting under way again and being out of contact for so long. She saw no reason to add to his misery by placing hers on his shoulders.

"What'll we do tonight?" Joanne asked, tracing a line from his belly button to his chin.

"More of this!" Mike replied, hugging her close.

"I mean when we're not doing this," Joanne chuckled.

"Well, man and woman can't live without food. We'll have to eat sometime," Mike commented.

"The apples!" Joanne exclaimed, sitting up in the bed.

"What?"

"I was on my way to my mom's when you appeared. I stashed apples in the trunk of my car for a pie she promised to make for me. I forgot all about them," Joanne said as she returned to her spot on Mike's shoulder.

"That's what we'll do tonight. Your mom makes a mean pie. She might even feed us if we look hungry enough," Mike suggested without releasing his hold on Joanne's shoulder.

"She'd be upset if we didn't stop by. I'll phone her. She must be wondering what happened to me," Joanne commented, trailing her finger along the line of Mike's jaw and cheekbones and burning the passage into memory.

"But first, you've awakened a sleeping tiger. Come here, woman," Mike said, lifting Joanne's chin so that her mouth pressed against his.

Again, Joanne and Mike abandoned themselves to the sensations that flowed through their bodies. Their fingers and lips retraced sweet paths. Their minds recorded every minute as the time slipped away. By the time they took a quick shower and dressed, the sun had set.

Joanne's parents were thrilled to see both of them. Angela Crawford noted that Mike had grown too thin from submarine life, with Mr. Crawford disagreeing, saying that the young man looked wonderfully healthy for someone who spent so many hours under the sea. Regardless of the reaction, Mike felt loved, sitting in the Crawford kitchen as Mrs. Crawford sliced the apples for the neglected pie and prepared dinner.

"How is life in the sub service really, Mike? Joanne's not here, so you can tell me," Mrs. Crawford said, sliding the pie into the oven.

"It's not an easy life, Mrs. C," Mike replied, using

the familiar nickname he had given Joanne's mother as soon as they had become engaged.

"Explain," Mrs. Crawford demanded, taking a seat at the table opposite him and presenting him with a plate of sugar cookies.

Allowing his mind to walk the decks of the sub, Mike replied, "The sub's small and cramped. Living conditions are tight. The food's good on our boat because the cook's top-drawer, but not that great on others. We work long shifts and are really always on call. Some of the work's really boring, but sometimes we do something exciting. It wouldn't be too bad if I had heeded my parents' admonitions and not fallen in love. The hardest part is being away from Joanne."

"It's always difficult being away from loved ones," Mrs. Crawford consoled, placing her hand on his arm. "This trip to the Mediterranean will be your longest time away from the States. You'll have shore leave, won't you?"

"Sure, but it's not like being at home, especially at holiday time. It's a foreign area, and not everyone likes Americans. We'll have to be very careful not to call attention to ourselves. These aren't the days when people welcomed the US with open arms. Even worse, I'll see all these great places but without Joanne," Mike replied with a shrug of futility.

"You can always return. Maybe even take her there for your honeymoon," Mrs. Crawford suggested, rising to flip the chicken.

"Marriage and a life with Joanne seem so far away. I know the time will pass quickly once I'm involved with the work, but right now, six months away, most of it without phone or computer contact, seems like a lifetime," Mike responded glumly, as he munched the cookies without really tasting them.

"How's Joanne taking the news?" Mrs. Crawford asked, returning to her place at the table.

"You know Joanne. She's being braver about this than I am, although I know it's only a face. At least, I hope she isn't glad to be rid of me," Mike chuckled sadly.

"You know she'll miss you. She's just trying to make it easier on both of you. It's been hard for her not being in the flight-training program. She really had her heart set on becoming a pilot. This long distance is just one more thing she'll have to endure," Mrs. Crawford said consolingly.

Shaking his head angrily, Mike complained, "That's another thing. When I'm under way, I don't know what's happening to the people I love. I didn't even know that she had been reassigned until two days ago when I returned to Norfolk. The e-mail service to the sub is iffy. Cell phones don't work most of the time. It's like living on a different planet, or at least a parallel universe."

"Maybe you shouldn't get married until after you finish your sea tour. Think of how awful it would be if you were married with kids," Mrs. Crawford offered.

"When we first became engaged, I didn't want to believe that," Mike confessed, shaking his head at his youthful foolishness. "Youthful naïveté, I guess. Just think about it. I've only been on short cruises until now, and I've already missed out on so much. I haven't said anything to Joanne, but I know that I don't want to be separated from my wife. It's hard enough being away from my girl. We'll have to wait until I finish this ordeal."

"Or you could ask for reassignment. Any way it

shapes up, she'll understand and probably agree with you," Mrs. Crawford said, serving the plates with steaming vegetables and deliciously aromatic spiced chicken.

Placing them on the table, Mike replied, "I know she will, although leaving subs isn't really an option. I feel the same way about submarines as Joanne did about flight. She understands that, too. Joanne's one in a million. I'm a lucky guy to have fallen for a woman like her."

Smiling, Mrs. Crawford said, "I know you are, but then, so is she to have a guy like you."

Joanne and her father entered the room at that moment. Seeing the serious expressions, Joanne asked, "What gives? Are we interrupting something? We're starving."

Kissing Joanne on the cheek, Mrs. Crawford replied, "We've been having a mother-son conversation. I've missed not having a son. Mike's a neat guy. I think you can keep him."

"Oh, thanks! That's why I fell in love with him," Joanne replied, hugging Mike's shoulders.

Feigning weakness, Mr. Crawford complained, "Before this mushy love stuff completely ruins my appetite, can we eat? I haven't had anything since breakfast, despite working like a slave around here. By the way, Joanne and I completed every item on your extensive to-do list. And in record time, I might add."

"You're too good to me," Mrs. Crawford teased with a wink.

As the foursome sat down to dinner, Mr. Crawford reached over, patted Mike on the shoulder, and said, "Glad to have you home, if only for a short time, Mike. We've missed you."

"Thanks, sir. I've missed being with all of you,"

Mike replied, feeling comfortably warm basking in the Crawford family's love.

Joanne's smile spread from ear to ear. She could hardly remember the time only a short few months ago that she had almost dreaded moving back to Washington and giving up her dream of flying. Being near her parents had filled her with so much joy that her disappointment at having to abandon her dream of being a pilot had quickly faded. Instead of feeling stifled by her job in Intel, Joanne had learned to appreciate the methodical nature of it. Rather than experiencing a sense of confinement from living in the same town as her parents, she relished being able to spend time with them as they aged. Having Mike at the table completed an idyllic family picture.

Now, with Mike seated at her parents' table, Joanne could not have been happier. Their union would be short, but it would be far richer than it would have been if she had not been able to include her mother and father in the moments. The old adage was true: Things do work out for the best.

"We'll do kitchen patrol," Mike offered in thanks for the delicious meal.

"You'll do no such thing!" Mrs. Crawford exclaimed. "You're only home for a week and have much more important things to do than clean a kitchen. My husband will keep me company. This is a perfect fall evening. Go to a movie. Take a walk. Sit and look at each other. Go! Enjoy yourselves."

Placing a quick kiss on her parents' cheeks, Joanne said, "I learned as a little girl never to disagree with my mother. Thank you for dinner. We'll come back tomorrow for the pie."

"See you tomorrow," Mrs. Crawford agreed as she and her husband vanished into the kitchen.

The sound of Mr. Crawford singing at the top of his voice as he helped his wife drifted toward the front door as Joanne and Mike stepped into the delicious evening air. The smell of autumn crispness mingled with the aroma of smoke from neighboring fireplaces. Taking her parents' suggestion and linking arms, Joanne and Mike strolled around the old familiar block.

"I hope we'll be as happy as they are after we've been married for thirty years," Mike commented, hugging Joanne tightly.

"We will be," Joanne replied confidently. "Success in a marriage comes from the willingness to compromise and support each other. If we ever have a chance to live together for any period of time, we'll learn each other's strengths and weaknesses and carry that knowledge into our day-to-day lives."

"I know it doesn't seem like it now, but we won't always be apart," Mike commented wistfully.

Sighing, Joanne said, "I know, but I'm so lonely when you're not with me. The chaplains at the Academy warned all of us against getting married, saying that the separation produces a hardship that often leads to divorce. They didn't mention the pain that comes with having fallen in love with someone who isn't around. They should have warned us about that."

"That's the drawback of this way of life, I guess," Mike responded with a shrug.

Joanne remarked thoughtfully, "True, but it's still the hardest thing I've ever done. I'm not exactly complaining, since my former career path made the same demands of me. It's just that I have experienced the stress of separation more now as the one who stays home and doesn't travel. It must really be tough on civilian significant others who don't have any firsthand knowledge of the Navy."

"Now that this phase of our training is out of the way, the time will pass quickly. In less than two years, I'll have finished my sea tour and be ready to spend some time on land. I was thinking of requesting assignment to the power school, or maybe a college ROTC program. The college location would give me time to work on another degree. What do you think?" Mike asked as they approached the car.

"Great idea, but don't forget the Pentagon. Lots of Academy grads work there. I might like to leave Fort Meade for a slot there myself one of these days," Joanne suggested.

Pointing the car toward Joanne's apartment, Mike said, "I'll check it out. It would be nice to live here for a while. Close to our parents and in the thick of activity. At least I'd keep informed of the events in the lives of the people I love and in the world. That's the problem with the sub service. I'm really out of touch when we're under way. The exchange of information is limited."

"The good thing is that the underways don't last forever. You will come home eventually. And when you do, I'll be waiting on the dock for you like in one of those old movies," Joanne commented with a little smile.

"And I'll rush off the boat, drop my duffel bag onto the walk, and pull you into my arms as the cheesy music swells in the background," Mike added to the little vignette.

"I'll make a note of it: Hire a string ensemble for the playing of cheesy music," Joanne said, pretending to write on an imaginary pad in her hand.

As their laughter faded, they drove in silence for a while and listened to the oldies-but-goodies station on the radio. Forcing themselves to think of nothing in particular, they were happy to be together and free from the demands of military life. The week would pass quickly, especially since Joanne would not also be on leave. They would spend their evenings together, giving Mike time to visit friends and family. Both knew that every minute would be special even if they did nothing at all.

Fortunately, Joanne's roommate was not at home when they returned. Tossing the bag he had left in the car earlier into Joanne's room, Mike made himself comfortable on the sofa while Joanne stowed the container of food her mother had given her in the refrigerator. Mike smiled as he watched her move around the kitchen and thought about the house in which they would one day live together. He knew that he was old-fashioned, but Mike liked the sight of a woman in the kitchen. But he was definitely not the kind of man who would deprive a wife of a career if she wanted one. After all, his mother had always juggled a successful career and domesticity so seamlessly that he had not realized her fatigue until he was ready to leave for college when she finally let down her guard and sat for a while. She had always been available when he needed her with cookies, milk, and advice. He wanted his children to have the same warm memories and hoped that Joanne would want the same.

"You know we haven't discussed the wedding. I thought you'd be overflowing with details by now," Mike commented as Joanne joined him on the sofa.

"I know," Joanne acknowledged, snuggling into the crook of his arm. "Actually, I don't have too much to share with you. Relocating from Florida and changing career paths set me back a bit. I had a few things to work out in my head that took precedence over anything else. I haven't made any real progress except for tentatively deciding on the menu for the reception."

"And what fabulous fare have you selected?" Mike asked, pulling her close. He needed to hear that their life, despite the Navy's control over it, was making forward progress.

Snuggling close, Joanne responded, "Melon balls with proscuitto for openers, followed by a salad of mixed greens with a vinaigrette dressing, baked salmon in a raspberry sauce, duchess potatoes, and green beans. For dessert, either baked Alaska, cherries jubilee, or bananas Foster."

"Wow! Sounds delicious and expensive," Mike commented, stroking her arm gently.

"It's not too bad. The officers' club on the Yard quoted us a really good price . . . much lower than other caterers," Joanne replied with a yawn.

"I've been thinking about our honeymoon trip," Mike said with a dreamy tone. "How does Hawaii sound to you?"

"Great! I've always wanted to play golf there," Joanne replied, thinking about the many tournaments she had watched.

"Then it's settled. We'll be married on the Yard, have the reception there, and then off to Hawaii we go. I think we've made a lot of progress. What's next?" Mike asked, not wanting the discussion of their future to end.

"I guess you're right," Joanne responded, stretching lazily. "Having the wedding at the Academy cuts out a lot of the running around. Let's see, I need to find a gown, order the invitations, and arrange for the carriage."

Mike's mind, lulled by the warmth of Joanne's body, did not register her last comment. Slowly, however, he shook his head and asked, "Carriage? What carriage? Don't you mean limo?"

"No, carriage," Joanne chuckled. "We'll ride through the Yard in a horse-drawn open carriage. I've wanted to do that ever since I saw a wedding at the Academy while we were plebes. A dark carriage with white horses, if possible. The bride looked so elegant stepping down from the carriage into the arms of her new husband as they entered Bancroft Hall. The sun was shining. It was a fairy tale come true."

Staring at Joanne, Mike demanded, "Won't all of our friends think we've flipped?"

"No," Joanne replied, "but I don't care if they do. It's our wedding, and I want a carriage. Anyone can have a limo. I want something different and memorable. I've already contacted a company, but I can't actually book it until we know the exact date. He's holding June twenty-fourth for us with the understanding that we might need to change it."

Settling into the sofa cushion again, Mike said, "A carriage. Humph. That's a new one. I like it. It'll definitely be something to share with our kids. Not many people ride in a carriage on their wedding day."

"I knew you would. It's unique and original. Actually, it's my favorite part of the wedding," Joanne replied.

They sat in silence for a while before Mike said, "Let's go boating tomorrow. The weather promises to be perfect. We can rent one in Annapolis."

"Okay, and fishing. I'd like to do both," Joanne said eagerly.

"Fine. We'll rent gear, too. And my folks are expecting us for dinner," Mike commented, happy that the weekend was shaping up so well.

"No problem. I love your mom's cooking. Let's spend every minute together this weekend. I have to work this week, you know," Joanne replied.

"I can always meet you for lunch," Mike suggested.

"True. I'm sure everyone in the office would love to meet you. They've heard so much about you that they probably feel like you're an old friend," Joanne chuckled, snuggling closer.

"I hope you haven't built me up too much," Mike commented, stroking her arm.

"No, not at all. I've told everyone that you're tall and handsome with a wonderful sense of humor and great personality. However, I've also told them about your many bad traits, too," Joanne replied with feigned seriousness in her voice.

"What bad traits? A woman's supposed to think that her fiancé's perfect," Mike demanded, twisting to study Joanne's smiling face.

"Oh, things like snoring, occasional soup-slurping. That kind of thing," Joanne laughed, kissing Mike softly on the chin.

"Oh, that. I can't argue with the truth," Mike chuckled.

Sitting quietly wrapped in each other's arms, Joanne and Mike did not speak for a few minutes. Only the sound of the beating of their hearts filled the space between them. Neither felt the need to speak now that they had completed the wedding plans, arranged the weekend, and set in motion Mike's visit to Joanne's office. Life was perfect without discourse.

"Where's your roommate? Shouldn't Gail have

come home by now?" Mike asked as he rose, stretched, and pulled Joanne to her feet.

Allowing him to lead her toward the bedroom, Joanne replied, "She left a note in the kitchen. She decided to fly to Connecticut to see her boyfriend. It's a good thing you're here or I'd be all alone this weekend."

"Wow, we have the apartment to ourselves. I like that. It's almost like being married," Mike responded, stopping in the hall to pull Joanne into his arms.

"I like it, too. This is my favorite part," Joanne sighed as she melted against his strong chest.

Stretching, the cat leaped from the bed as they entered the room. Uttering its usual nightly meow of disdain, it sauntered into the hall. Closing the door behind it, Joanne and Mike soon forgot about the sulking animal, the marriage plans, and the shortness of their time together. All that mattered was the here and now.

Chapter Nine

Autumn swiftly changed to winter with Joanne busy in her Intel work and Mike under way on the submarine. Communication between them was almost nonexistent. Although Joanne knew that he could not call or e-mail, she found herself listening for the phone to ring and frequently checking for a message. When neither happened, she would shrug and turn her attention to the routine of life.

Joanne's life had become a series of disjointed events held together by Mike's appearances. Her work at Intel had become part of her daily routine, neither exciting nor boring, simply an element of her life. She visited her parents on the weekend or took day trips with her roommate when the weather allowed. Despite a lonely ache, Joanne forced herself not to wait for Mike's return to enjoy her life. She missed him, but she had to live. Life was too short to put it on a shelf when he left to pick it up again upon his return. She hated the loneliness of his underways, but knew that the separation would not last forever.

A few months after Mike's departure, Joanne's chief called her into his office with news that ordinarily would have made her very happy. Under other circumstances, she would have been proud of the recognition that her work had received. She would have relished the opportunities that a transfer would bring. However, with Mike away, she could take little joy in it. She had hoped to make Washington her home for a while, but that would not happen. Living close to her parents had become very important to her now that her position in the family had changed to that of an adult child. To her dismay, Joanne had been reassigned.

Returning home that night, Joanne broke the news to her roommate, saying, "It looks like you'll have to find another new roomie."

"You're kidding! You're been reassigned, too," Gail wailed.

"Too? You mean that you're moving?" Joanne demanded, leaning against the kitchen wall while the cat rubbed against her shins.

"I just found out this morning. I'm headed for San Diego," Gail replied without looking up from the chicken dish she was preparing for their dinner.

"I beat ya. I'm going to Hawaii," Joanne stated with a little grin.

"I'll change with you. Hawaii! I'd love that assignment. The beach, the sun, the beach," Gail quipped.

"I can't deny that it's a prime assignment, but it's so far away from my folks and Mike. It's just that Mike and I had planned to honeymoon there. We'll just have to find a different place, I guess," Joanne remarked, leaning over to stroke the cat's ears.

"Have you told your parents?" Gail asked, smiling at the reluctant friendship that had developed between her roommate and her feline friend.

"Not yet. I'll tell them after dinner. They won't be too happy about it, but they'll understand. That's

Navy life for ya. Have you told your boyfriend?" Joanne asked, setting the table for two.

"Uh-huh," Gail replied with a grin. "The San Diego transfer works great for us. He's being reassigned there, too. We'll see more of each other than we do now. As a matter of fact, we're getting married as soon as we get settled. Nothing fancy. Just a little ceremony with the justice of the peace. This transfer's ideal for us. I'm sorry that it's not working out the same way for you and Mike."

"Congrats on the wedding! It'll work out for us one of these days, too," Joanne said with a touch of sadness in her voice.

"Have you been able to tell Mike?" Gail asked, placing their plates on the table. Both women had decided that, regardless of the demands of their jobs, they would always spend quality roommate time together at dinner. They felt that they needed something to give them focus.

"No. I sent him an e-mail, but it's anyone's guess when he'll receive it. I'll be in Hawaii by then. I leave in two weeks. I've already made plans for the movers," Joanne responded, diving into the delicious meal.

"Me too. Let's have as much fun as possible in the time we have left. Who knows when we'll see each other again?" Gail stated.

"I'm game, and I don't have anything else planned," Joanne said.

"Then let's use some leave, shop 'til we drop, see movies, catch exhibits at the museum, and do all the things we've put off for another day. It's our time now," Gail suggested, ticking off all the things that she had planned to do while in DC but had postponed.

"I need to spend time with my parents, too.

Hawaii's a long way from DC, and my mom doesn't like long flights. I don't know when she'll get up the courage to make the trip," Joanne said as they cleaned the kitchen.

"She'll change her mind with seeing you at the end of the journey," Gail commented.

"Eventually, but it might take her a while. The way things are with the Navy, I might leave Hawaii before she ever arrives," Joanne chuckled at the reality of their military life.

The ringing of Gail's cell phone put an end to their conversation. Suddenly missing her parents, Joanne grabbed her car keys and headed out. She knew that home would be wherever she hung her hat for a while, but she still missed the comforts of the stable life her parents' house had given her. For a few hours, she intended to return to the bosom of her family.

The Crawford house even at nine at night looked inviting with light streaming from all of the windows. As she pulled into the driveway, thoughts of her childhood flooded through Joanne's mind. She had made such wonderful memories in that house, the only home she had ever known. Now, because of the Navy, she could never spend enough time in the house of her childhood. She was so busy doing these days that she had little time for dreaming.

Dreaming in her father's sunroom had been one of Joanne's favorite pastimes. She loved to sit by the window with the sun warming her skin. When she was a little girl, she'd imagined life as a teenager with a driver's license, boyfriends, and parties. Her romantic side had always included that special someone in her reveries. He was always tall and handsome with a ready smile.

As she grew older, Joanne's thoughts had turned to college and the challenges of study and exploration that the Academy offered. When she dared to think past the glow of college days, Joanne had imagined herself as a successful officer, married with children and a house of her own. She never factored in the reality of constant relocations, sea tours, dashed dreams, and distant lovers. Reality had made itself an uninvited element in her life.

Joanne had said good-bye to her parents and family home for the first time when she left for college. Four years later, she had kissed them farewell when she traveled to Florida for flight school. In two weeks, she would leave them again. This time, her journey would take her to a state connected not by the interstate but by an ocean.

"Joanne!" her father exclaimed as he opened the front door. "What's wrong? Why are you here?"

"Nothing's wrong. I missed you, so I came over," Joanne replied, knowing that her father would not believe her.

"Okay, now what's up?" Angela Crawford asked over her husband's shoulder.

Standing in the living room in which she had made so many memories, Joanne sighed and said, "I've been reassigned to Hawaii. I'll leave in two weeks."

"Oh my!" her mother cried as her eyes filled with tears. "Not again."

Without taking his eyes from his daughter's sad face, Mr. Crawford said bravely, "She has to go where the Navy sends her. She's only a phone call away."

"Thanks, Daddy," Joanne whispered as she

melted against her father. "I knew I could count on you."

Squaring her shoulders, Angela Crawford said, "I know where we'll go for vacation this year. Hawaii, here we come. I've always wanted to visit, but the islands were too far away. Now, I have a reason to go."

Hugging her mother, Joanne stated, "Just think, Mommy, I'll be able to show you around the island like a native by the time you come to visit. I'll take leave, and we'll really do it up."

As Joanne joined her parents in the family room, she thought about the separation that was to come. For the first time since learning of the transfer, she was glad that she would not be leaving Mike in DC, too. She found it difficult enough to leave her parents and could only imagine the longing she would feel if she had to leave the man she loved in another state. Mike's assignment to the submarine service and his constant travel had saved her that heartache. Although Mike was stationed on the east coast, the reality of his service community meant that he was at sea as often as he was in port. An apartment for him was simply a place to stash his gear.

"I'll cook all your favorites for your last meal at home," Mrs. Crawford announced, serving her husband and daughter tall glasses of milk and cookies.

"That's what you did when I went away to college and to Florida. I'll get really fat if I have too many more transfers," Joanne chuckled, sipping the cold milk.

"You know that your mother has always opened and closed every major event in our lives with a big meal," Craig Crawford teased.

Smiling at her little family, Angela Crawford said, "Can you think of a better way to mark memorable events? I filled the freezer with prepackaged home-cooked meals before you were born. I've prepared special meals for holidays, birthdays, and transfers. I'll prepare something wonderful for your wedding, Joanne. That's who I am and the way I mark events."

"I'm not complaining," Mr. Crawford remarked proudly. "Other men go out to eat or order carry-out. I don't have to do that because my wife's the best chef I know."

Feeling warm and sad at the same time, Joanne added, "Well, Mom, I guess you'll be very busy two weeks from now."

"Two weeks? That's all? I'll start planning the menu tomorrow," Angela Crawford remarked.

For the next week, Joanne revisited all of her old favorite sites with Gail at her side. She crammed memories into her heart that would fill the lonely nights of separation from her family. Although she knew DC like the back of her hand, everything suddenly looked new and sparkling, as if wanting to give her a fond farewell. Joanne had been very homesick when she first arrived in Florida and knew that she would experience it again. However, this time she was better prepared for the separation and knew that she would survive the loneliness.

Joanne thought about Mike constantly and missed him more than she had ever thought possible. Knowing that he was doing his job and serving his country did not make the longing any less. She would have liked to see him before leaving or at least have been able to tell him of the transfer.

Turning off the computer in her father's study for the last time as her parents waited in the car for the trip to the airport, Joanne finally resigned herself to the fact that she would be securely ensconced in Hawaii before Mike would ever know that she had moved from DC. He had neither called nor responded to her e-mails. Joanne had always known that contact with a submarine would be difficult, but she had not realized the total feeling of disconnection until now.

The family chatted with a strained gaiety as they traveled the short distance to the airport. For her parents, forty-five minutes just was not enough time to say good-bye and to tell someone all the things she should know before leaving. For Joanne, they barely had time to squeeze in all their love for each other before arriving at the terminal.

"It seems like only yesterday that we tricked you into thinking that we were meeting you at your arrival. Instead, it was Mike who brought you home. Now, it's our turn to take you back," Mrs. Crawford said as they hugged Joanne good-bye again at the drop-off.

"I'll see you as soon as school closes, right? I'll take leave, and you can stay as long as you want. We'll have a great time," Joanne encouraged her parents as she bravely fought off tears.

"Nothing will keep us away," Mr. Crawford remarked, kissing his daughter.

"Take good care of my car. Sell it to the boy next door if you can. It's a good car and deserves a good home," Joanne instructed.

"He's probably waiting on the front step now. His dad wouldn't let him make us an offer until after you left," Mr. Crawford interjected, hugging Joanne under that watchful eye of airport security.

"I'd better go. Checking in takes forever these days. If Mike shows up on your doorstep, tell him where he can find me," Joanne said, giving her parents a last hug.

"We will. Good-bye, baby," Mrs. Crawford whispered as Joanne turned sharply and vanished into the terminal.

Looking at each other sadly, the Crawfords returned to the empty car. Their dearest daughter was off on an adventure that would take her far from home across an ocean to an island paradise that they would not be able to share with her. They missed her already and knew that Joanne was doubly sad at having to leave.

While Joanne headed toward a new assignment across the Pacific Ocean, Mike worked onboard the submarine somewhere under the Atlantic off the coast of the US. At first, although Mike missed Joanne, he was so busy and excited to be under way that he could put the pain of being away from her into a neat little compartment in his heart. He had so much work to do on the little underways that he mostly thought of Joanne as he lay exhausted on his berth just before falling into a deep sleep.

However, the long underway had proven to be different from the shorter ones that he knew. Mike was no less busy and exhausted, but routine had soon set in, giving him a chance to feel the loneliness that lay just under the surface. He wondered what Joanne was doing and was frustrated by the enforced silence. Mike knew that he would feel better if he could only hear her voice.

"We'll surface sometime tomorrow," the captain announced at officers' mess as he ran through a sheet of reminders. "Have your e-mails ready. It's been a long time. You'll want to contact your family and friends to let them know that you're okay."

The buzz around the table was loud and excited at the thought of communication with home. Even the experienced officers looked relieved that they would soon break silence. They had not communicated with their families since the underway began.

"Remind your men of the limitations. Keep 'em short, and no attachments," the captain continued.

As they left the mess, one of Mike's roommates commented, "It's about time. My girl has probably given up on me by now. I didn't think being under way would be like this, did you? Lack of communication is tough."

Mike replied, "I'm glad to know that I'm not the only one who hates the lack of contact. It's worse than I expected. I know Joanne will understand, but it's asking a lot of a woman to love a man she can't see or talk to."

"At least your girl is in the Navy, too. Mine's a civilian," Mike's roommate stated. "Joanne knew about military life before making her commitment. My girl tries to adjust to the separations, but she's having a hard time. All of her friends, who graduated two years ago also, are planning weddings for the summer, and we're still waiting. It's hard for her because they don't understand this life. They keep hinting that I'm not as serious about her as I should be. It's tough."

"Joanne's a real trouper about it, but she's had a hard time," Mike said, shaking his head. "Not making it through flight training was tough on her. I think, all things considered, that she's adjusted well. Still, I wish I could have shared more of it with her. I was under way when she relocated from Florida to Naval Intelligence Headquarters at Fort Meade, MD.

For all I know, she's not in DC now. We've been out of communication for so long that she might have transferred by now. Worse, she might have sent me a 'Dear John' e-mail and I wouldn't even know it."

"Nah, she wouldn't do that," his roommate replied with a worried chuckle. "At least, I hope she wouldn't. Darn, don't make me think things like that. I can stand a lot, but one of those e-mails would be too much."

"Don't worry. They wouldn't do that," Mike responded, hoping that his quip would not become reality.

Mike had no way of knowing that, at that moment, Joanne was standing in her new apartment on Oahu. The view was spectacular. The mixture of ocean breezes and ethnic cooking was tantalizing. She would have indeed felt that she had set foot in paradise if Mike had been at her side.

Rather than deal with the unpacking and positioning of furniture, Joanne sprawled on the sofa in front of the window and quickly fell asleep. She was jet-lagged from the long flight and sleep deprivation. Even the loneliness she felt for home and the longing she battled for Mike could not keep her awake.

The next morning, after spending hours putting her apartment in order, Joanne ventured into the streets of her new home. Immediately, she was entranced by the fragrances from the shops, the feel of the breezes, and the caress of the sun on her skin. Wearing only a light sweater and a pair of capri pants, she sauntered through the shopping area and wandered down the main street, looking into shop windows that displayed colorful summer clothing.

Purchasing an agi sandwich and a bottle of tea, Joanne slipped off her shoes and walked onto the beach. Unlike the lonely Atlantic Ocean beaches, this one teemed with people, playing volleyball and lounging in the Hawaiian sun. Strolling along the warm sand, Joanne munched her sandwich and breathed deeply of the salty breeze. She would have to return to the confinement of an office soon enough. For the moment, she would enjoy her leisure and the island.

Playing tourist, Joanne stopped at the Pearl Harbor monument. Taking the short ferry ride to the fallen ships, she thought of Mike and their trip to Fort Sumter. It seemed as if an eternity had passed since the days of South Carolina and Florida. She missed him terribly.

Standing on the walk overlooking the sunken *Arizona,* Joanne sighed and wiped a tear from her lashes. So many had died and lay entombed at the bottom of the sea. So many more had struggled to make a life without a beloved husband, son, or brother. Military life and wartime . . . realities that had seemed so alien until Joanne joined the navy.

As the respectful silence washed over her, Joanne once again understood her reason for choosing a career in the military. She needed to serve the country that had endured despite attacks, had thrived during depressions, and had risen above a history of discrimination to offer the potential for a promising future to its citizens. Despite setbacks for women and blacks, Joanne could see progress. She hoped that her efforts as a navy officer would continue to place the struggles and successes of women and blacks in the front of people's minds.

Even if she had to fight insurmountable obstacles, she would do her part to leave an enduring legacy.

Regardless of her hard work and sacrifice of a military career, Joanne was dedicated to doing her part, and so was Mike. They both knew that they would face racial and, in Joanne's case, gender biases, yet they had decided to try to make a difference. Having been a brigade officer while a midshipman had been historic in that primarily male bastion. Being an officer had added another dimension to her efforts. She had been forced to deal with racial and gender issues that arose among the members of the brigade.

One day, she would look back on the struggle and smile with the satisfaction of knowing that she had tried to make a difference. For the moment, Joanne was content to wander the streets of Oahu and take in the sights. The view of Diamond Head, the blue of the ocean and sky, and the fabulous colors filled her with an indescribably sense of peace tinged with a unique melancholy. The assignment in Hawaii would be good for her. The island breezes would do much to blow away her sadness. The stunning vistas would feed her soul. If only Mike had known where to find her, Joanne would have been content.

Chapter Ten

Like any other job, the Intel center suffered from Monday-morning blahs. Joanne reported to duty with the expectation that working in Hawaii would be different from working in DC. She had thought that the magical surroundings would fill people with an energy unfelt in other parts of the country. Instead, she encountered the same sleepy people who would rather be doing anything other than wearing uniforms that restricted movement, shoes that pinched their feet, and belts that cinched their waists. The most noticeable difference was the warm, inviting sun streaming through the windows, calling them to surf and sand rather than sitting at their desks, rooting through reams of paper, and preparing yet another report.

Joanne's small cubicle was next to that of a young woman who had graduated from the Navy ROTC program: Sylvia was engaged to a navy officer with whom she had gone to college and who was stationed aboard a carrier. She offered coping suggestions that Joanne readily added to her arsenal. Joanne was happy to incorporate anything that would make her miss Mike less.

Joanne soon discovered that most people in that office had a friend or loved one stationed far away, serving the country and the world. Everyone seemed to listen to the radio that played in the background while bravely going about their jobs with smiles and guarded laughter. Their lives continued as they waited to be reunited with the person they loved.

The office environment suited Joanne's mood perfectly. Everyone appeared to enjoy the work and the companionship. They lunched together, enjoyed the beach together, and supported each other in difficult times. More than simply the assignment held them together. Their common bond was loneliness and ever-present worry. Joanne was content despite missing Mike and her family.

The days passed with Joanne slipping into the routine without difficulty. She walked to work every day even in the rain for the exercise and the joy of being in Hawaii. The sunshine on her shoulders made Mike's continued silence somewhat more bearable. The splendor of Hawaii's blue sky helped to life her spirits. The richness of Hawaii's colors warmed the cold spot in her heart left vacant by the distance that separated her from Mike.

When they returned from lunch one day, the unusual stillness in the office shocked Joanne and Sylvia into silence. In the hour that they had been away, the mood had changed from lighthearted to heavy and ominous. Tossing her cover and purse onto her desk, Joanne walked toward the gathered group standing by the director's office. From the stiff shoulders and brave expressions, Joanne could tell that something very serious had occurred.

Joining the silent group, Joanne whispered, "What happened?"

"A sub's lost," one of the men replied without taking his eyes from the computer screen that flashed the news.

"Which one?" Joanne breathed with difficulty, trying to quiet the pounding in her chest and the tightening of her throat.

"We don't know yet. We're waiting for the details," the man replied, trying to smile to ease Joanne's worry.

"I'm sure it's not Mike's," Sylvia said softly. "The fleet has hundreds of subs. It can't be his."

Joanne could only nod. Her throat was too tight, too constricted to allow her to speak. A sub was missing. Mike was an ensign on a submarine somewhere far away. Joanne had not heard from him in ages. Mike might be missing. The reality of the equation was too horrible to face.

The silence and the accompanying sense of impending disaster was so huge that Joanne felt as if it would squash her and suck the life from her body. Her shoulders rounded at the weight as she stood with the others. Her heart pounded and her head ached. A submarine and its crew were lost. Mike was on a submarine. Mike might be lost. She might not see him again. The refrain repeated in her head, filling her entire body with an intense sickness that threatened to buckle her knees.

Joanne told herself that she should be brave. She was navy. The Academy had prepared her to be an officer, to command, to take orders without question. Her friends and classmates had scattered over the globe. Many were facing danger. Many more would soon face the enemy. She knew that their names might appear on one of the bulletins that passed as a courtesy through the Intel office. She knew the reality of military life. The chaplains had prepared them to deal with loss in the line of duty.

However, Mike was on a submarine far from the action in the Middle East. He had told her that nothing could happen to him. He had said that he was safer underwater on a submarine doing routine maneuvers than she was crossing a busy Oahu street. Mike had laughed at her fear, saying that she was being irrational in her concerns.

And Joanne had believed him. But nothing had prepared her for the possibility that he might die while on duty. The reality surrounded her in its cold, clammy grip and tried to pull her apart. Joanne would not allow herself to speculate on life without him. Mike could not be in harm's way. It was not possible. Mike would not lie to her.

Standing silently with the others, Joanne struggled to maintain her composure. Not even the reassuring pressure of Sylvia's hand on her shoulder could make her feel better. She was a woman of action. She had led the brigade and graduated at the top of her class. She had managed her life perfectly. Her career, despite a blip on the screen, was now on a steady course. Joanne was a take-charge kind of person. Life could not possibly have thrown her this curve.

But it had. In a matter of minutes, news had entered the security of her life and shattered it forever. She was just like all the other people in that room who listed for information and pretended to live a normal life. She was military, and she was vulnerable. She was a woman in love with a man whose career choice might have placed him in danger. If not now, then it could one day. She might escape reality this time, but it would try to strike her down again.

Slowly, sensation started to return. Joanne's body

no longer seemed to hover over the room, looking down on itself. She could feel her fingers and toes again. She squared her shoulders to adjust the weight that had rounded them from her perfect posture. She was Navy. Mike was Navy. They were ready for all conditions and circumstances.

Joanne was angry. The initial fear and dread had faded, leaving behind anger so intense that she could hardly control the hot tears that threatened to flow down her cheeks. She had initially been too shocked to cry, but the overwhelming anger had freed her. Mike had promised her that he would be safe. He had lied, and Joanne was furious.

Mike had selected a service community that carried intrinsic dangers and long separations. He had chosen to live on a submarine, a relatively small vessel propelled by nuclear power. The submarines carried men under the sea to staggering depths. The men lived elbow-to-elbow in a space so small that most people would become claustrophobic simply thinking about it. Yet they chose to work and live in those conditions. And Mike was one of them.

Mike had sampled the life of the submariner as a midshipman during a required summer cruise. He had lived it and still selected that life. He had chosen a life that put him in danger and subjected her to pain beyond belief. Anger was her only choice for survival . . . the only thing Joanne could control.

"Are you okay?" Sylvia asked, seeing the rigidity of Joanne's shoulders.

"Yeah. I'm fine. I'm so angry I could spit," Joanne replied through clenched teeth.

"I can understand that," Sylvia replied gently.

"I feel betrayed and abandoned. Mike lied to me. He chose this life. He decided to do this to us. No one made him do it. It was his choice. I'm so angry that if he walked in that door at this minute, I'd smack him silly," Joanne said as she walked toward her desk with Sylvia beside her.

"It might not be his sub, you know," Sylvia counseled carefully.

"It doesn't matter," Joanne replied firmly. "Even if it's not his, this has burst my bubble of security. I can't deny to myself any longer that Mike might get killed. I allowed him to convince me that submarines were safer than flight or surface. I know I'm sounding hypocritical since I started my career in flight school, but I didn't enter it thinking that life would be rosy. I acknowledged the danger. I didn't promise my parents or Mike that I'd be safe and out of harm's way. I knew the reality of my life as a pilot. I loved Mike so much that I allowed him to sweet-talk me into oblivion. I didn't let myself think the same way about him. Everyone knows that planes crash and ships sink, but no one ever hears about a US sub being in trouble. It's only Russian subs that sink. Mike would be safe as long as he didn't transfer to the Russian navy."

"Are you angry with Mike or yourself?" Sylvia asked softly.

Shaking her head sadly, Joanne replied, "Both . . . equally. I convinced myself that he'd be safe so that I wouldn't have to worry about him and myself. After leaving flight school, I started thinking that we'd both be okay. Now, this has forced me to see the reality. No sea tour is safe. I'm in love with a man who might not return to me. My competition isn't another woman; it's the sea. I don't know how to prepare myself for this. I can't fight the sea. I can't scratch out her eyes or pull out plugs of her hair. She's bigger than I am. Her attraction has been luring men to their deaths for ages. This is a no-win sit-

uation for me. If I insist that Mike leave the sub community, I'm depriving him of his dream. If he stays,
I'll live in terror. This sucks!"

Smiling sympathetically at Joanne, Sylvia said, "I
felt the same way when my boyfriend left. I can't say
that I'm used to the separation or the constant
worry, but my heart doesn't stop every time the
news comes on television or we get one of these
bulletins."

"How do you do it?" Joanne asked, shaking her
head at the hopelessness that consumed her heart.

"I've hardened. I love him, but I can't give up living because my boyfriend has chosen this career
path. I still worry, but I have to live, too. My life and
career are as important as his. I can't allow his
choice to overpower my own. I guess I've learned to
maintain my individuality. I'm me regardless of
whatever happens to him. We're together but separate," Sylvia shrugged.

"I think I worry more about Mike than I ever did
about myself. I always felt in control while flying except for the airsickness. I'm not in control of anything now. He's out of reach, out of contact, and
out of my control."

"You'll find that work will help, too. It'll keep you
focused on something other than Mike. You can
make yourself crazy worrying about him. Trust me.
The first time something like this happens is the
worst," Sylvia said as she turned toward her desk.

"I hope you're right. I'm ready for a distraction.
This is a nightmare," Joanne stated, watching the
others return to their work. Each of the women
smiled sadly at her as she walked past, and the men
averted their eyes in sympathy.

Joanne spent the rest of the afternoon caught in
the middle between work and worry. No new bul-

letins or updates arrived. No one knew the identity or the location of the downed submarine. No one even knew the reason for the sub's failure or the status of the crew. She could only wait, worry, and pray.

Joanne put on the bravest front she could. She squared her shoulders and went about her work with a clear and distinct sense of purpose. Only the sadness in her eyes and the occasional slump of her shoulders belied the façade.

The buzzing of the phone startled Joanne from her work in the late afternoon. A familiar but sad voice met her ear. Despite the time difference, her parents had heard the news on the radio and wanted to share the worry with her.

"Hi, baby girl," Mr. Crawford said in his usual greeting. "Have you heard anything about Mike?"

"No. Nothing. No news at all about the sub. Silence is tight for obvious reasons," Joanne said, trying to sound braver than she felt.

"Mom and I know Mike's okay. I'm sure it's not his sub."

"We'll keep saying that until it's true, Daddy," Joanne replied, trying not to dissolve into tears.

"Do you think we should phone Mike's parents? Do you think they've heard anything?" Joanne's mom asked from the extension.

Bravely, Joanne said, "If you'd like, but they won't know anything you don't. The wire service has only the information the Navy has released. If I haven't learned anything in this office, they don't know anything either."

"The Navy'll identify the missing submarine soon," Mrs. Crawford commented and added, "Someone has to communicate with the families.

It's not fair for all of the families of all the sub-mariners to worry like this."

"The Navy works in its own time, Mom, but let's hope we'll hear something soon. I'll call as soon as I hear anything," Joanne replied.

"Anytime . . . day or night. If it's Mike's sub, don't go through this alone," Mr. Crawford advised sadly.

"I won't. Thanks for calling," Joanne replied as she tried to return to her work.

For a long while, Joanne just stared at the padded wall of her cubicle. She sat in a room surrounded by people, yet she felt completely alone. Thoughts of Mike flooded her mind. She remembered their first days together at the Academy, the day they first realized that they loved each other, and their graduation day. Joanne reflected on the first time they made love and the stroll through the streets of Charleston. She smelled the fragrance of his skin and hair and felt the touch of his hands on hers. Joanne saw him in her apartment and in his. She touched his face and pulled him close. She ran her fingers over the flatness of his stomach and smiled into his loving eyes. She felt the sweetness of his kisses and heard his laughter.

Joanne sat alone and remembered.

The afternoon passed without further information and without laughter. After two calls from her parents and one to Mike's family, Joanne reluctantly left the office after the director turned off his light and closed the door. There was nothing more she could do. Until Mike called or the Navy released the name of the downed submarine, she could only pray that Mike was safe and that the crew would be rescued.

* * *

"Let's have dinner together," Sylvia suggested as she and Joanne stepped into the warm early evening air.

"I'm not very good company," Joanne replied, shaking her head.

"I understand. You shouldn't be alone. Not tonight," Sylvia responded, hooking her arm through Joanne's.

"And tomorrow night? And the night after that? As long as Mike's in the submarine service, I'll have many nights of waiting and worrying. This accident destroyed my false comfort level," Joanne stated, smiling at her friend.

"I know all too well," Sylvia replied. "Let's go out to eat anyway."

"All right. You're a glutton for punishment," Joanne chuckled.

The women strolled down the street to one of their favorite lunch spots that also offered a fantastic dinner menu. To avoid the wait, they sat at the outside bar overlooking the water that lapped around the wide wharf. Seabirds soared overhead and dove skillfully into the waves for their dinner. The last of the beachgoers straggled back to their homes and hotels. Boats of every description dotted the horizon with their sails billowing in the wind. It was a beautiful sight, spoiled only by Joanne's deep sadness.

While discussing Sylvia's wedding plans and sharing family anecdotes, Joanne caught snatches of conversation from the other diners. Every discussion contained a reference to the lost submarine, causing Joanne's emotions to roller-coaster between the joy of planning for the future and fear of possibly not having one with Mike. The presence of the navy was too real in Oahu, where the legacy of the attack on Pearl Harbor during World War II was more than a history item.

To distract her attention, Sylvia asked, "Tell me about golf. I've always wanted to play but haven't tried it yet. I usually just run for exercise. Gotta keep in shape for the physical readiness test, you know."

"Thanks for trying to cheer me up. You're a good friend," Joanne smiled. "Do you really want to hear this?"

"Yeah. Really. I bought golf shoes on sale a few weeks ago but haven't made progress past that," Sylvia replied, sipping a specialty frothy beverage.

Sighing, Joanne began, "Well, golf's more athletic than most people realize. It requires coordination of the upper and lower body, plus a sense of balance. However, anyone can practice and learn these skills. People get frustrated because they can't hit the ball like Tiger Woods as soon as they pick up the club. They don't realize that he's a natural athlete who practices constantly. If you've ever played tennis or softball, you won't have any trouble adjusting to golf. If you haven't, you'll have to practice a bit more, but you can still learn the game. I love it and play every chance I get. Now that I'm living here, I play every weekend."

"I was the captain of the women's softball team in college, if that counts for anything. Can I come with you this weekend?" Sylvia asked.

"Sure, I'd love to have the company. I'm not an instructor, but I can set you up with the basics. You might want to take lessons if you really like it," Joanne agreed. "You can rent clubs at the course. They won't be the perfect match for you, but you'll find out if you like the game without investing money in your own set. But let me warn you that this game is addictive. If you like it, you'll want clubs, a bag, a hat, and more clubs every time a manufacturer brings out new ones."

"I'm game. It's a sin to live in this paradise and not spend every minute outside. Do you hike? I'm going with a group from work next Saturday. Would you like to come?" Sylvia asked while munching a delicious chicken with pineapple kabob.

"I saw the flyer. Yeah, I'll go. It should be fun. At any rate, it'll keep my mind off Mike," Joanne replied with a weary smile.

Joanne and Sylvia ate in silence for a while, only punctuating it with comments about the food, restaurant, and view. When they had paid their tab, they left just as someone switched on the television at the far end of the bar. The headline blazed across the screen as the door closed behind them. Mike's submarine, the *Montpelier*, lay crippled somewhere under the Atlantic Ocean.

While Joanne walked to her apartment after spending the evening with Sylvia, Mike made arrangements either to float the submarine or evacuate it. Although the crew had practiced the lifesaving techniques against the possibility of needing them, this time the drill was for real and very frightening. As an officer, he had a job to set an example for his men, to remain calm in the face of danger, to follow the captain's orders precisely, and to respond to the ever-changing conditions seamlessly. However, regimentation and training did not eliminate the fear.

"Is everyone ready? The captain says we'll try to float her in five minutes," Mike commented to the sergeant major at this side.

"We're ready, sir," the seasoned veteran of the sub service replied.

"We have our supply of hoods if that doesn't work?" Mike asked, trying to sound braver than he felt.

"Yes, sir. The men are ready," the sergeant major replied.

"The captain wants to see me. I'll return as soon as I can. Keep the men together on task and calm," Mike instructed, showing a calm demeanor he did not feel.

"Yes, sir," came the crisp reply. Both men knew that each one was playing the required role that training made second nature.

Walking down the quiet, narrow corridor that lead to the officers' mess, Mike briefly thought of Joanne. He knew that having her on his mind was the worst thing he could do at the moment, but the vision of her face floated before him without his bidding. He had to keep his mind clear for orders and his emotions under control. Thinking of Joanne only distracted him from the work at hand.

However, Mike could not put aside the vision of her smiling eyes and inviting lips. He could feel her hand in his as he made his way down the corridor by the glow of the emergency lights. He could smell her skin and perfume above the sweat of nervous men. He could hear her voice over the sound of men scurrying to complete the last-minute tasks necessary to a successful emergency surfacing.

Mike missed Joanne and knew that he might never see her again. If they could not float the sub, an emergency evacuation using a mini sub or the swimming hoods would be necessary. Any maneuver that placed men in contact with the freezing temperature of the ocean could be fatal. The Navy seldom lost submariners, but there had been fatalities in the past. The danger was real.

The silence on the sub frightened him the most. The men talked in whispers as if they wanted nothing, not even the sound of their own voices, to interfere with the work that lay ahead. They had practiced the emergency maneuver countless number of times, but they had always known that it was a drill. They had prepared for the worst and known that it would never happen. But it had.

They'd had faith in their submarine. The reactor had just been serviced. The computer had been updated. Nothing could have gone wrong, but it did. A steam pipe had developed a leak so severe that they could not fix it, resulting in the need to shut down power to all but the most essential life support features of the sub. At the time, they had not realized that their communications equipment had suffered from the spray of hot water that had filled the compartments. Without communication, they would have to surface and wait for orders. If they could not fill the ballasts, the submarine and her crew would have to wait to be rescued from the ocean's depths. Command knew their coordinates. It was just a matter of time . . . if all went well.

The tension in the officers' mess was palpable. Rather than standing with cups of steaming coffee in their hands, the men carried clipboards of instructions. Their faces wore expressions of worry and concern. They trusted their submarine and their captain. They hoped that it would be enough.

"Ensign?" Mike's department chair greeted him.

"All's ready, sir," Mike replied crisply.

"Stay for a bit," Mike's superior officer instructed.

Standing quietly to the side with the other junior officers, Mike tried not to allow the memory of days with Joanne to enter his mind. The here and now would dictate his future with her. If they could not float the sub, they would have to undertake more drastic and dangerous measures. Only time would tell their fate.

Mike listened carefully as the captain laid out the emergency plans for the last time. Each task needed to be executed in the proper sequence for the good of the submarine and the safety of the men. Nothing could be done out of step if they were to succeed. Their lives depended on the faithful execution of their training.

While the clock in the officers' mess slowly ticked away the minutes until the emergency plans became practice, Joanne struggled from her sleepless bed to face another day of worry. The late news had provided the identity of the missing submarine. The *Montpelier*, Mike's sub, was out of commission somewhere. Although she did not know the details, Joanne could envision the sub lying helpless and the men wondering about their fate. She knew the hours of practice, testing, and drills that submariners underwent to enable them to live that life. She had listened to Mike's stories of the arduous training that would not only make him an officer but eventually save his life. He had told her about the feeling of adventure that he had experienced as a midshipman when the submarine on which he sailed had popped to the surface during a drill. Joanne knew that he had been well prepared for the worst, but she still worried . . . and waited.

Turning on the television while she pulled on her uniform, Joanne listened for any new information about the submarine and Mike. Instead of hearing anything encouraging, she only heard a replay of the previous evening's special report. By now, the newscasters had lost interest. For them, the *Montpelier* was old news. To her, it was her only connection with the man she loved.

Chapter Eleven

Walking to her office, Joanne tried to capture the Hawaiian sunshine and warm her spirits. She stopped at her favorite shop but ignored the newspaper that carried the alarming headline. Purchasing her usual cup of latte, she chatted briefly with the owner. Fortunately, he did not know that her fiancé was onboard the crippled submarine. The shop owner had noticed the dark circles around her eyes but had said nothing, probably thinking that she was working too hard. He did not know that her heart was breaking and her nerves were raw. Sleep was the last thing on her mind. In fact, Joanne had begun to wonder if she would ever again have a good night's sleep, the kind that children enjoy, knowing that their parents look after and protect them.

"Any news?" Joanne asked Sylvia as she tossed her purse into the bottom drawer of her desk.

"The chief's expecting something shortly. How are you?" Sylvia inquired, studying her friend's face.

"Holding up," Joanne replied with a little smile, and added, "I never at any time in my life thought that I would spend every waking minute waiting for news about the man I love. While I was at the Academy, I was so involved in studies and the excitement of the fleet that I didn't give the reality of life a thought. This is the toughest thing I've ever had to do."

"Folks, gather around, please." The chief's summons interrupted their conversation.

Breathing deeply, Joanne squared her shoulders and joined the other members of the staff in a semicircle around their boss. The silence in the room was almost overwhelming. Although Joanne was the only one who had acknowledged having a personal connection to the ailing submarine, they all shared the worry for those in peril on or under the sea. One day, a sea tour might lead them into dangerous waters, too.

Clearing his throat, the chief began, "First, Joanne, our thoughts and prayers are with you and your fiancé. These are very difficult times for all of us when a ship and her crew are in danger, and even more so for him. Second, we have the latest status report on the *Montpelier* and her crew. The sub is at a depth that will not allow emergency surfacing. The captain will need to fill secondary ballast tanks to bring her up before he can begin the emergency measure. The crew has been fully trained and readied for all conditions. The captain is a man of considerable experience. The men are in very capable hands. I'll keep you informed as the information crosses my desk. Any questions? If not, you're dismissed. Joanne, I'd like to see you in my office for a minute."

As Joanne entered the sterile office with its government-gray walls and utilitarian vinyl floor, the chief closed the door behind her. Although a seasoned officer, he was always uncomfortable with delicate situations like this one, especially when he might have to deal with a woman's tears.

He did not consider himself a chauvinist, but he had been much more at ease dealing with un-nerving situations when he had commanded only men. Women's tears made him feel helpless, not a desirable trait in an officer of his rank.

"Take a seat, Joanne," the chief instructed, pre-ferring the informality of the new Navy to the rigid standing at attention of the old one. "I know this is tough on you. If you need to take leave, I'll under-stand."

"Thank you, sir, but I'd rather be here. I don't trust television coverage. Besides, I have a job to do. Mike would want it that way. We're Navy, sir," Jo-anne replied, swallowing hard.

"Good." The chief smiled with relief that the tears had not fallen. "Have you been in touch with his parents?"

"Yes, sir. They don't understand the extent of the danger although they suspect that it's greater than the Navy contact led them to believe. It's difficult consoling them from a distance, but I'm doing my best," Joanne replied, squaring her shoulders under the heavy burden.

"Tell them that they're in our prayers, also. These are trying times for all of us. My son is also an en-sign on that submarine. I'd appreciate it if you wouldn't share that with the others just yet. These are difficult times for his mother and me," the chief commented stoically as he turned his attention to the papers on his desk.

Feeling tears burning behind her lids, Joanne rose and said, "I won't, sir. Thank you, sir. If there's anything . . ."

"I'll be sure to call on you," the chief interrupted. "You're dismissed."

"Let's get some air," Sylvia suggested, seeing the strain on Joanne's face.

Nodding, Joanne followed her friend into the warmth of the Hawaiian morning. The light blue sky with only the puffiest of clouds was in sharp contrast to the heaviness of Joanne's heart. Children on the way to school rushed past them without noticing the day that they took for granted. Until now, Joanne had been almost as oblivious, the splendor of the constant warmth having become an expected part of her life. Having Mike in danger had sharpened her senses and made her more aware of every nuance of life.

"It seems as if I've lived here forever. I was so homesick when I first arrived, but now I can't imagine living anywhere else, although I know another move is always in the works. This is a beautiful island," Joanne commented as they meandered along the sidewalk past the shopkeepers who were just opening their doors.

"I love it, too," Sylvia said and added, "My tour's almost up. I've asked to remain. I can't think of any place that would compare to Hawaii."

"So much history and beauty. To think that only a few decades ago, an enemy tried to destroy this island paradise. Life's full of unexpected turns," Joanne commented, buying a tiny orchid for her desk.

"The island survived, and so will you," Sylvia stated gently. "Mike will be okay. He's with a good captain and on a great sub. The crew's received many decorations for outstanding performance in combat situations. He'll come home."

"I hope you're right. I keep telling myself that he'll make it, but the risk is great," Joanne sighed.

"Keep sending him positive thoughts," Sylvia suggested. "He'll need all the energy he can muster for this ordeal."

"If constantly thinking about him can save his life, Mike has all my thoughts and prayers," Joanne replied, allowing the Hawaiian breeze to fill her soul.

Joanne and Sylvia returned to the office in silence. Although Joanne did not really feel any more at ease, she relished having someone with whom to share her thoughts, even the unspoken ones. She hoped that Sylvia would not have to transfer out. Good friends were hard to find, and she needed a good friend now more than ever.

Mike, surrounded by people in whose hands his life rested, had needs, too. He needed to breathe fresh air again, to leave the confinement of the ailing submarine, and to hold Joanne in his arms. He knew that her job in Intel had provided her with information on the plight of the *Montpelier*'s crew. He thought that she would find comfort in her parents' support, and he did not worry about her. Mike did not know that she was more than a continent away from them.

The captain's voice boomed over the sub's internal communications system, interrupting his thoughts and saying, "Man your stations, men."

Quickly leaving the officers' mess for his post in the aft of the submarine, Mike barely saw the strained expressions on the faces of the crew and fellow officers. He did not need to see his reflection in their eyes, knowing that he wore the same deep circles and heavy lines. He was young, but this experience had added years to his soul. Fatigue, worry, and dread had become his constant companions.

"All men accounted for, sir," Mike reported to his department chair.

"This is it, Shepherd. We'll know in a few minutes if we'll float or swim," the lieutenant stated. His face was also heavily lined with worry. It was one thing to practice lifesaving drills and another to need to enact one.

Before Mike could reply, he felt and heard water moving through the ballasts. At first, nothing happened as the compartments slowly filled. Then, almost imperceptibly, he felt pressure on the soles of his feet and a tremulous upward motion. Peering at the gauges, he watched the needle move by fractional increments, indicating that the submarine was, indeed, rising against the pressure of the ocean. Yet the question remained about the safety of the sub and depth of the water. Only time would tell.

His heart raced. His skin tingled. His eyes scanned the dials. His mind prayed.

Mike knew that this was only the first step to safety. If it did not succeed, he and the rest of the crew would have to follow more drastic measures. Mike hoped that safety, home, and Joanne would soon be within his grasp. Until he heard the all's clear from his captain, Mike would not be able to take comfort in the possibility of being safe. He needed assurances that, as yet, had not come. His men needed them, too, as they went about their work in silence as deep as the sea itself.

At that moment, Mike thought about the many ships that were buried in the depths of the sea. Ocean liners, sailing vessels, and submarines alike had found eternal rest at the bottom of the sea.

The melody of "Eternal Father, Strong to Save," the
navy hymn, played continuously in his mind, giving
him comfort and hope.

Despite the hours of waiting and the slow ascent
that lay ahead, Mike knew that he would see Joanne
again . . . someday.

The long hours without further news passed
slowly for Joanne. She knew that rescuing the submarine and her crew would be a lengthy process
fraught with danger at every step. The ballasts
might not fill. The pressure from the depth of the
sea on the submarine's shell might be too great to
overcome. The men might have to expose themselves to the chilling water, increasing the risk and
chance for fatalities. Anything could happen.

Yet Joanne was anxious for any tidbit that the
navy might decide to release. She dreaded the calls
to and from her parents and Mike's, knowing that
she had nothing to tell them that would allay their
fears. Her own were so great that she could not
think of a plausible lie to ease their worry.

The silence of her apartment seemed especially
foreboding that evening after a day spent at the office. Joanne usually enjoyed returning to the peace-
fulness of her home after being in the company of
other people all day. She liked being alone or with
only Mike at her side. She enjoyed solitude. Now,
however, she almost decided to go to a movie so
that she would not have to be alone. She did not
want to have time on her hands to think and worry.
She was slowly driving herself sick with thinking
about Mike and the future they might never enjoy.

Since the first news of the submarine accident,
Joanne had taken to keeping a photo of Mike in

front of her as often as possible. She did not need it to remember his expressions or the sparkle of his eyes, but she felt closer to him when she could see the smiling face in his Academy senior yearbook photo. Somehow, he did not seem so far away when Joanne could almost kiss his lips and hear his voice.

Joanne remembered the day of the photo session. They had been first-semester seniors with the end of their tenure at the Academy still months away. Yet they had been as excited as if they were ready to receive their diplomas that day. As usual, the photo session had occurred by company, with theirs being among the last. As a company officer, Joanne had sat for those photographs separately and requested the second session with her friends. Mike had been one of them, of course. She wanted the yearbook informal photo to capture their relationship for all posterity. At the time, however, neither of them had known the importance of that day and the shared memories. Neither had spoken of their emotions for each other. They had yet to share the love that had built over the years at the Academy but remained unspoken until their senior year, second semester.

Joanne had felt Mike's eyes on her face as she had sat for her photograph. Her dress white uniform had sparkled from recent cleaning. She had smiled happily, knowing that the end was near. All of the hard work would pay off in May. She only had to finish two semesters of work, pass two physical readiness tests, and complete reams of battalion paperwork.

Looking at his photo as she ate a bowl of tasteless, canned chicken-noodle soup, Joanne remembered that Mike had looked especially handsome that day. He had lost a little weight that summer and added

a healthy glow to this skin from months on the
water. The angles of his cheekbones accentuated
the laughter in his eyes. He could see the end of
the lessons and the drudgery of the Academy, too.
Soon he would live a regular life in the fleet, away
from pettiness and juvenile squabbles.

Now, they were free of the Academy's restrictions
and knee-deep in life. They saw less of each other
than while they were at school. They worried more
about each other. True, they no longer lived under
the watchful eye of the honor code and overly am-
bitious roommates who would try to turn even the
tiniest glance between man and woman into an in-
fraction. Instead, one of them lived in danger of
death and leaving the other behind to live in loneliness. At that moment, Joanne almost wished for
the return to the Academy life.

Clearing away the remains of her meager dinner,
Joanne reached for the cordless telephone, picked
it up, and then returned it to the charger. The timing was not right to phone her parents. Calling
them now would only make them think the worst.
Joanne knew that it might be days before she would
know anything about Mike's safety. She was lonely,
but she would not disturb Sylvia's evening either.
Her friend needed a chance to deal with her own
problems and wedding arrangements. After all, she
and her fiancé were also navy officers.

Thinking that a little mindless television-viewing
would make her sleepy, Joanne settled into her favorite chair. Switching on the set, she flipped
through the commercials to find one of her regular
shows. Unfortunately, rather than the usual pro-
gramming, she found a special on the plight of
Mike's submarine, complete with information on the

building of the structure, the number of crewmen and officers, and the safety features of the vessel.

Joanne was on the verge of turning off the set when photos of the crew began to fill the screen. An industrious reporter had acquired shots of all of them from the captain to the lowest-ranking enlisted man. Glued to the set, Joanne watched as Mike's smiling Academy photo slowly faded from view. Her heart broke as it vanished. She almost felt as if contact with him had broken once again. An overwhelming loneliness and helplessness washed over her. Tears that she had bravely forced to remain unshed ran down her cheeks. Burying her face in her hands, Joanne wept until her sides and stomach ached.

Wiping her tears and sighing, Joanne flipped off the set and headed toward her bedroom. She was exhausted and in need of rest. Yet she felt disloyal even thinking about closing her eyes. Mike and the crew of the *Montpelier* would not have that luxury as long as they were aboard the crippled submarine. Part of her felt that she had to stay awake until she heard his voice again. The more rational side demanded sleep. She knew that she would not be able to stand the stress of worry if she did not sleep.

Clutching Mike's photo, Joanne flipped off the living room light and checked the apartment door. Dragging her tired feet, she passed through the short hall that separated her bedroom from the living room. Placing Mike's photo on the night table, Joanne undressed and turned back the covers. Slipping between the lonely sheets, she looked one last time at the face that she loved above all others and smiled wanly. Sleep would come, and work would resume the next day. Her life in this ragged form had to continue. Mike would want it that way.

Chapter Twelve

The days passed without further news about the submarine. The news channels and the newspaper had stopped publishing the crew's photos. To her relief, once again, Joanne could numb her troubled brain in front of the television, the news channels having moved on to more immediate events. Even her parents and Mike's resumed their less-frequent calling pattern, knowing that Joanne would phone as soon as she learned something new. Life, or some form of it, continued as Joanne and her boss joined the other families of crewmen and officers of the *Montpelier*, waiting for information that did not come.

Joanne found herself working longer and longer hours. She received a strange comfort from the office routine and the company of the members of the unit. Sylvia was a particularly reliable support, although she was now heavily involved in making wedding plans.

"I thought you wanted to keep it simple," Joanne said as she watched her friend parade around in yet another elaborate wedding gown. They had stretched their Friday lunch hour to incorporate several wedding-related stops for Sylvia.

"I did and I do," Sylvia replied, "but my parents

want a big blowout. Ben doesn't care; he'll do whatever keeps the peace. So we're having a medium-to-large affair."

"Far cry from a trip to the justice of the peace," Joanne commented, frowning at the exorbitant price for wedding gowns.

"If you think this is bad, take a look at the menu. It's in my briefcase. You know, I carry that thing with me everywhere now. I have samples of this and that, a list of appointments, and a full menu in there. It's become a mini office," Sylvia chuckled as the wedding consultant slipped the veil onto her head.

"Wow! Fifteen, twenty, thirty bucks a head!" Joanne exclaimed, reluctantly giving in to the wedding fever that possessed her friend. "This is really expensive. I'm glad Mike and I decided to make use of the officers' club option at the Academy. It's not inexpensive, but I don't have to promise my firstborn to pay for it."

Sylvia shook her head and moaned, "If my parents hadn't said that they'd pay for this shindig because they want to invite all of their friends, I wouldn't have changed my plans. As it is, Oahu will be overrun with my folks' buddies. They're all planning to attend . . . a much-needed vacation for all of them. I'd still rather just get married in front of a justice of the peace and get on with it."

"There's a lot to be said for a small ceremony. It's looking better to me the longer I watch your preparations. I don't want to go through all of that on top of all of this. I just want to hold Mike in my arms forever," Joanne explained, trying to push away the sadness that had crept back into her heart.

"You'll change your mind after Mike's been home for a while. According to my mother, a woman's wedding day is her time to shine and look her best. Do you think I'll manage to shine while dragging along this heavy gown?" Sylvia quipped, trying to lighten Joanne's mood.

Smiling gratefully, Joanne replied, "You'll be the most gorgeous bride the people of Oahu have ever seen."

"And you'll make a stunning maid of honor. Now, get in there and try on that mauve number," Sylvia directed, pretending to be the bossy type.

"Aye-aye, captain," Joanne saluted as she disappeared into the adjoining dressing room cubicle. Within a few minutes, she emerged in a slinky gown that hugged her curves, exposed her thighs, and revealed her bosom while cinching her waist.

"Maybe that's not the right dress for you," Sylvia said, looking with dubious pleasure at her friend. "If you wear that, no one will notice me."

"It does draw attention to all the assets," Joanne laughed, viewing her image in the mirror.

"I didn't know you had those assets. The uniform is not your best friend. Neither is the baggy Tee shirt and two-sizes-too-big shorts you live in on the weekends," Sylvia remarked as she pointed to another gown for Joanne to try on.

"I like that outfit. It's comfortable and broken in," Joanne retorted with a chuckle.

"Broken down is more like it," Sylvia quipped gaily.

Quickly shedding the mauve creation, Joanne emerged in a gown of the same color but consisting of more fabric and a higher neckline. Gossamer fabric kissed her throat and wrists and danced around her ankles. Although it hugged her waist and billowed into a full skirt, the gown managed to accentuate Joanne's athletic figure rather than making her appear chunky.

"Oh, much better!" Sylvia exclaimed. "You're still stunning but not distracting."

"You're a nut," Joanne laughed. "Anyway, I like this one better. The other one showed way too much cleavage."

"Good. It's settled. I think we're done," Sylvia announced. "I'm happy with both of them. Let's change and grab some lunch."

Walking toward one of their favorite restaurants, Joanne and Sylvia marveled at the plethora of seabirds that fluttered and swooped overhead. Although Joanne was not new to Oahu, she was no less impressed at the many species that lived together in seeming harmony. Back home, she often saw gatherings of birds that fought over seed and scraps of bread.

Everywhere Joanne looked, she saw tables on the sidewalk and along the walks leading to the beaches. Living in Hawaii had given Joanne a greater appreciation for dinning alfresco. Everyone did it. At home in DC, a few of the restaurants offered outdoor seating, but most stuck to the more traditional arrangements. Frequent summer thunderstorms, noisy traffic jams, and pesky dogs greatly reduced the desire to eat outdoors for all but the die-hard devotees. Even picnics had become part of the past, due to rising stream and creek pollution. The smell of rotting garbage dulled the appetite.

Grabbing salads and glasses of tea, Joanne and Sylvia found a table with an open umbrella for shade and a fabulous view of the ocean. The fresh air smelled sweet and warm. Joanne really would have felt that she was in paradise if Mike had been at her side.

"I don't need to spend a penny for your thoughts," Sylvia commented, watching melancholy spread across Joanne's face.

"I'm sorry. It's just so beautiful here, and I miss Mike. Did I tell you that we had planned to honeymoon in Hawaii? Now, I'm here, and he isn't. To make it worse, he doesn't even know that I'm here, and I don't know if I'll ever see him again," Joanne replied, smiling through the sadness.

"There are other islands for your honeymoon. Lanai is breathtaking, and so is Kauai," Sylvia suggested.

"We'll see," Joanne replied, trying to be upbeat.

"While we're out, let's go to the florist. We still have time. The shop's around the corner," Sylvia said, changing the subject back to her wedding plans.

"I'm game," Joanne replied, feeding a persistent gull the last of her roll.

Joanne had expected a regular flower shop, the kind that populated certain neighborhoods back home. They carried a limited selection, although they could order anything that the patron desired. She was surprised at the assortment of flowers and ferns that greeted her as they entered the huge warehouse facility.

"My goodness!" Joanne exclaimed. "I've never seen so many flowers. I don't think I'll buy a sad little bunch at the grocery store ever again."

"This place is famous for its selection. It's really not open to the general public except for wedding planning, and that's by appointment only. If a bride can't find what she wants here, the flower doesn't exist," Sylvia whispered knowingly.

"Are these all indigenous flowers?" Joanne asked, gazing around the massive building.

Stepping toward them, a sales representative replied, "Yes, ma'am. We specialize in providing native flora for every occasion. With so many varieties on the islands, we see no need to import even a single bloom. Now, how may I help you, ladies?"

Joanne breathed deeply of the heady scent as Sylvia detailed her requirements. She wanted creamy white and mauve orchids that matched the fabric swatches from their gowns. The majority of the flowers would adorn the altar of the little church, but many would find their way into her bouquet.

"I'll return in a few minutes with some suggestions. In the meantime, help yourselves to the champagne and cookies." The sales representative nodded slightly.

"Champagne!" Sylvia mouthed as the man walked away.

"I don't know any flower shops that serve champagne at home. Soda, maybe coffee and tea, but not champagne," Joanne whispered.

"I can only imagine the price of the flowers. Someone has to pay for the drinks," Sylvia said.

Joanne and Sylvia nibbled and sipped as directed until the man reappeared. Pushing a cart laden with more varieties of orchids than Joanne had ever seen in her life, he began to fashion sample nosegays and boutonnieres. His fingers danced among the wires and ribbons until the table contained twelve stunning miniature creations from which Sylvia could select her bouquet.

"You make it look so easy," Joanne commented, picking up a nosegay and placing it next to the swatch of fabric from her gown.

"Perfect!" The man beamed at the praise for his work.

Fingering a darling boutonniere with trailing satin ribbon, Sylvia declared, "And this one matches my gown. I'd appreciate learning the price of these two, plus two single-orchid boutonnieres for my fiancé and his best man."

"Excellent choice, ladies. You may keep these samples. I'll take those two and start a file for you. If you'll excuse me," the man stated and left them to admire the little treasures.

"It's not every day that I get to see a master at work. These are lovely," Joanne gushed.

"I can hardly wait to see my bouquet. I'll have a hard time giving it up. I might have to toss silk flowers," Sylvia stated.

"If I catch it, I'll store it in the refrigerator for you," Joanne commented, patting her friend's hand.

"I'm so excited!" Sylvia beamed. "I'm actually doing it. I'm getting married with all the trimmings. Even though all this fuss isn't my style, I'm so glad my parents convinced me to do this. A trip to the justice of the peace wouldn't have been enough. Just think, in a year or two, you'll be up to your ears in plans, too."

Trying not to allow her mood to change, Joanne nodded and said, "I won't find any florists in Annapolis or DC like this one. I'll have to put away my champagne tastes and settle for coffee."

Sylvia finalized the arrangements as Joanne discreetly browsed the display cabinets. Moving from one ornate creation to another, she marveled at the artist's talent in transforming loose stems of blossoms into magical arrangements, corsages, and bouquets. Just as Joanne thought that she had seen the best the shop had to offer, she would step in front of yet another case to find more wonders. The assortment was so extensive that Joanne found it difficult to leave the shop.

Walking to the office in the bright sunshine, Joanne and Sylvia made one more stop at the photographer's studio. He had promised to show Sylvia a montage of his work from which she could draw inspiration for her wedding portraits. As they entered, a very impressive binder sat on the front counter surrounded by smaller samples. Looking at each other, Joanne and Sylvia lifted eyebrows as an indication of their satisfaction.

"If he can make me look that good," Sylvia said, pointing to the photograph of a stunningly beautiful June bride, "I might just leave the navy for a modeling career."

"Piece of cake!" Joanne commented with a snap of her fingers. "You're gorgeous already and won't need those special filters to brighten your complexion."

"I'm so glad you got this assignment. You're a great ego-booster," Sylvia chuckled.

While Sylvia made the final arrangements with the photographer, Joanne continued to flip through the binder. Page after page of beautiful, happy people in wedding finery greeted her. Because of the military bases in Hawaii, many of the grooms in the photos were in uniform, looking especially handsome. Picturing herself in the photos, Joanne wondered if she and Mike would ever sit and reminisce over wedding photos. At this point, she would happily abandon plans for a formal wedding just to have him safely on land.

Joanne's delayed return to the office went unnoticed as she and Sylvia slipped quietly into the cubicles. They had done so much in a little over an hour that Joanne's head reeled from the rush.

Pushing aside thoughts of flowers and menus, she retuned to the work on her desk that would keep her mind occupied and distracted from thoughts of Mike.

By late afternoon, Joanne had become so engrossed with her work that she barely noticed a man enter the suite. Lifting her head from the stack of papers that littered her desk, she glimpsed a uniformed person rush up the aisle toward the chief's office. Thinking nothing of one more visitor to the popular office, Joanne returned her attention to her work.

Minutes later, the door opened again. This time a voice announced, "There's a deliveryman here looking for Joanne Crawford."

Thinking the person was the UPS man delivering the new telephone for her kitchen, Joanne raised her hand above the short partition and shouted, "Here!"

"You'll have to sign here, ma'am," a voice behind her stated.

Joanne sat upright as a chill ran through her body. The voice was so like Mike's that she had to swallow hard to compose herself before turning to face the man. The pain of missing Mike threatened to consume her. She had not cried at work and did not want to start now.

"You can put it right here," Joanne stated as she turned toward the man.

Expecting to see a brown UPS uniform, Joanne was startled by the presence of a pair of white shoes, trousers, and matching shirt. Following the uniform buttons to the face, Joanne blinked hard as her throat constricted. Her hand flew to her mouth to stifle the cry that rose unbidden.

"Mike!" Joanne whispered as she flew into his

arms on legs so wobbly that she barely managed to close the distance between them.

Crushing her to his chest, Mike buried his face in Joanne's neck and breathed deeply of her sweetness. During the worst moments on the submarine, he had not expected to see her again. Now, as he held her, Joanne's warmth filled him with indescribable happiness. He was home. He was safe. Being with Joanne made everything right.

"Joanne! Joanne!" Mike muttered, kissing her cheeks and lips.

"I didn't know . . . the news didn't say . . . why didn't you . . . How did you find me?" Joanne sputtered as his lips silenced her attempts.

"Don't talk . . . nothing matters . . . I'm here now," Mike replied, too busy to answer any questions.

Joanne and Mike did not see the shy smiles on the faces of their fellow officers. They did not hear the soft prayers of thanksgiving that many of them offered. They only saw each other's face and heard the wild beating of their hearts.

After a reasonable interval, Sylvia cleared her throat noisily. When that did not break the embrace, she lightly tapped Joanne on the shoulder. Although they were no longer at the Academy or in ROTC, public displays of affection seldom happened in the stiff-upper-lip world of the military.

"I assume this is Mike," Sylvia said jokingly.

"Oh, yes! This is my fiancé, Mike. He's home, and he's safe," Joanne gushed as the tears streamed without warning down her cheeks. She had been brave for so long that she could no longer control the emotions that burst to the surface.

"Nice to meet you, Mike," Sylvia stated, blinking back her own tears and extending her hand.

"Nice to be here. It's nice to be anywhere that isn't under the sea," Mike exclaimed, shaking her hand enthusiastically.

Seeing the department chief approaching with a younger officer who looked just like him in tow, Joanne said, "Sir, I'd like for you to meet my fiancé, Mike Shepherd."

"Glad to meet you, son. My boy's been filling me in on all the details. You're lucky men," the chief said as he greeted Mike.

"Sir. We are that, sir," Mike acknowledged, smiling broadly.

Turning to Joanne, the chief said, "Take your ensign and go home. I don't expect you to concentrate on this stuff with him here. I'm leaving with my son right now. My wife is throwing a big bash to welcome him home. Everyone's invited, but I don't expect to see either of you two. I'll see you on Monday."

"Thank you, sir," Joanne replied as one of her coworkers approached.

"Sir, we feel that an appropriate welcome is in order for the ensigns. If you will, sir," Joanne's coworker stated.

"At your leave, Miller," the chief replied with the smile of a happy father.

Turning to the others, the man instructed, "Ladies and gentlemen, raise your coffee mugs and join me. Hip, hip, hooray! Hip, hip, hooray! Hip, hip, hooray! Oh rah!"

Joanne's eyes filled with tears again as she looked from the chief's son to Mike and smiled. They both looked extremely tired. She could only guess at the fear that they had endured. Once Mike had relaxed a bit, she would ask him for the details, but not now. The present belonged to the reunion for which they had so long waited.

Joanne happily followed the chief's instructions and walked with Mike into the Hawaiian sunshine. The brilliant sun shone more brightly with him at her side. The fragrances of the island were even headier as Joanne linked her arm through Mike's. Suddenly, the world seemed brighter and the gulls' cries more demanding. Even the laughing children seemed to play more vigorously on the sand.

"Are you hungry?" Joanne asked as they passed her favorite restaurant.

"Only for you," Mike replied, smiling down at her.

"You'll see so much of me this weekend that you'll get tired of looking at me," Joanne replied, laughing happily. She felt light for the first time since the plight of the ailing submarine made the news.

"Never! The memory of your face kept me alive," Mike stated softly.

"Was it awful? You don't have to tell me all the details. I don't think I'm ready to handle that yet anyway," Joanne said as she held tightly to Mike's arm.

"There's nothing worse than being trapped in a dead submarine at incredible depths of the ocean. When we're both ready, I'll tell you all about it. Let's just say that the experience has made me a changed man. It changed all of us. I'm not young anymore," Mike replied with a depth of emotion that Joanne had never heard.

"Your face looks different. It's not that you have extra lines or anything, it's just that even when you smile, your smile has lost something," Joanne commented as they stood with their backs to the pounding surf.

"I doubt that I'll ever get it back," Mike replied, studying her face for compassion and finding it. "I've faced mortality. It's not a good feeling knowing that only two ways to save your life exist and neither is safe or foolproof. It's a very sobering experience."

"Then you'll put in for reassignment? Maybe even join me in Intel?" Joanne asked hopefully.

Studying her face, Mike tried to assess the depth of Joanne's comprehension of his new self-awareness. Thinking that she might understand, he decided not to avoid the question but to face it directly. Tilting her face to his, he kissed her deeply and held her close for a long few minutes, not wanting to break contact with the energy that had sustained him through the harrowing experience.

Finally, looking deeply into Joanne's eyes, Mike replied, "The sub service is where I belong. The guys are the best in the world. I'd put my life in their hands again any day. I'm a submariner. I found an inner strength that I didn't know I had. I'm not afraid anymore of anything. The way I feel now, I know that I'll stay in this community and in the Navy until I'm ready to retire."

"I don't understand," Joanne whispered. "Make me understand, Mike."

"I will, or at least I'll try, but not now," Mike replied with a smile of wisdom. "Right now, all I want is to enjoy being with you on this beautiful island. I want to feel the sun on my face and your hand in mine. I want to hear the cries of the gulls and the sound of your voice until I fall asleep. I want noise and life. I'll tell you everything later . . . maybe not today and perhaps not even tomorrow, but one day. Today, I'm home with you and very happy."

"I can wait. All that's important is having you with me," Joanne replied, kissing him softly.

As they walked toward Joanne's apartment, she began to see the depth of Mike's transformation. The old Mike would have bubbled over with the excitement of sharing his adventures. The Mike she knew would have found it difficult to keep his thoughts to himself. Joanne thought that the other Mike would have wanted to change his billet and might even have already submitted the paperwork. This Mike was calm and composed even after a harrowing experience. This Mike carried his shoulders with a new determination and a new sense of purpose.

Almost against her will, Joanne realized that Mike had changed even as she had kept the memory of him alive. The man who had returned to her from the depth of the sea was more confident and self-assured. He was someone on whom others depended for their safety and life. The Academy training had given him the foundation to be a successful officer, and necessity had transformed him into a leader of men. Mike seemed to have put aside his youthful exuberance for a maturity that she had never expected possible of the man she loved. Joanne would need time to get to know this Mike. She would gladly give both of them the time and space they needed to rediscover themselves and their love. For now, she was just happy to have him home and safe.

Chapter Thirteen

Joanne and Mike spent the weekend rediscovering each other and enjoying Hawaii. They visited all of the tourist spots on Oahu and then took a commuter flight to Maui. Once there, they played golf like the old days when they were carefree midshipmen, ignorant of the real world and in a hurry to experience it. However, this time, Mike won. They rented a boat and went sport fishing. Mike caught the largest number of fish, including one that he had stuffed and mounted for Joanne's apartment wall. Their positions had changed from Joanne being the dominant leader of the duo to Mike taking the assertive role.

Lying in bed Sunday night, Joanne and Mike snuggled close. He had lost weight during his ordeal, making her usual spot against his collarbone less than comfortable. Her fingers could trace the outline of his rib cage and easily feel the six-pack beneath the taut skin.

"The weekend's over too quickly," Joanne sighed with a tinge of sadness.

"I'll be here for another week and can meet you for lunch every day," Mike replied, gently stroking her cheek.

"And then what? We'll return to seeing each

other when we're on leave, living separate but parallel lives, seeing each other when duty allows?" Joanne asked.

"Yes. That's the only way for us for a while. We knew the reality of this life before graduation," Mike responded softly.

"You could request a change in billet," Joanne suggested, feeling hope beginning to fade.

"You know I can't do that," Mike stated firmly. "The submarine service is what I want. I can't leave it."

"We could be together more if you worked a land-based job. No one would fault you for changing after what you've experienced," Joanne insisted gently.

"I'm not staying in subs for anyone else," Mike said firmly. "This is for me. I wandered through college not really knowing what I wanted. I signed up for subs because my GPA was good and it sounded like fun. Now, after all this, I love it. It's dangerous, thrilling, and exciting. I found something within myself that I didn't know existed, and I found a bunch of guys that I'd die for. I want subs for me, not to impress anyone."

"And us? What about the strain the separation puts on us?" Joanne asked, feeling a bit like a nag and not liking the tone in her voice.

Speaking gently, Mike said, "This is the same reality we faced when we first started this journey. When you were in flight school, you didn't see the danger, but now you do. We selected careers with built-in stress factors. You're living a calmer life now and can appreciate the stress and danger more fully. The stress of separation is the same now as it was before the sub accident. You're just reacting to it. You'll get over it."

"And if I don't?" Joanne asked as her fingers froze on his chest.

"You will. You're Navy," Mike insisted proudly.

Sitting up in bed, Joanne replied, "I'm also a woman who had to live with the fear that the man I love would never return. I lived in terror of the phone ringing with the news that you had died on that submarine. I waited for news that my life had ended. I know I didn't think, feel, or react the same way when I was facing the reality of life as a pilot and its dangers. I was too caught up in the adrenaline and the excitement. I see life more clearly now without the thrill of the danger staring me in the face. I can understand the way my parents felt when I first entered flight school. They were horribly frightened for me. Now, I'm frightened for you . . . for us."

Silent for a few moments, Mike struggled with the need to find the right words to convince Joanne that he would be safe and that they would weather the separation. He knew that he could never convince her that submarine service was safe; Mike could not convince himself that he would never find himself in a life-threatening situation again. Somehow, he had to make Joanne see that she would change her mind and become accustomed to the life as a submariner's fiancée and wife.

Pulling her into his arms, Mike explained, "We'll survive. We love each other. I can't promise that there won't be another accident on board. I won't lie to you about that. Anything's possible. But let's face reality for a minute. My reality's no different from yours. Submarine accidents don't happen that often. Cars are more dangerous. You're just worried because this is new to you. You never thought that you'd be sitting at home waiting. You had plans to fly. My danger's small compared to that of a pilot. We'll survive the transition. You'll get used to being the one left behind, the one who waits."

Relaxing a little against his warmth, Joanne replied, "I know it's not only the distance or separation that's weighing me down. You're right; I wouldn't have seen the danger in your job if I were still in flight school; I would have been too absorbed by my own sense of conquering the altitude and the thrills. I know that many more flying accidents occur every year than ones involving submarines. You're right; I'll just need more time to adjust to the changes in my life, to being the one who stays home and listens to the radio for updates. I'll try not to transfer my issues to you, but it's hard."

"You're doing okay. This was simply a blip on the radar," Mike chuckled, feeling as if they had already weathered a potentially disastrous storm.

Mike needed for Joanne to understand on a gut level that he had to remain in the submarine service. He knew that she comprehended his love of the sea and the metal fish that sailed beneath its waters on an intellectual level. However, Mike was aware that contentment and peace in their relationship would not come until Joanne fully embraced his decision to remain in the submarine service despite its dangers.

Lying in his arms, Joanne breathed deeply and tried to calm her pounding heart. She did not want to sound like a nag and take the chance of driving Mike away, but she could not keep her reservations to herself. She had lived through a hellish experience with only friends to comfort her. She needed him to understand that his career decisions also impacted her life. Mike had to understand that she shared the dangers he faced. She loved him and lived the experience with him.

Joanne silently agreed with Mike that she might be overreacting to the devastation she had experienced. However, she knew herself, too. Mike had changed, but so had she. Their lives would never be the same again. They both needed to bend and to compromise, but they were both strong people with equally strong opinions. Joanne wondered if they could.

The week passed much too quickly, with Joanne trying to survive the morning until she could meet Mike for lunch, and then the afternoon until she would rush home for dinner. Mike prepared delicious meals to delight her palate, after which they would take long walks along the beach. Holding tightly to each other, they would pick up shells, run along the wet sand, or simply sit and watch the sunset. Each night Joanne fell asleep in the comfort of his arms, and each morning she awoke to the fragrance of freshly brewed coffee. Although she knew the heavenly days would soon come to an end, Joanne enjoyed every minute and filled her mind with memories that would have to feed her until they could be together again.

While Joanne struggled with nagging questions and self-doubt, Mike had never been happier. The submarine ordeal had given him a new perspective and a confidence that he had not felt while a student at the Academy. While in college, he had not sought out command, preferring to follow rather than lead. However, during the submarine crisis, he had discovered an inner strength that had enabled him to remain externally calm as he dealt with the life-threatening sequence of events. Although he had been afraid for his life, Mike had reassured his men of their safety and performed his duties without hesitation.

Mike knew that he would miss Joanne when his leave expired, but he found that he actually looked forward to returning to the submarine. There, he did not have to explain his reasons for returning. Everyone felt the same way. They had shared a bond created by danger and survived. Never would he be able to make Joanne understand the camaraderie and the oneness he felt with the *Montpelier*'s crew. Mike still sensed that she did not fully comprehend the effects of the ordeal on his psyche and the changes in him. He often found her studying him with a quizzical expression on her beautiful face. Mike needed to be in a place in which words were not necessary, an environment in which all had shared a common experience.

During his brief hospitalization at Bethesda Naval for mandatory post-trauma review before joining Joanne in Hawaii, Mike had visited his parents and hers. All of them had remarked at his new maturity and sense of self. They noted that he had grown up in the short time since his last visit. Rather than shaking his foundation, the experience had strengthened it. It was that resolve that made him want to stay in the submarine service. The *Montpelier* was home, and the crew was his family.

The morning of his last day in Hawaii, Mike dressed in his uniform for the first time since his arrival. His shoulders were square and his back straight as he adjusted his cover and hooked

Joanne's arm through his. They made a handsome couple as they walked through the busy streets.

Standing on the sidewalk with his duffel bag at his feet, Mike kissed Joanne lightly and smiled into her upturned face. The time had passed too quickly. With luck, their work would keep them busy and help to lessen the pain of separation.

"I'll miss you. You'll have to come to Norfolk next time," Mike said, gazing into her eyes.

"When? Tomorrow?" Joanne joked, but only slightly.

Laughing, Mike replied, "No, not tomorrow. I'm getting under way again at the end of the week. We'll be out for at least six months this time, probably longer. As soon as I return, we'll plan your visit."

"Under way? Is the sub safe?" Joanne asked with her heart pounding loudly.

"Completely," Mike reassured her. "I called the base yesterday. They've replaced the steam pipe. Everything's working just great."

"Why didn't you tell me?" Joanne demanded gently.

"I didn't want to ruin our time together. I knew you'd worry. I know how you feel about my sub duty," Mike replied, studying her face.

"You didn't give me a chance to get used to the idea of your getting under way again. You should have told me. I wouldn't have collapsed," Joanne objected, feeling the Navy coming between then again.

Studying her face, Mike replied, "I didn't want to take that chance. Besides, you don't really understand what I've gone through. I'm not complaining or criticizing; I'm simply stating a fact. When you do, you'll know that I have no choice but to return to the sub."

Joanne stood quietly for several minutes. She had been trying to be brave about the dangers that Mike faced at sea. She had analyzed her objections and hesitations. She had come to terms with the reality of not living her flight dream while he lived his of being a submarine officer. She had faced the realities of their life together and apart. Joanne had fought her silent battles all week and had thought that she had won.

Looking into Mike's eyes, Joanne said simply, "I can't do this. I thought I could, but I can't. I can't have my heart torn out of my body every time I hear that you're under way or that a submarine's in trouble. I'm being selfish, but I can't help it. It's not because I'm not flying. It's because I love you more than I ever thought possible. The constant fear's just too much to bear. I can't do it."

"Then where does that leave us? I can't leave the sub service. I won't leave it, not yet. When my sea tour is over, I'll have a land job, too. But now, this is my life," Mike said, holding her hand tightly.

"I guess it means that we need to reconsider being engaged at this time in our lives," Joanne whispered as unshed tears burned her eyes.

"Would that make a difference? Would you stop loving me if we weren't engaged? Would our love die? I don't see the point in ending something this good. We'll still have time together. Granted, not as much as other people, but as much as others in the military," Mike said calmly as the pain jabbed at his heart.

"I'll never stop loving you," Joanne replied, looking deeply into his eyes at a resolve that stimulated and frightened her. "But not being engaged to you might help me to survive and not worry about you and our future as much. If something happens to my fiancé, my life is over. If something happens to the man to whom I used to be engaged, I'll ache and I'll cry, but I won't die. It's a selfish difference, but I have to protect myself."

"I'm not willing to end it because of my love of the sea," Mike replied firmly. "You're still haven't come to terms with the realities of my life. I have because I live it. You haven't because you're one step removed. You didn't see the respect in my men's eyes as we worked together to save our lives. You didn't hear the cheer of elation as we breathed fresh air for the first time. You don't know how it feels to be so completely together with a group of people that you walk in the same shoes. I can't explain it. I'm living life on a different plane and it's intoxicating. I can't give it up. I won't give you up either."

Twisting the ring from her finger and holding it out to Mike, Joanne responded, "You're right. I don't understand. I've tried, but I can't. All I can see is the man I love marching back into imminent danger at the bottom of the sea. I don't like it, and I don't want to live with it."

"I won't take it," Mike said as he stepped back from her outstretched hand. "Keep it until we see each other in Norfolk in six months. We'll discuss ending it then. You'll have had more time to digest it by then. You'll see that the danger's not as big as you think it is. Talk with our parents; they understood. Talk to a chaplain or a doctor, but don't give up on us yet. I love you, Joanne. Nothing will ever change that. Not you . . . not the sub service . . . not the months away from each other . . . nothing.

Wear the ring on your right hand until we see each other again. Good-bye."

Joanne watched as Mike picked up his duffel bag and walked away. She wanted to run after him to say that she had changed her mind. She wanted to return the ring to the third finger of her left hand. She wanted him to stay. Joanne wanted so much but could have none of it. Not Mike . . . not his safety . . . not a life of days and nights together. They were Navy. He had his duty, and she had hers.

Slipping the ring onto her right hand, Joanne squared her shoulders and entered the building. She would wear it as a friendship ring until she could return it to him, but she would not consider herself engaged to him. She loved Mike, but she could not accept the lifestyle that took him away from her and placed him in danger. In her heart, Joanne knew that she would have given up flying to be with Mike if he had asked her if airsickness had not grounded her, but he never did. She had always known that she would not fly once they started a family. Yet Joanne would not come any closer to asking Mike to abandon his dream for her. She had suggested and he had resisted the change. He had to make the move for her, not because of her. He would stop loving her if she made him give up his career choice. It was easier for her to give him up to save their love.

Opening the top folder on her desk, Joanne looked at the naked spot on her finger. It would take time for the color to reappear and the emptiness to fill in, but it would. Maybe Mike was right when he said that not being engaged would not stop the worry and fear. Only time would tell. For now, Joanne knew that she had to put emotional as well as physical distance between them. She would not be able to face another period of agony, of not knowing whether Mike was alive or dead. She might be deluding herself, but it was a delusion with which she wanted to surround herself.

Just as Mike had to do what was right for him at this time in his life, Joanne had to do the same. She would love Mike no less but from a safer distance. This time, a news flash would not make her legs go limp and her heart stop beating.

Chapter Fourteen

The months passed with Joanne hard at work and deeply involved in Sylvia's upcoming wedding. While under way in the submarine, Mike e-mailed when he could, but usually she did not hear from him. Although her feelings had not changed toward him, Joanne found that she could sleep better and listen to the news less, knowing that their relationship had moved to another level. Her parents' visit to Hawaii added another element to her days.

"But Joanne," her mother exclaimed, "I just don't understand your reasoning. You still love him. Mike's crazy about you. What have you accomplished by breaking up with him?"

Joanne only smiled and replied, "I've set myself free, Mom. I can't explain it. You'll just have to trust me on this. It's what's best for me. I'm happier now. Maybe one day Mike and I will rediscover each other, but I'm not marking time until that happens. I'm happy with life as it is."

Mrs. Crawford could only shake her head at this new generation's ideas. Try as she might, she could not understand the arrangement that Joanne had with Mike. The idea of a platonic relationship between people who loved each other was alien to her. In her day, when people were as perfectly matched as Joanne and Mike, they married. Even if they had to commute, they made the commitment.

Applying suntan lotion to Joanne's shoulders and back, her mom sighed and changed the discussion to news from home. Several of Joanne's high-school buddies had married their college sweethearts and settled down to raise their families in DC. Others had moved away from home, following their jobs. Although Joanne had not continued her friendship with them, she was always happy to hear of their successes.

"Did I tell you that your high school friend John Franklin married a woman who operates a very exclusive boutique in Georgetown? They met while on a Caribbean cruise. John was with his buddies, and she was with hers. Bingo! They fell in love, became engaged, and set the date. Whirlwind courtship, but they're happy."

Smiling, Joanne replied absently, "I'll have to visit the shop when I come home."

"When's that?" her father asked, taking his eyes from the latest mystery novel by his favorite author.

"Next month. I didn't tell you guys, but I've been reassigned to the Pentagon. I'll have to exchange this paradise for traffic congestion and air pollution," Joanne responded with a mixture of sadness and resignation in her voice.

"You're coming home! That's wonderful! We got this vacation in just under the wire," Joanne's mother gushed.

"It'll be nice to see more of you, but I'll really miss Hawaii. I love it here," Joanne said, spreading her arms as if to embrace the island.

"I'd find it hard to leave if I lived in a place like this. Beach, sun, fish, natural beauty. It's perfect," her father commented, returning to his book.

"You're just like your father—a romantic. Hawaii's a great place to live for a while, but you need a place where you can really make a home for yourself. An island paradise isn't it," Joanne's mother advised.

"All the people who live here on a permanent basis would disagree with you, Mom," Joanne rebutted. "Besides, what's so special about the DC area that it's more home than this? Just because I grew up there doesn't make it a more desirable place for me to live."

"Maybe not, but DC's closer to the center of activity . . . and Mike," her mother added.

"Mom, give up. Okay? That chapter of my life has closed—perhaps permanently, but at least for a long time," Joanne commented firmly.

"Humph! Then why do you still wear the ring?" her mother demanded.

"One, I haven't seen Mike to return it. Two, he wouldn't take it before he left. Three, it's pretty," Joanne replied with a chuckle.

"I think it's more than that," her mother insisted.

"Think whatever you like, Mom, but it'll never represent more as long as Mike's in the sub service. Let's discuss something else," Joanne replied.

This time, her mother acquiesced and changed the subject to Sylvia's wedding the next day. She had seen Joanne's gown and heard about the arrangements but was always interested in hearing more. She loved the details of wedding preparations and longed for the day that she could help Joanne with hers.

"Has Sylvia said where they're going on their honeymoon?" Mrs. Crawford asked.

"No, but I think they're going to Kauai. It's much more secluded than Maui," Joanne replied.

"Weddings are so exciting! I remember ours as if it were only yesterday," Mrs. Crawford sighed.

Lifting his head from his novel, Mr. Crawford said, "I do, too. It rained the whole day. The outdoor ceremony moved inside your parents' house. People stood shoulder-to-shoulder in the living room and hall, trying to catch a glimpse of us. I had to squeeze down a tiny opening to reach the hearth. My shoes squeaked from the puddles I'd walked through getting to the front door. My brother-in-law, the best man, arrived in the nick of time—I was on the verge of drafting my father for the job. The flowers wilted from the heat in the house. Your little nephew pigged out on sandwiches and refused to leave the table until someone carried him away. The limo got a flat tire on the way to the airport, and the honeymoon flight had to detour to another airport due to fog. But the cake was really good. Rum!"

"See, even your father remembers. Good or bad, messy or organized, a wedding produces memories," Mrs. Crawford commented, leaving her desire to see Joanne happily married unsaid.

Avoiding the obvious discussion trap, Joanne stated, "Sylvia has planned everything perfectly. She hasn't forgotten a single thing. We're not likely this time of year to have excessive rain to ruin the wedding. Everything should go off without a hitch."

"We'll see. Something strange happens at all weddings," Mrs. Crawford said in her voice-of-experience tone.

Joanne's father looked at her and raised his eyebrows, a signal that further discussion with her mother on this subject was a waste of breath. Once his wife dug in, nothing, no amount of logic or contradicting examples, would change her mind. He had been married to her for over thirty years and had learned from experience.

"I know you'll enjoy the rehearsal dinner tonight," Mrs. Crawford stated. "What will you wear?"

"It's really informal—more a beach party–clam bake kind of thing rather than anything else. Sylvia instructed all of us to wear bathing suits under our clothing. It seems we're going for a splash after the actual rehearsal," Joanne replied.

"Young people!" Mrs. Crawford muttered.

Joanne chuckled and rose to her feet. The surf was too inviting to ignore any longer. Pushing her hair beneath a cap, she trotted to the water. Testing it with a toe, she slipped into its warmth. For a few moments, nothing mattered. Joanne put Mike, work, and relocation far from her thoughts.

The next day, Joanne rose early and dressed quietly so as not to awaken her parents, who slept on the sofa bed in the living room. Gulping a bagel and juice, she headed toward the door with her shoes in one hand and her keys in the other. Although the wedding would not take place until noon, Sylvia had instructed Joanne and the two bridesmaids to arrive at the little church by ten for the formal photo session. For someone whose plans had started small, Sylvia's wedding had blossomed into an extravaganza.

By the time Joanne arrived, the photographer had set up his camera and lights in the nave of the little church. Orchids in shades of white and mauve decorated the altar and the pews while an off-white cloth surrounded by matching rose petals covered the center aisle's carpet. Joining the bridesmaids, Joanne allowed Sylvia's mother to adjust her minimal makeup and smiled for the camera.

When Sylvia entered the church, a chorus of

oohs and aahs erupted. Joanne's friend was a vision in the splendid gown that accentuated her figure and skin tone. Seeing her friend's happiness, Joanne was even more pleased that they had changed her gown from the one with the more revealing neckline to the one that she wore so easily. It was Sylvia's day. She did not need to be upstaged by her maid of honor.

The lengthy photo session over, Joanne and the rest of the wedding party retired to the minister's office. With only a few minutes to spare, they waited as the two ushers seated the last of the guests and the organ started to play. Sylvia looked nervous but happy as she stepped aside for the bridesmaids to begin their walk down the aisle.

"This is it," Joanne whispered to her friend.

"I'm so glad I allowed my mom to do this. I'm so happy I could burst," Sylvia grinned.

"You should be. You worked hard to pull this together. There's my cue. All the happiness in the world, my friend," Joanne stated as she blew a kiss to Sylvia.

"You'll find yours one day, too," Sylvia commented.

"One day," Joanne replied with a slightly sad smile and stepped onto the white runner.

As she walked down the center aisle, Joanne struggled with thoughts that pressed their way into her heart. She wanted all the trimmings, the music, the flowers, the gown, and the waiting bridegroom, too. Life could be so trying at times. She wanted Mike. No other man would ever suit her needs as well. She could not imagine making a life with anyone else; however, a future with Mike was definitely not in the plans.

As she approached the altar, Joanne's heart took

a momentary lurch. For just a second, the best man in his dress white uniform looked so much like Mike that Joanne took a misstep and had to recover quickly. Her heart pounded as she forced herself not to stare at him. He had missed the rehearsal, making this the first time that Joanne had ever seen him.

Taking her place to the left of the altar, Joanne breathed deeply. Mike was far away. Their life together might never happen. She had to face that reality and make a new but different life. Joanne told herself that she had to stop looking for him in the face of every man she met.

Glancing at the best man, Joanne chuckled inwardly. He was handsome and tall with the same complexion and hair color as Mike, but the similarity stopped there. This man's eyes did not sparkle with mischief, and his smile did not turn upward at the left corner. Although his uniform fit him perfectly, he was not Mike.

Taking Sylvia's bouquet, Joanne turned toward the waiting minister, who intoned the familiar words of the wedding ceremony. Within minutes, her friend had sealed her life to that of the man she loved. The music blared, signaling the end of the ceremony, and the happy couple turned toward the assembled family and friends.

Slipping her arm through the best man's, Joanne left the church and its ritual behind. Stepping into the Hawaiian sunshine, she sighed. The handsome man at her side looked at her with an inquisitive frown. Joanne merely smiled happily for her friend's joyous day.

"Anything wrong?" the best man inquired.

"Nothing. Weddings just do that to me. Romance,

flowers, love. I guess I'm a hopeless romantic at heart," Joanne replied.

"Nothing wrong with that. I felt a little twinge of something, too, but I decided it was indigestion," the best man laughed.

"Funny!"

"Sorry I didn't get a chance to meet you last night. The name's John. Sylvia has all but handed me a copy of your résumé. I feel as if I've known you for ages," he added as he helped Joanne into the waiting limo.

"It's nice to meet you, John. I hope she hasn't built me up too much. I'm just a hardworking maid of honor," Joanne said, smiling.

"I think she was honest in her description, except that she omitted the part about your being a romantic," John chuckled.

"Drat! That's my best quality," Joanne quipped as the limo transported them through the busy streets.

The reception was a jumping affair with a string quartet, shimmering silver, sparkling crystal, and orchids everywhere. Sylvia appeared on the arm of her new husband to cheers and whistles. Looking a bit shy from all the attention, she joined Joanne, the bridesmaids, the best man, and their parents at the head table.

Joanne found that she could not stop smiling. Despite missing Mike, she was so happy for her friend that her heart felt strangely light. Dancing with John, Joanne glided across the floor, remembering the steps to the waltz that she had learned at the Academy during one of the long freshman weekends without liberty. She had thought that the lessons would come in handy one day, although her original thought had been to dance at her own wedding. In the arms of this handsome man, Joanne was glad that she had practiced relentlessly.

Holding her a little closer, John said, "You're one of the most beautiful women I've ever met. There's something distant about you that's very appealing. It makes me want to know you better."

Laughing, Joanne replied, "I bet you say that to all the maids of honor wearing mauve silk."

John chuckled and responded, "No, only to the ones with a touch of sadness in their eyes."

"Who could possibly be sad at a wedding like this?" Joanne hedged.

"I'd like to find out. I'll be here for the weekend. May I see you again?" John asked, as they returned to the table.

Smiling slowly, Joanne replied, "I think I can squeeze you in among the packing chores."

"Packing?"

"I'm being reassigned to the Pentagon," Joanne stated.

Chuckling, John responded, "Ah! I should have known that the wistful woman who has instantly stolen my heart would be in and out of my life too quickly. Well, that's even more reason to live life quickly. I'll pick you up early tomorrow morning. We'll spend the day together. Swap a few stories and sail off into the sunset. Literally."

Laughing at his easy wit, Joanne said, "I'd like that. I'll give you the twenty-five-cent tour, but my parents are visiting, so I'd like to make it an early day."

"No problem. I have an early flight the next morning. We'll start and end early," John agreed.

Joanne and John were inseparable for the rest of the reception. They danced together exclusively and chatted nonstop. Sylvia, busy with her new husband, managed to lift her eyebrows in recognition of the pair. By the time of the bouquet toss, everyone had noticed the shared laughter and instant compatibility.

"Do you have any plans for that?" John asked, motioning to the bouquet that Sylvia had neatly tossed to her friend.

"At the moment, no. I'll put it in the refrigerator and save it for Sylvia's return," Joanne replied, laughing at her friend's pitching skills.

"I was wondering if there's a man in your life," John said, obviously interested in Joanne on first sight.

"There was. He's a submariner. I broke it off. I don't want a long-distance relationship," Joanne replied with a touch of sadness in her voice for the first time in hours.

"I can understand that. Too much stress. You're heading for the Pentagon?" John asked as he walked Joanne to her car.

"In a week. I'll miss it here. It'll be hard leaving this paradise," Joanne commented wistfully.

"I'll see you there soon. It's a big place, but I'll find you. See you at eight tomorrow?" John asked.

"I'll be ready," Joanne replied and headed home.

Driving home with the fortune-telling bouquet on the seat next to her, Joanne wondered at her fate. A new man was knocking at the door, but she did not know if she wanted to open it. Mike had been all-important in her life for too long, and she still wanted him in it. Only time would tell if Joanne would change her mind.

Joanne spent the next day showing John around the island that she had learned to call home.

Watching him revel at the splendor of Hawaii, she wondered at ever having felt homesick or thinking that she would not become accustomed to this tantalizing land. Now, with her departure imminent, Joanne wondered how she would ever get used to being away from the blue sky and slapping waves that she loved so much.

Seeing her reaction to the island, John commented as he skillfully piloted the small craft that he had rented, "You love this place, don't you? I can see that it would be easy to fall in love with Hawaii."

"It's not at all like I expected when I first arrived. It has become more glorious with each passing day," Joanne replied, gazing at the distant horizon.

"The Pentagon's not a bad assignment," John remarked. "It's definitely the center of activity—a real plus on your résumé."

"I know, and I'm glad to have the opportunity to work there. I'm looking forward to going home, too. It's just that Hawaii's special and always will be," Joanne replied with a smile at the memories.

Studying her expression, John asked, "Was the guy you were involved with ever stationed here?"

"No. He only visited once. He's always been assigned to subs. That was his choice at graduation and his love," Joanne responded, shifting uncomfortably at the mention of her former love. She had been feeling a little self-conscious about being out with another man, albeit only a social outing, not a date. Mentioning Mike had only made the feeling stronger.

"If I may ask, why'd you break up with him?" John inquired.

Adjusting the blue- and white-striped shell, Joanne

said, "I couldn't handle being in love with a man who daily faced the danger of life on a submarine."

"Is he on the sub that ran into trouble a while back?" John asked.

"Yeah. He loves what he's doing and doesn't want to change. I appreciate his dedication, but I just couldn't live a life of constant worry. I sleep better now," Joanne replied, smiling.

"Then you're open to other possibilities?" John asked, lightly placing his hand on Joanne's.

Chuckling, Joanne liberated herself and said, "I'm not over the submariner yet, and I need to see what this job at the Pentagon has to offer. I don't want any complications at the moment. I need time to sort through my feelings."

"Okay. I can appreciate that. I'll give you the time you need, but I very much want to see you again," John smiled. His eyes twinkled, but not as brightly as Mike's.

Not wanting to give a false impression, Joanne stated, "I'm a slow study. We'll take it one day at a time. I might as well tell you up front. I might not ever get him out of my system. I've loved him for a long time. We were classmates at the Academy. We survived four years together. We slogged through the horrors of plebe summer together. Our relationship turned from friendship to something more during our senior year. I don't even know if I'm ready for another relationship. I'm still in mourning for this one. I don't want you to waste your time."

Pulling into the slip, John responded, "I like an honest woman, but I won't be wasting my time. I'll be spending it with a delightful woman who I'd like to know better. We'll take it slow and see what develops. We can both use more friends."

"Friendship is good as long as we understand that I might not be able to offer more," Joanne commented as she tied up the boat.

Walking toward the wharf's parking lot, Joanne stopped for one last look at the boats along the pier. She would not return to this spot and probably not to Hawaii for a long time, if ever. She loved the island, but like so many other beloved memories in her life, Joanne knew that the time had come to leave.

"I'll find you at the Pentagon as soon as I report for duty," John said as he closed Joanne's car door. "I've found a jewel that I don't intend to let go of."

"Have a safe trip back. I'll see you in a month," Joanne replied and pulled away.

Driving back to her apartment, Joanne thought about the unexpected curves that life can throw at a person. Just when she thought that she would never find another man even remotely attractive, John appeared in her life. Joanne knew that she loved Mike and still wanted him in her life, but she might never have him again. His love for the submarine service might outweigh his love for her. She had to move on even if it meant putting her love for Mike safely in one of the many compartments in her heart. Joanne needed to have someone to love. Maybe John would be that someone.

Chapter Fifteen

A week later, Joanne followed the tide of humanity that flowed inside one of the largest office buildings in the world. Standing on its threshold, she could only gasp at its size. Like most people, she had only seen photos of the structure. Now she was about to join the masses who worked in this structure in defense of the United States.

The Pentagon with its seventeen and one-half miles of corridors was more impressive than Joanne had ever imagined. The structure, completed in 1943 and listed among the nation's historic landmarks, occupied over two hundred acres of land and housed the headquarters of the Department of Defense. Often called a self-contained city, the Pentagon was the work location for twenty-three thousand employees, the physical plant for two hundred thousand telephones and one hundred thousand miles of telephone cable. With its many corridors dedicated to the different divisions of the military and those who have served in the Armed Forces, its massive libraries, its ability to combine seventeen distinct buildings into one, and its location on the Potomac outside the city limits of the nation's capital, the Pentagon was truly a structure of monumental proportions.

Feeling overwhelmed, Joanne stood near a display of women in the military and tried to get her bearings. She needed to report to an office in the Navy corridor, but had managed to take a wrong turn despite the well-marked halls. Knowing that she would become lost in the massive structure, she had arrived early for her first day on the job. The ID that hung from a chain around her neck gave her access to the building despite the heavy post–September 11 security.

Retracing her steps, Joanne successfully located the Navy corridor and found her way to the department chief's office. One of the many secretaries looked up as she entered and smiled briefly before returning to the task of opening the massive pile of mail on her desk. Reading the nameplates on each desk, Joanne quickly found the one that identified the secretary who would act as her liaison to the new job.

"I'm Ensign Crawford to see Captain Marks," Joanne announced. Smiling slightly, Joanne waited until the woman looked from the memo she had been typing.

"He's expecting you. I'll show you to your cubicle," the woman replied with a smile that already showed fatigue despite the early hour.

Following the secretary toward a bullpen of cubicles, Joanne tried to memorize her way back to the captain's office. The gray walls and vinyl floors made it difficult for her to get her bearings. Feeling overwhelmed, Joanne longed for her cubicle in Hawaii or even her cramped dorm room at the Academy.

"Here's your cubicle. I've ordered the standard array of supplies for you. If you need anything else, let me know. You have an appointment with the captain in one hour. There's a map on top of the stack. You'll need it," the woman added with a grin.

"Thank you," Joanne called to the retreating back.

Sinking into the gray chair behind the gray cubicle walls, Joanne tried to push Hawaii from her mind. In this windowless environment, she would have to rely on her watch rather than the sun that had always warmed her former office. Although it had been the standard, government-issue gray office, the sun's rays had washed the walls with a pale yellow hue. Now, everywhere she looked, Joanne saw only gray.

"Hi, Joanne. I'm Brenda Parks. I'll show you around for a while. We'll become friends. One of us will get transferred. It always happens," a pert young woman with short brown hair stated, standing inside the opening of Joanne's new office.

"I definitely need someone to show me around. I could always use a new friend. I promise, we'll keep in touch if one of us transfers," Joanne replied, accepting the handshake.

Laughing, Brenda said, "The best way to learn this place is to study the map and keep it with you at all times. I still carry mine, and I've been here eighteen months. I'll take you to lunch after your meeting with the captain. Along the way, you'll see the restrooms. That should do it for the important places. When we have time, I'll take you on the tourist tour of the building."

"That would be great. I'd like a few more copies of this map. Where can I find the copier?" Joanne asked, looking around the constantly repeating décor.

"It's next to the restrooms and the coffee room. I'll show you later on the way to lunch. If you attach this slip to the item you want copied and put it into that bin against the wall over there, one of our assistants will return it to you within a few minutes. You don't have to do it yourself," Brenda said.

"That's a change. In my former office, we did everything," Joanne added, following Brenda's instructions.

"You're in the Pentagon now, dear!" Brenda retorted with a tone of feigned smugness.

Laughing, Joanne tossed the paper into the appropriate bin and returned to her cubicle. Surveying the area, she smiled and said, "I don't think I've ever seen so many people in one place in my life."

"This is nothing. Just wait until we go to lunch. That's a real experience," Brenda said and added, "You might want to familiarize yourself with the organization chart for our department, its mission, and its goals before your session with the chief. He likes for people to dive right in."

"Thanks, Brenda. I'll do that," Joanne replied as she set her watch alarm for ten minutes prior to her appointment time.

Turning her attention to the welcome folder on her desk, Joanne pored through the sheets of information that detailed everything she would need to know in order to perform the tasks laid out for her by the chief. Photographs of each member of the team dotted the pages. The only thing missing was the actual personality profile for each one. However, from the serious expressions on their faces, Joanne decided that this was a no-nonsense group. As she plowed through the pages, members of her new division stopped by to welcome her and then disappeared down the corridor.

Rising, Joanne adjusted her uniform and started retracing her steps to the chief's office. Carrying the binder under her elbow, she marched with a confidence she did not feel down the long corridor. Without a single wrong turn, Joanne finally arrived at her destination. With a sigh, she identified herself and then settled into the indicated chair.

Watching the parade of uniformed humanity, Joanne was impressed with the efficiency of their motions. She could imagine that life in the massive structure of the Pentagon could be chaotic, but everyone she saw seemed to go about business with purpose and determination. A missed step would have sent the entire drama out of sync. Joanne was impressed by what appeared to be a carefully rehearsed panorama.

To her surprise, the department chief greeted her himself. Life seemed so regimented that Joanne expected someone to show her into his office. Rising and extending her hand to take his, Joanne felt relieved to find that real people existed within the gray, sterile walls.

Not surprising, however, was the barren atmosphere of the chief's office. Casting a quick glance around the room, Joanne saw nothing personal or decorative other than the few family photographs on his desk. It was clear that, on a moment's notice, the chief could pack his briefcase and move to another assignment.

"Welcome. Your reputation for hard work has preceded you, Joanne. You'll be able to put everything you've learned from the Pacific experience to good use here but on a much larger scale. Our intelligence work is global in scope. I know you'll make a good member of the team," the chief said, motioning toward a straight-backed chair.

"Thank you, sir."

"I see that you've familiarized yourself with the

binder. You're under Commander Clarke's subdivision. He's waiting for you now. Again, welcome," the chief stated in dismissal.

"Good-bye, sir."

Joanne moved from one brief session to the other all morning. In each office, the conversation was the same, a handshake, quick welcome, and dismissal. Formal, direct, and concise. Navy.

"I see you survived," Brenda greeted Joanne upon her return.

"Barely. Thank goodness for photos. Otherwise I wouldn't be able to tell one person from the other. Thanks for telling me about the binder," Joanne added, slipping into her chair.

"We stick together around here. Ready for lunch?" Brenda asked, fitting her bag onto her shoulder.

"Starving," Joanne replied, following her down same hall that led past the chief's office and deeper into the maze of corridors.

"Grab your map and follow me. Stay close," Brenda advised.

"I don't intend to let you out of my sight," Joanne said nervously.

"If we get separated," Brenda laughed, "I'm the one in the uniform."

"Funny!"

"Just a touch of Pentagon humor," Brenda chuckled.

Although she never could have found it on her own, the walk to the cafeteria did not take as long as Joanne had anticipated. Along the way, they passed corridors dedicated to each service, and to the African Americans, women, and Native Americans who served in the military. Displays, austere and simple in design, highlighted the contributions of each group and marked the transition from one corridor to the other.

One display of a submarine caught Joanne's attention as she passed. Stopping briefly, she saw that the model was of the same class as the sub on which Mike was an officer. The photographs vividly displayed the cramped quarters, the intricate system of pipes and wires, and the racks of torpedoes. Even in the multifaceted Pentagon, she could not escape reminders of Mike and the danger in which he lived.

Stepping into the cafeteria, Joanne stopped short at the impact of seeing so many uniformed and civilian people. As a member of the brigade of midshipmen of the Naval Academy, she had taken her meals in a dining room populated by approximately four thousand people. Here, however, the count was much greater and the size of the room dwarfing.

Turning toward her, Brenda said, "If we get separated, meet me under the clock."

"Which one?" Joanne demanded, spotting at least ten of them at regular intervals along the wall.

"Just kidding!" Brenda quipped. "It's something, isn't it? You'll get used to the size. Most of the time, you won't even eat here."

"Where do people eat around here?" Joanne asked.

"I usually brown-bag to save money and time, but I knew you would report today and wanted to show you around. If I go out, I head to the mall," Brenda replied, handing Joanne a tray.

"I saw the entrance when I got off the Metro this morning," Joanne commented, adding a salad and bread to her tray.

"It's the only way to travel. The parking lot's massive and congested. The subway's an easy ride," Brenda said, paying her bill and moving toward a very distant table.

Following closely, Joanne remarked, "My apartment's a short walk from the Silver Spring Metro stop. It's great. Out one door and in the other. No fuss. I doubt that I'll drive very often. I walked to work in Hawaii, but I'll enjoy the reading time on the subway, too."

"When we're in a crunch, that'll be the only free time you'll have. Enjoy it," Brenda stated.

"What causes a crunch situation?" Joanne inquired, following her new friend.

"The events of the U.S.S. *Cole* bombing and September 11 definitely had people around here scurrying. I was still in college, but I've heard stories. Any last-minute, top brass request for intelligence can send blood pressures soaring, too. It's part of the job," Brenda replied, shrugging her uniformed shoulders.

"It seems pretty quiet today," Joanne observed, looking around the room.

"Good. Don't jinx it," Brenda responded, digging into a big Caesar salad with chicken.

The two women ate in silence for a while as the swarm of people changed on the quarter hour. Uniformed military types mingled with civilians as they searched for tables, exchanged pleasantries, and returned to their tasks. The flow of traffic in the massive room never seemed to dwindle.

As they ate, Joanne noticed that everyone seemed to go about business in a purposeful way, even while at lunch. No one lingered over dessert or conversation. It seemed as if everyone wanted to nourish the body and get on with more pressing issues. Soon, she and Brenda joined the wave of people that flowed from the cafeteria, making way for the next group to enter.

Everywhere she looked, Joanne saw men who reminded her of Mike. Uniforms, clean chins, and short haircuts were definitely in vogue. Many of them walked with the same spring in their step, the crispness that came from hours of marching.

Returning to her cubicle exactly thirty minutes after leaving it, Joanne discovered an even larger stack of folders and binders on her desk. The brief honeymoon of being new had ended. She tossed her purse into the drawer and got to work. She was so engrossed in her work that she did not feel the passage of time.

"Quitting time!" Brenda declared, standing in the opening of Joanne's cubicle.

Looking at her watch, Joanne was surprised at the rapid passage of the day. She had only just opened the second folder of the many marked for her immediate attention. Despite Brenda's announcement that their day had ended, she had actually worked an hour past the stated workday. Already Joanne had discovered that work at the Pentagon followed no set time limit.

As Joanne and Brenda joined the flow of people exiting the building, Joanne decided that she would like working in the Pentagon. It was not the informal office in Hawaii, but it certainly had a distinct ethos. The order and regimentation reminded Joanne of her days at the Academy, days filled with more than enough to do and few minutes to waste. Perhaps she would not miss Mike so much while working under the demands of strict deadlines.

* * *

Mike, however, was so busy that he had little time to think. In addition to his duties as a junior officer, he had a ream of certification questions to answer. The portfolio would be his ticket to his dauphins and true acceptance as a submariner.

Noting the time, Mike switched off his light and stowed the assignment on which he had been working since the end of his shift under his pillow. Settling into his small berth, he yawned and for a few minutes thought about Joanne. She had looked so heartbroken the last time he had seen her that he had to struggle to keep that picture of her from coming to his mind. He preferred the images of her laughing, swimming, or beating him at golf.

Mike knew that Joanne understood his passion for submarines, just as he had comprehended her need to fly. They had been afraid for each other but accepting of the decisions that led them into their chosen professions. However, now that her airsickness problem had forced Joanne to change her direction, she was acting more like a civilian than a naval officer. Although the sub accident had shaken her badly, Mike was confident that Joanne would recover her composure and adjust to the conditions of their life.

Yawning, Mike closed his eyes and listened to noise coming from the berth beneath his. Of the four men who occupied the tight quarters, one was a terrible snorer. Despite the racket, Mike had learned to ignore it, study by it, and sleep without hearing it. It was only at times like this when he wanted peace to think clearly about Joanne that the raucous blasts that threatened to shake him from his berth disturbed him.

"Turn over, Frank. You're rocking the boat with that noise," Mike shouted over the trumpeting.

Without awakening, his roommate shifted and momentarily stopped the racket. Knowing that the respite would not last, Mike quickly returned to thoughts of Joanne. In the brief lull, Mike decided that he would buy her something special as soon as they made port. The e-mails he had sent had so far received only brief responses to his equally brief messages. It was not easy to communicate with someone from a submarine. The sub rarely rose close enough to the proper depth to receive messages and never rose close enough to the surface to permit telephone calls.

Normally, Mike would not have minded the silence, knowing that Joanne was safe and busy at her job in Hawaii. However, with the unpleasantness of her decision to end their engagement hanging over him, he would have liked to have been able to reassure Joanne of his love for her. Being far away and out of contact would not help to convince her that they should make a life together.

As Frank's snoring began again, Mike turned on his side and slipped into a deep sleep caused by long work hours and sleep deprivation. As his lids fluttered down, he could almost feel Joanne's warmth against his body and her head on his arm. Sighing, Mike sank into a slumber as deep as the sea and as silent.

Chapter Sixteen

The months passed quickly with Joanne slipping seamlessly into the fabric of life at the Pentagon. Every day, she read while riding the Metro, melted into the flow of employees in the building, performed her duties, and returned home. When she had extra time, Joanne went shopping at lunchtime or after work, visited with her friends and family on the weekend, and pushed nagging thoughts of Mike into their proper compartment in her mind. The routine and demands of her day helped Joanne to survive the loneliness of missing him.

Although during the day she forced herself not to look for information on his submarine, Joanne often found herself searching the files for reports of ship accidents and feeling relieved when she did not find them. Joanne told herself that ending the engagement had liberated her from worry, but her heart did not agree. She had to keep reminding herself that distancing herself from Mike emotionally was for the best.

The nights, however, were different. At night, the longing magnified without the demands of work to keep it in check. As she lay in her bed waiting for sleep to come, Joanne prayed for his safety and missed him terribly. Her body remembered the nights spent in his arms and the touch of his hands. Her lips recalled the feel of his kisses and the taste of his skin.

When she could not calm her fears, Joanne would rise and do sit-ups and push-ups until her abdomen and arms ached. Exhausted, she would fall asleep, too tired to think and too lonely to cry. The dawn would soon rescue her from the dreams that brought Mike's face close to hers only to fade with the blast from her clock radio.

One morning, rushing from yet another meeting, Joanne rounded a corner and bumped into an oncoming officer. Scrambling to pick up the dropped binder and the papers that spilled from the folders, she hastily apologized and prepared to leave until something familiar about him stopped her in her tracks. As he returned the last folder to her arms, recognition flashed across her face and his.

"I've been trying to find you," his deep baritone voice said.

"This is one way to do it," Joanne replied with a smile.

"You bumped into me," John stated with a big grin.

"Only because you're on the wrong side of the corridor," Joanne responded, chuckling.

"Let me buy you lunch to make up for my clumsiness," John offered.

"Fine. Meet me at the clock at noon," Joanne commented, preparing to dash away.

"Which one?" John asked, placing his hand on her arm.

Realizing that she could not give him the brush

with the customary Pentagon humor, Joanne replied, "The one over Halsey."

"I'll be the guy in the uniform," John responded.

Chuckling, Joanne dashed away. Her heart pounded not only from the rushing that she had been doing all morning but from John's sudden appearance. He had promised that they would meet again and they had.

"Who was that? Your cheeks are flushed. Another amorous admirer who loves the sight of you in a uniform?" Brenda demanded.

"That's from running all over this place. My feet hurt, too. I don't think he did that. No, he's not one of my groupies. This one is different," Joanne replied, laughing at her friend's comments about her single male following. "I met him at a wedding in Hawaii. He was the best man; I was the maid of honor. Candlelight and roses, or in this case, orchids, followed by sailing and sunshine, but it didn't work out. The timing wasn't right . . . the recent breakup with Mike, the imminent transfer, his short leave. Now he's here. I tried to brush him off with the clock routine, but he didn't buy it. I'm meeting him for lunch."

"Smart and handsome. You might not want to let this one get away," Brenda suggested. "He's new but not green. That's refreshing."

"You know I'm not interested in a romance. I've had more than enough opportunity, but I just don't want to get involved. I'm happy with my life right now," Joanne said, reordering the pages of her file.

"You've definitely been in demand since you reported here. Just the same, you might want to rethink your determination to spend your life and career unattached," Brenda suggested.

Shaking her head, Joanne commented, "The last

time I got involved with a fellow officer, I found heartache and worry. No thanks. No military men for me. Besides, I'm not over Mike. I dreamed about him again last night. I guess it's because he's probably back in port by now. He's probably prowling the streets of an exotic Mediterranean city, eating pasta by the bowlful, and having a great time."

"He still thinks you're still in Hawaii, doesn't he?" Brenda reminded her friend.

"Probably, since the e-mails take forever to process. I haven't received confirmation that the last one reached the ship. He can always find me if he's interested in accepting life on my terms. Remember, he has my parents' phone number. They know where I live," Joanne replied, adding a touch of lipstick.

"I thought you weren't interested in this guy. Lipstick?" Brenda observed.

"I'm not, but this white does nothing for me. He should have bumped into me on a blue day," Joanne joked.

"It's a good thing I have plans for lunch. You've certainly kicked me to the curb," Brenda complained good-naturedly.

"Get off it," Joanne objected. "We had already decided that you'd make this trip to the mall alone. I can't afford either a long lunch or a spending spree. I have too much work to do and too little money."

"You could have lent your support to my efforts to add to the GNP," Brenda replied, as they walked toward the confluence of corridors.

"Another time. I'll give you all the details over dinner tonight. It shouldn't take long," Joanne said and waved good-bye.

"Don't be surprised if this one is a keeper," Brenda said. "It's time for your luck to change."

"Whatever."

As Joanne entered the cafeteria, her eyes immediately sought the clock and the Halsey photograph. Despite the crowd, John's gaze met hers and held it. Against her wishes, Joanne's felt a smile tugging at the corners of her mouth. Something about lunching with a new man appealed to Joanne's sense of adventure.

John was even more handsome against the drab décor of the Pentagon than he had been amidst the flowers of Hawaii. His smile was quick and his wit even faster. She had liked his first impression and was looking forward to seeing if there was more to the man.

Yet he was not Mike. Although John smiled warmly at seeing her and his eyes sparkled gaily, they did not ignite a fire in Joanne. Handsome as he was, the sight of him did not make her want to run to him. His voice was mellow, but it did not make her knees buckle. John was a perfectly wonderful guy, just not Mike.

From the very beginning of their relationship, Mike's presence in the same room had sent her emotions on a roller-coaster ride. She only had to hear his voice and see his smile to forget time and place. Not even the crowd in a room could keep her from feeling the magnetism. Mike cast a spell that no man, not even one as handsome as John, could equal.

"The uniform becomes you," John commented as they moved through the cafeteria line.

"This old thing? It's the first outfit I put my hands on this morning," Joanne joked.

"You're a stunningly beautiful woman, Joanne," John stated seriously.

"I bet you say that to all the ensigns," Joanne quipped.

"Only to the ones whose sparkling eyes have been on my mind since my trip to Hawaii. Strange, I don't remember anything about the island, but I remember everything about you," John commented softly.

Slipping into her seat, Joanne asked, "Do you always come on this strong?"

"No. I guess I've rehearsed what I'd say to you so many times that I can't help myself," John replied honestly.

"We hardly know each other. We met at Sylvia's wedding and spent a day together touring the island," Joanne replied, tasting her salad.

"I know enough to be sure that I want to learn more," John responded quickly.

"Look, John, I'm still not over the breakup. I'm not really looking for a relationship," Joanne stated, studying his gentle face.

"I hear you, but you never know what you might discover without looking for it," John said.

"You've been warned. You're a grown man. It's your decision," Joanne shrugged.

"Do you have any plans for this weekend?" John asked with a grin.

"I'm going wedding-gown shopping on Saturday with one of the women in my unit. Yes, another of my friends is getting married, and yes, I'm a bridesmaid again," Joanne replied with a roll of her eyes.

"Take careful notes. It'll be your turn soon enough," John said, smiling.

"You're either a dreamer or a romantic. Either

way, there's something strangely charming about you," Joanne stated with a grin.

"Good. I'm already breaking down your defenses. So, I guess you'll let me take you out to dinner on Friday and Saturday. We'll spend the day together on Sunday, too, if you can put up with me that much," John decided with a contented smile.

"You are a pushy person, aren't you?" Joanne laughed.

"Life's too short when you're in the military not to be," John replied seriously.

Swallowing hard as thoughts of Mike rushed through her mind, Joanne replied, "I know. Let's take it one day at a time. Dinner Friday night's a go. The Saturday wedding shopping thing includes dinner with the other ladies in the bridal party. Sunday I almost always spend with my parents."

"I'll take what I can get and book next Friday and Saturday in advance," John declared.

"We'll see. We might discover that we have nothing in common and can't wait to get away from each other. One dinner might be enough," Joanne replied, studying his face.

Looking directly into her eyes, John said, "I knew when I first saw you at the wedding that you were the right woman for me. I'll take it slow and give you plenty of time to get to know me. I'll pick you up at seven. How's Japanese food?"

"Perfect. I've missed it since leaving Hawaii. I can't find a place that's as good here," Joanne replied.

"Leave it to me. I discovered a gem the other night. I've only sampled the oyako domburi, but it was top-drawer," John commented as they settled into a comfortable silence.

After a lunch punctuated by casual discussion of

job duties, Joanne returned to her division, leaving John to turn left from the Navy's main corridor. Before Joanne could toss her purse into the drawer, Brenda slipped into her cubicle with hands on hips and waited for the details. Joanne realized that she would not be able to return to the stack of folders on her desk unless she shared the lunchtime scenario with her new friend.

"Well?" Brenda demanded.

"He's a nice guy, but I knew that from the wedding. He's witty and genuine. I could like him . . . " Joanne replied with a shrug.

"It's Mike, isn't it? Don't you think you should put him out of your mind? You have a life. It's time you lived it," Brenda advised.

"I haven't stopped living simply because Mike isn't here and our engagement fell apart," Joanne insisted.

"Loving is part of living. You need a man in your life. Fate has dropped this guy at your feet. Go for it. Don't let him get away," Brenda insisted.

"I don't know, but I can't stop comparing every man I meet to Mike. I don't think I'm ready," Joanne sighed.

"You won't know unless you try. You've told John about Mike. He's willing to invest the time in a relationship that might not happen. What have you got to lose?" Brenda asked.

"Nothing. I could use the company. Now that you're getting married, I won't see as much of you on the weekends," Joanne commented.

"I knew you'd see the light," Brenda smiled.

"I haven't committed to anything. We're having dinner together Friday night and then again next weekend if all goes well. I'm taking it one step at a time . . . very slowly," Joanne reminded her friend.

"That's all I ask," Brenda remarked.

Frowning, Joanne said, "I feel as if I'm being unfaithful to Mike."

"That's silly!" Brenda exclaimed. "You're not engaged to him any longer. It's over. You haven't seen or heard from him in months. He's happily sailing the seven seas. You're here. You're doing nothing wrong."

"I can't help the way I feel," Joanne insisted, leafing through a folder.

"You'll get over it. John's charm will make you forget all about Mike," Brenda promised.

"That's a tall order," Joanne declared as the phone rang, putting an end to the conversation.

By the time the week sped to an end, Joanne had spent another lunch with John. Try as hard as she could, Joanne was unable to find anything about him that she did not like. They reminisced about the brief time they had spent in Hawaii together and discussed their military plans like old friends.

When John picked her up for dinner on Friday night, Joanne felt none of the first-date jitters. In fact, she was amazed by the ease with which he had slipped into her life. Lunch discussions and evening phone conversations had set the stage for their blossoming friendship.

Without knowing it, John had selected one of the area's newest and trendiest restaurants, according to the *Washington Post* and *Washingtonian* magazine. It was a bit pricey, but well worth the money. Everyone said that the chef was a creative genius. From the lines at the door, it looked as if the establishment was off to a good start.

"Ah, oyako domburi, as promised!" John exclaimed as he scanned the menu.

"You like that, too? You're the only other person I know who has ever tasted it. It's so hard to find around here. I ate it all the time in Hawaii. I've been dying to come to this restaurant but couldn't find anyone who liked Japanese cuisine." Joanne smiled.

"It's the best chicken casserole I've ever tasted. I guess it's the combination of pickles and seaweed," John commented.

"Most people think that eating Japanese means feasting on sushi and aren't willing to explore. They miss the other great dishes," Joanne stated, sipping her sake.

Chuckling, John explained, "When you've lived as many places and in as many countries as I have, you learn to eat everything. My dad was in the navy, too. I've lived in Guam, Japan, the Philippines, and every state in the union that has a naval base. He retired from a post in Brussels, NATO actually, but I only visited that one once. I was at the Academy by then."

"I met a lot of military kids when I was in college. In a way, I envied them. They lived in so many exciting places," Joanne sighed.

"And some not so wonderful ones, too," John stated. "You never know what you'll find. Some of our housing was great, others were in shambles. The higher my dad's rank, the better we lived. That's why I'm determined to rise as quickly and as far as possible. I like the idea of having household help and not having to pay for it. If I'm going to uproot my wife and kids every few years, I want them to live well. It's hard on a woman to abandon her career because of her husband's transfer. Kids hate changing schools and friends all the time. There have to be some perks with rank."

"Is that why you decided on this way of life?" Joanne asked.

"I don't know any other. Besides, I love travel. The long hours and hard work give me a sense of purpose that I don't think I'd find in other walks of life," John explained.

Shaking her head, Joanne said, "It's not always easy to find a spouse that wants the life of packing and unpacking and making and leaving friends. None of my high-school friends would even look at a military man. We'd visit Annapolis on the weekends, but they just weren't attracted to the mids. Most of them couldn't believe it when I chose this way of life. It's too demanding for them. They wanted careers and normalcy."

"I know. My civilian buddies thought I was nuts, too. They said I should have gotten the wanderlust out of my system as a kid, but I haven't. I love it," John said, smiling happily.

"Me, too, although I haven't been too far from home . . . Florida and Hawaii," Joanne added.

"You will," John said from experience. "You haven't had a sea tour yet. I've finished two of them. Each one seemed more demanding than the preceding one. I guess it was the added responsibility of extra rank each time. Whatever the reason, the tours weren't half bad. Now that I'm no longer a college man, time seems to pass quickly wherever I am. It was really slow during the dark ages; those long winter months with nothing to do but study were bad. Remember those days at the Academy when winter seemed to last forever and the sky was always gray? It's good to be a graduate and not a midshipman. Life in the fleet, for all its demands, is better than that."

Nodding in agreement, Joanne said, "I don't miss the trivial stuff of the Academy, that's for sure. However, I do miss the feeling of expectation that hovers over everything. As midshipmen, we didn't know about life in the fleet. It was a promise. For me, it hasn't exactly been fulfilled as I expected."

"I'm sure not being able to fly has been tough on you, but you seem to be adjusting well. Flexibility is a good trait in an officer," John commented, studying her face for secrets beneath the surface.

Chuckling softly, Joanne replied, "Sometimes, the ability to adapt is thrust upon us along with the responsibility of command. We certainly grow up fast in the military. I don't know if civilians face the same demands."

"They probably do, in their way. It's different from our life, but probably just as demanding," John responded. "I'm sure some of them travel often, too. Upheaval is rough whichever way it presents itself."

Joanne and John ate in silence for a while as they thought about private elements of their lives. Joanne knew that she had needed to adapt both professionally and personally. She wondered if John had experienced the same turmoil in his plans. She wanted to know more about the handsome man who sat opposite her.

As if reading her mind, John said, "You were right about not being able to find partners who're willing to live the military life. I was involved with a woman who changed her mind about us at the last minute. She just couldn't move with me to the tropics. She's an attorney and wouldn't leave her life for mine. I don't blame her; it's a lot to ask. She had worked hard to become a partner in the firm and couldn't turn her back on it. We ended the relationship as friends."

"I'm the one who ended my last relationship. I couldn't live with the fear of his submarine service selection. I'm not that strong," Joanne stated.

"I know several guys in the sub service. They love it, and they're still single. They won't bring a woman into that life. As a matter of fact, a couple of them are in pretty serious relationships and planning to change communities. One's headed to meteorology so that he can have a normal life. The other's not ready to settle down. He likes the bonuses too much to give it up," John said, studying her reaction.

Wistfully, Joanne replied, "Maybe one day your friend will fall in love so hard that the sub service won't mean anything to him anymore."

Studying her closely, John stated, "Any man with half a brain who meets a woman he can love and who loves him back would be a fool not to leave subs behind. Not to put too sharp a point on it, but a woman whose man won't do that for her should walk away and never look back."

Smiling bravely, Joanne said, "I did."

Again, Joanne and John ate in silence. Against her will, Joanne found herself comparing John to Mike. John was older and more settled and a good listener. He appeared to have learned a few life lessons along the way, as opposed to Mike, who had only just started living.

Mike, on the other hand, was barely able to contain the energy that made it difficult for him to stay seated for more than a few minutes. His mind often jumped from one topic to the other. Joanne knew that having a conversation with him was often like playing ping-pong as one thought bounced off the other. Mike was busy exploring life and learning to live it.

However, although John's mellow, laid-back personality was engaging, Joanne liked Mike's spontaneity and his energy. He was exciting and refreshing.

Physically, the men were similar. Both were tall and muscular. Their gaze was direct and steady. Their voices were deep and comforting. Joanne could find nothing that she did not like about either of them. The primary difference was that John sat across the table from her, and Mike sailed the seas.

"Let's take in a movie after dinner," John suggested, eating the oyako approvingly.

"Sounds like fun. Which one do you have in mind?" Joanne asked, relieved for the opportunity to put the comparison from her mind.

"Unless it's too much navy for you, I'd like to see the new Denzel Washington movie—the one in which he's a SEAL on a dangerous mission," John suggested.

"I think I can handle it. As if there's any other kind of mission for them," Joanne chuckled.

As they left the restaurant, Joanne noticed that a touch of fall had kissed the air. Soon they would enter the holiday season . . . her first one without Mike or someone special in her life. She felt the cool air kiss her cheek along with a touch of sadness.

Joanne knew that she should have been happy and felt blessed for the many gifts that filled her life. Everyone she loved was healthy. She had a job she enjoyed, surrounded by people with whom she liked to work. Her career had finally settled into a niche from which she could plan a life.

However, even with John at her side, Joanne knew that something was missing. She did not have someone with whom to share the love that threatened to overflow and consume her in its unspent passion. She needed to feel, to care, to worry. Perhaps this man who understood her thoughts so completely would be the one to take her mind and heart away from the man she loved and could not have. Perhaps she could learn to love someone new, but only time would tell.

While Joanne watched a movie about submarine life, Mike lived it. The submarine had surfaced to collect messages, providing the men with time for calls and e-mail. Seizing the moment, Mike quickly dialed Joanne's home number in Hawaii. Frowning, he listened to the message that told him the number was no longer in service. Remembering that she always carried her cell phone, he punched in the familiar number. This time, instead of a mechanical voice, Mike heard Joanne's sweet tones advising him to leave a message.

Shouting against the lapping of the waves, Mike said, "Hi! I hope you're enjoying Hawaii. What's up with the phone-number disconnect? We've surfaced for messages. I sure am glad that I sprang for the international calling plan. Without it, I wouldn't be able to make this call. As it is, the transmission's scratchy. I hope you can hear me. I thought I'd call you to say that I love you and think of you all the time. Life's hectic, boring, and exciting. My waking hours are too long, and the sleeping ones too short. My mates snore, but I've learned to sleep through it. We'll make port one of these days. I'll call again when I have time. Bye."

As he returned his cell phone to his pocket and left the tower, Mike frowned. He wondered why Joanne's home phone would have been disconnected. Deciding that she must have been on some kind of economizing venture, he pushed the thought from his mind. Since she used that line as a computer connection most of the time, he decided that she had decided that accessing her e-mail from work would suffice. Whatever the reason, he knew she was okay.

As the submarine prepared to dive, Mike returned to his duty station near the nuclear reactor. He had become accustomed to the rocking that ceased as soon as they reached cruise depth, although the motion reminded him that he had selected wisely. A surface ship was not his cup of tea. Mike liked smooth seas in his career and his personal life.

Pushing the thought of Joanne's sweet face and the feel of her body against him from his mind, Mike returned his attention to his certification sheets. Although he could take up to eighteen months to complete the tasks, he wanted to finish early so that he could enjoy liberty in port both in the Mediterranean and back home in Norfolk. More freedom would give him a chance to visit Joanne in Hawaii. Feeling Joanne's lips on his one last time, Mike focused his attention on the gauges that maintained life on the sub. The mini break had ended.

Chapter Seventeen

The holiday season always put Joanne into a festive mood. She loved the smell of cookies and cakes fresh from the oven, the aroma of pine needles, and the excitement of opening presents. She relished sitting with her parents at dinner and feeling the joy in being at home again. However, this holiday was different; Mike was not in her life. In a short period of time, so much had changed.

Joanne awoke in her old bedroom, having spent the night so that she could help her mother prepare the Christmas meal. She stretched and yawned lazily, not wanting to leave the warmth of her bed. Not even the insistent meowing of the family cat could make her move.

"All right. Just give me a few more minutes," Joanne muttered to the tiger cat sitting on her pillow. In response, the cat lay its head on her shoulder and purred loudly into her ear.

"I guess I don't have any choice now. There's no way I can sleep with you in here," Joanne said to the cat as she scratched its ears.

Rising, Joanne rushed to the bathroom for a quick shower. If she hurried, she would be able to peel the apples for the pie, or maybe cut up the stuffing ingredients. At the very least, she would be able to rescue her father from the task of setting the table.

Hearing her mother singing from the kitchen, Joanne knew that the preparations were well under way. Her mother always rose early to prepare the turkey and start the breakfast. Once she had cleared the kitchen, she would start the baking. Every Christmas followed the same familiar pattern, and nothing ever changed. Christmas in the Crawford home was perfect, a holiday to store in memory for a rainy day.

Pulling on jeans and an oversized blue sweater, Joanne dashed down the stairs as she had done every Christmas for as long as she could remember. The tree in the living room announced the importance of the day. Gaily wrapped gifts waited under its boughs for the time when anxious fingers would rip open the paper, toss the ribbons onto the floor, and pry up the tops. Everyone would exclaim in delight at the carefully selected gifts that reflected both the giver's and the receiver's personality.

Kissing her mother lightly on the cheek, Joanne surveyed the kitchen. The stack of clean breakfast dishes still sat on the table, indicating that her father was in hiding in the sunroom. Carrying them to the dining room, Joanne quickly set the table for four and laid out the usual number of trivets. Double-checking to make sure that everything looked perfect, she returned to her mother's side.

"That's done. What's next?" Joanne asked, nibbling a slice of orange.

"It's so nice having you home. Your father's a great help, but he's not one to volunteer. The dishes have been sitting on that table since seven this morning. I think he's reading every article in the *Post* to keep from having to help me," Mrs. Crawford chuckled.

"Didn't he do that last year, too? Daddy's very predictable. Anyway, I'm here, so what can I do?" Joanne asked again.

"Slice the apples for the pie," Mrs. Crawford replied. "The pie plate is ready. Toss them with the ingredients in that mixing bowl and then cover with that extra crust."

"Done!" Joanne responded with youthful enthusiasm for a task that would reap tasty results.

For a while, neither of them spoke. Mother and daughter felt that the joy of being in the warm kitchen together was sufficient. Joanne's growing up and moving away had created a huge void in Mrs. Crawford's life that having her home for the holiday helped to fill.

"Do you and John have any plans for after dinner?" Mrs. Crawford asked, finally.

"No, not really," Joanne replied without looking up from the apples. "His parents live in Florida, so he'll phone them. We'll probably just stay here underfoot. We're leaving early tomorrow for a weekend of skiing. We won't exactly be alone, since we're part of a big group from work that's going. I'm sharing a room with my friend Brenda, and John's rooming with her fiancé. We're even driving up in separate cars. He wants as much time on the slopes as possible, and I'm in no hurry to get frostbite."

"He seems to be a very nice guy. I'm glad you met him," her mother commented casually.

"So am I. He's almost perfect, but he's no M—" Joanne stopped in mid-statement.

Looking at her daughter, Mrs. Crawford said, "No one will be. He was special . . . your first real love. He wasn't one of the many crushes you had when you were in high school. It's hard to replace a love like that, but you will."

"But I shouldn't compare them. It's not fair to John. He is a really great guy. I just don't love him," Joanne replied with a touch of sadness in her voice for the absent Mike and for John, the man she could not love.

"He has certainly tried hard enough to win your heart," Mrs. Crawford commented.

Smiling, Joanne said, "I know . . . probably too hard. We've seen every art show that's currently running downtown. I've seen more theater with him than with anyone else. We've played racquetball and tennis until I think I'm developing tendonitis. He plans everything. I never have to lift a finger. He thinks of everything. No girl could ask for more. He's terrific."

"Well, give it time," Mrs. Crawford advised. "He'll grow on you. That's what happened to your Aunt Susan. She met your uncle after a painful breakup. He was perfect, just like John. He was willing to give her the time she needed. One day, she looked at him and knew that he was the one for her. She couldn't recall exactly when she fell in love with him, but she knew that she wanted him in her life forever. To her surprise, she couldn't remember the way the other guy looked, and she had thought that she'd die from missing him. They've been happily married for thirty years."

"Maybe that'll happen for me one day, too," Joanne replied wistfully. "At any rate, I'm giving it a try. I'm not sitting around waiting for Mike to decide that it's time for him to leave the sub service. He might never get tired of it. I'll miss too many opportunities if I wait for him. He's living the life he wants, and I'm living mine. I just wish he were still in it."

Entering the kitchen with the folded paper under his arm, Mr. Crawford stated, "Something sure smells good! Anything I can do to help?"

Joanne and her mother looked at each other and burst into gales of laughter. While her confused husband looked from his daughter to his wife, Mrs. Crawford composed herself enough to hug him tightly. He was and had always been the love of her life, despite his minor flaws.

"No, Daddy. We've just about finished here," Joanne replied, dabbing the happy tears that clung to her lashes.

"You're so predictable, my dear husband. You always make your entrance once everything's done," Mrs. Crawford stated as she returned to drying the last of the mixing bowls.

Beaming at the reception from the women in his life, Mr. Crawford replied, "It's a skill I've honed over many happy years of marriage. If you need me, I'll be in the living room shaking my presents."

Tossing her apron onto the nearest chair, Joanne followed him saying, "No, not yet. Breakfast is ready."

"Let's eat fast. My curiosity is getting the better of me," Mr. Crawford replied, sinking into a dining room chair.

"Don't gobble. I've spent too much effort on this meal for you not to enjoy it," Mrs. Crawford commented, serving her husband's plate.

"Yes, dear."

As they inhaled the delicious aromas, the Crawfords thanked God for their blessings, the food, the hands that had prepared it, and the joy of being together during turbulent times. They discussed nothing in particular as they devoured the fried apples, scrambled eggs with corn, thick buttery biscuits, and slices of Smithfield ham. When they had finished, they quickly cleaned up the kitchen and retired to the living room.

Shaking a long thin box, Mr. Crawford announced, "I think this is a tie."

"Safe bet, but wrong!" Joanne rebutted.

"Gloves?" her father tried again.

"Don't guess. Open it," Joanne instructed as she watched her father rip off the paper.

"Be careful! We can save that paper," Mrs. Crawford instructed, as she did every year.

Raising their eyebrows at each other, the father and daughter ignored her pleas. Long ago they had decided that the gift-wrap paper from the presents of a family of three was hardly worth cluttering the top of closets to keep. Besides, careful unwrapping took too much time, and they were anxious to open their gifts.

"What is this?" Joanne's father asked as he opened the portfolio.

"You'll see," Joanne replied, waiting for him to finish reading the brochure.

Clearly impressed, Joanne's father exclaimed, "Wow! Listen to this! 'This ticket entitles the bearer to a golf trip for two to Williamsburg including cart, greens fees, practice range, balls, club cleaning, bag tags, and commemorative shirts. Accommodations include two nights at the Williamsburg Inn, two dinners at historic inns of the bearer's choice, all breakfasts and lunches during the stay.' This is great!"

"Beats socks," Joanne's mother commented, smiling.

"Looks like we're finally going to play golf in

Williamsburg. Thanks, baby. All right, wife, open yours," Mr. Crawford instructed his wife.

Mrs. Crawford slipped her nail carefully under the tape and slid out the thin box. Lifting the top, she gasped and looked at Joanne with a genuine expression of surprise on her face. She had decided against purchasing the bracelet for herself because of its price, but now the cherished trinket glistened from her wrist as if it had been fashioned for her.

"Joanne, you really shouldn't have spent so much on us this year. The golf trip and this wonderful bracelet must have taken all your money. It's just too much," Mrs. Crawford advised as she snapped the bracelet's clasp.

"You're the only parents I have, and I wanted to give you something you really wanted," Joanne replied, pleased that her gifts had hit the mark.

"You did that," her father stated, kissing her gently on the cheek.

"Too extravagant, but I love it," Mrs. Crawford said as she added her kiss to the other cheek.

"Now open yours," Mr. Crawford instructed.

Lifting a huge package, Joanne settled on the floor with the cat at her feet. Trying to be careful with the paper, she unwrapped it gingerly and lifted the lid. Inside she found a new ski jacket and pants.

"You remembered that the movers lost some of my stuff. I was going to buy new stuff on the way to the slopes tomorrow. This is perfect," Joanne stated happily.

"You're not the only one who's attuned to the desires of family members. I helped your mother pick out the outfit," Mr. Crawford proclaimed proudly.

"You guys are the greatest. I'm so happy to be home again," Joanne replied, kissing both of them.

"Don't forget the other one. It arrived yesterday,"

Mrs. Crawford said, pointing to the shipping box leaning against the base of the tree.

"I wonder who sent it," Joanne mused. "John and I exchanged gifts last night. Do you think . . . ?"

"Open it and find out," Mr. Crawford urged, looking over Joanne's head at his nodding wife.

Ripping off the brown paper to reveal a box wrapped in silver and decorated with a big red bow carefully protected by rigid cardboard, Joanne read the gift card. She had decided against sending Mike a gift, since they had not spoken since their breakup months earlier. However, he had remembered her while in Naples, Italy.

"I feel awful. I didn't send Mike anything, and he's far from home," Joanne cried.

"That's okay. I'm sure he didn't expect anything. Besides, you didn't even know where to send it," Mr. Crawford consoled her.

"Open it!" Mrs. Crawford insisted. "Save the paper! The embossing is too pretty to toss into the trash."

Joanne's hands shook as she carefully slipped the box from its silvery wrapping. Inside, she found the most exquisite hand-knit mauve dress that she had ever seen. A slip attached to the seams with tiny stitches added coverage, and the scooped neck with fagoting made it youthful. Standing on uncertain legs, Joanne discovered that the hem of the dress reached to just above her knees. The long sleeves would kiss her wrists perfectly. The mauve brightened the color of her cheeks that had turned pale with the surprise.

"What does that say?" Mrs. Crawford asked as a note fluttered to the floor.

Picking it up, Joanne read, "'I saw it in a shop

window in Rome and couldn't resist it. It's so you. Wear it for me when I come home. Love, Mike.'"

Tears trickled down Joanne's cheeks and onto the paper. She was on his mind although she had broken off their engagement. Her image followed him through the streets of Italy.

"I'm a rat or at the very least a real witch. I love Mike, but not enough to accept his choices if they caused me hardship. I'm selfish and small-minded. But it's Mike fault, too. He shouldn't have put me in a position to feel this way," Joanne stated simply, wiping the tears with her trembling fingers.

"No, you're not," Mrs. Crawford said as she slipped her arms around Joanne's thin shoulders. "Mike made his choice, and you made yours. The timing just wasn't right."

"I should have stuck it out. I shouldn't have been so self-centered. I should have learned to live with the fear. Other military folks live with it all the time, and they don't end a good thing," Joanne sniffed.

Watching his suffering daughter, Mr. Crawford advised, "Don't beat yourself up. You're too young to make a commitment to a man who isn't at home with you. Don't blame yourself. Mike could have changed his choice at any time. He chose to stay in the submarine division. The breakup wasn't entirely your responsibility. If the relationship had been more important to him than submarines, he would be here now."

Looking thankfully at her parents, Joanne replied with a sigh, "You're right. Mike could have opted out. He could have changed his mind while we were still at the Academy or anytime during his training. He could be here now, but he's not. Just the same, I'll save this to wear when he comes home."

"And if he doesn't come to town to see you? Then what?" Mrs. Crawford asked.

"I'll wear it on my birthday in June. If I haven't seen him again by then, I'll know that I never will. I'll finally put Mike in my memory drawer and wear the dress a nice guy sent me for Christmas," Joanne replied with a thin smile.

"Good idea," Mr. Crawford commented.

"What did John give you?" Mrs. Crawford asked as she folded the dress and returned it to the box.

"This little necklace," Joanne replied, pointing to the delicate chain at her throat. "I gave him a pair of driving gloves. He'll be here soon. I'd better get changed."

Picking up the box containing Mike's gift, Joanne slowly climbed the stairs. Although she knew that her parents were right, she still felt sad and heavy. She could not deny that she missed Mike. Breaking off the engagement had given her the distance that she needed, but Joanne had not been able to remove Mike from her heart. She thought of him constantly and unfairly compared other men to him. Whenever she experienced something new or enjoyed a special moment, Joanne wished that he were with her. She had to stop herself from e-mailing the sub, knowing that contact would only bring increased pain and anxiety.

Placing the box with the dress carefully in the bottom of her duffel bag to take home after the ski trip, Joanne forced her mind from thoughts of Mike. Her father was right; she was too young to dote on an absentee lover. She needed to make new memories, not dwell on old ones. She owed it to herself and to John, whose life had become intertwined in hers.

Changing into a dressy pair of slacks and a fluffy

white sweater, Joanne studied her reflection in the mirror. Her eyes barely showed the signs of the tears that had traced down her face. A little concealer would cover the slight darkness under her eyes; carefully applied liner and mascara would make them appear more alert. Her lips needed a touch of color to disguise the slight downward turn at the corners. Her cheeks could use a touch of blush as a brightener. However, for a woman whose heart lay in the bottom of a duffel bag, Joanne decided that she looked pretty good.

Adjusting her appearance and squaring her shoulders, Joanne trotted down the steps to answer the doorbell. John's visit with her family for Christmas was about to begin. The house smelled wonderfully of all her favorite Christmas foods, giving it a welcoming air that would embrace John as soon as he entered. Everything looked perfect for a delightful day and making memories.

As Mike strolled the silent neapolitan streets, he stopped to admire a crèche and figures of the Baby Jesus and his mother Mary. Despite his family's strong religious background, he had let his career interfere with his devotion. Since the submarine accident, Mike had thought more about those religious beliefs that firmly grounded him to his family and their faith. As always, the holiday season made him feel the need to express his beliefs publicly. He had attended service on Christmas Day in a little church on the corner. The priest had delivered the mass in Italian, but Mike had enjoyed it anyway. Some things did not need translation in order to have meaning.

Now, Mike felt alone and lonely. He had noticed

a strange silence among the men on his submarine, too. They appeared more subdued and very homesick for their families. Many of them had phoned home. Earlier, Mike had spoken to his parents and had tried to phone Joanne, but he had decided not to leave a message on her cell phone. She was probably at her parents' house.

Stopping on a street corner, he checked his watch. Calling now would mean disturbing her. It was eight o'clock in the States. However, he would soon be on watch again and unable to phone. They planned to get under way the next day, making contact impossible again. He did not know when or where the sub would surface before returning to Norfolk.

Punching in the numbers, Mike waited. The connection was slow despite its touted high technology. When the familiar voicemail finally answered, he felt his heart sink with the realization that, once again, he would not be able to speak with her.

Remembering that Joanne usually turned off her phone when she did not expect a call, Mike said, "Merry Christmas! I guess you're with your parents or something. I really miss you. I hope you liked the present I sent you. The dress shouted, 'Buy me for Joanne!' from the shop window. I can hardly wait to see you in it. I'll call again the next time we make port. I love you."

Sighing, Mike shoved the phone and his hands deep inside his pockets. He was lonely and probably wore the same long face as his crewmates. This was his first Christmas away from the warmth and love of family. He hoped that it would be the last. Mike did not think he could stand being away from Joanne much longer. He missed her too much and needed her in his life. It was time to make a change if she would have him back in her life.

Chapter Eighteen

The hotel, decorated in the manner of an English country inn, gave Joanne the impression of stepping into one of the eighteenth-century novels she had read as a student. Massive area rugs dotted the sparkling wood floors. Seating in clusters encouraged conversation in front of the roaring fires warming the rooms from the numerous hearths. A game room encouraged the skiers to come in from the snow and enjoy pool and camaraderie. Books lined the library walls, while leather wing chairs provided perfect places to rest and enjoy them. Soft music played in the background.

The snow was perfect, the temperature cold, and the hot chocolate delicious. Although Joanne was not an expert skier, she quickly discovered that the skills she had learned the previous season had returned. She swooshed down the slopes with John, Brenda, and her fiance Jeff Greenway at her side, displaying a style that belied her limited experience. The rest of their group was impressed by her athleticism, despite the fact that Joanne was a golfer and not what they considered a true athlete.

Sitting by the fire and clutching a hot cocoa in her cold hands, Joanne said, "This is great fun! I'll have to ski more often."

"We do it every long weekend in the winter. Someone will post an e-mail reminding all of us. This is a relatively small group compared with the January and February outings," Brenda explained.

Jeff leaned over and added, "Even those of us who don't work at the Pentagon can enjoy this trip. It doesn't matter on the slopes that I don't know the latest office gossip. I'm simply a skier. Besides, Brenda fills me in on the personalities on the drive up here."

"I'll definitely keep my eyes open for the e-mail," John said, sipping his cocoa contentedly.

"Does anyone feel like going out for dinner?" Brenda asked. "I heard that the next lodge has the best restaurant in the area."

"I don't think I can move," Joanne yawned as the combination of a day in the cold, hot chocolate, and a roaring fire made her lethargic.

"Being the faithful fiancé that I am, I'm game, but I want to change first. I'll meet you down here in a few minutes," Jeff replied as he rose on stiffening legs.

Turning to John, Joanne said, "Don't think that you have to stay with me. I've heard about that restaurant, too. I'm about to fall asleep anyway and won't be decent company."

"I couldn't get up if the lodge caught fire. My legs turned to mush a half hour ago," John replied, casually slipping his arm around the back of her seat.

"Should I bring you anything? A big slab of beef? A slice of pie?" Brenda asked.

"No, thanks. We'll eventually find our way to the dining room. Hunger will win out," John responded for both of them.

"Speak for yourself. I'm rooted here," Joanne

yawned again and snuggled into the plush leather upholstery.

Joanne smiled lazily. John had taken on the role of boyfriend despite not getting any of the benefits. He was so understanding that she almost felt guilty for not being able to offer him more. He deserved a woman who put his interests first and cherished moments with him. He should be with a woman who returned his affection rather than only offering friendship.

Although she enjoyed his company tremendously, Joanne was not that woman. John was her friend. Since opening Mike's Christmas gift, Joanne had known that she would not be free to love again until she wore that dress. If Mike left the submarine service and came home to her, she would wear it the first time they went to dinner together. If that dream failed to become a reality, she would wear the dress on her birthday. Either way, Joanne would not be able to give John the relationship he wanted from her until she settled her feelings about Mike.

"Let me know when you get hungry. I'll carry you to the dining room," John stated half-jokingly.

"Right. Your legs are as rubbery as mine," Joanne laughed.

"True. Maybe we can crawl the short distance," John suggested, smiling into her eyes.

"That would require energy I don't have, too," Joanne replied.

"I guess we'll just have to stay here and starve," John said and added, "I don't mind spending my last minutes in the company of the most beautiful woman on the slopes."

"Are you flirting with me? How do you have the energy?" Joanne chuckled.

"I'm a man. It's second nature, like breathing," John admitted.

Grinning at his honesty, Joanne said, "In that case, Mr. Flirt, you can lend me your strong arm. I am getting hungry. Since it'll take me a while to cover the short distance to the dining room on these rubber-band legs, we should start now to arrive before they close the doors."

Rising, John pulled Joanne to her feet. For a moment, she stood close to him with his warmth filling the space between them. Although they had never done more than exchange friendly good night pecks, she could see that he would have liked to take their relationship to a different level.

Straightening her stiff body, Joanne declared, "I'm ready. Let's go."

"I'm at your disposal," John replied, holding her a second longer.

"Why is it that my entire body is so stiff, but you're not? I exercise regularly and even play racquetball with you. I don't understand," Joanne quipped as she limped toward the dining room from which all manner of delicious aromas emanated.

"Just luck, I guess. They say everything's in the genes," John laughed as Joanne struggled to cross the distance to the dining room.

"I feel like an old woman," Joanne complained.

"But you don't look like one," John replied.

"It's a shame that looks can be deceiving," Joanne laughed.

Standing inside the restaurant doorway that overlooked the tables set with white linen tablecloths, sparking silver, monogrammed china, and glistening crystal, Joanne sighed. If only Mike were at her side instead of John, the scene would be idyllic. She was growing weary of missing him and being incapable of putting him from her mind and heart. She was trapped on a treadmill that only promised more of the same.

From their table at the window, Joanne and John overlooked the illuminated bunny slope and could watch the cars on the lifts as they carried night skiers to their runs. The snow twinkled as if studded with diamond dust, almost causing Joanne to want to return to the slopes. However, the appeal of the warm indoors and the aroma of the mix of spices prevented her from moving.

"May I suggest the prime rib?" the waiter offered, handing them their menu. "It's the specialty of the lodge and fork tender. If you'd prefer fowl, the Cornish hens are very tasty. For the fish-lover, the rainbow trout is superb. No matter what you order, you will enjoy a tasty treat."

"Prime rib it is, and salads with blue-cheese dressing," John replied after catching Joanne's eye for her consent.

As the waiter left the table, Joanne stated, "This place is a delight. Our room is terrific, or it would be if Brenda weren't such a slob. She leaves her stuff everywhere. I feel sorry for the maid and find myself picking up after her."

"Jeff's not exactly Mr. Clean either," John chuckled. "Just image how their house will look."

"I hope the restaurant they went to is as beautiful as this one," Joanne commented, lightly touching the flower petals of the bouquet on the table.

"I have a feeling that it would be difficult to find an unattractive place up here. These ski resorts rely on positive word of mouth for their survival," John stated.

"Oh look! That little boy has fallen again! He's almost completely covered in snow," Joanne exclaimed as she watched the wintery panorama.

"He's having fun," John commented. "I remember making snow angels when I was a kid. My brothers and I would play in the snow all day and come in only when Mom called. My fingers, toes, and nose would be frozen, but I was happy."

"I remember the neighborhood snowball fights. Being an only child, I had a huge extended family to enjoy. We had great battles," Joanne reminisced.

"Those were the days before work and financial responsibilities gave us a different perspective," John added.

"We don't have as much playtime as we used to, or at least we don't make the time. We're afraid to appear lazy by using our leave for relaxation. We wait until we're so tired that we can't enjoy anything," Joanne stated.

Tapping the table for emphasis, John said, "We're too concerned about missing the office gossip or getting the crummy assignments. But I plan to change all that. When the spring thaw comes, maybe you'll play golf with me. We could play on Fridays and extend into the weekends . . . really make a statement by missing work."

"Sounds good to me," Joanne replied.

Looking at the family happily playing in the snow, Joanne felt a pang of loneliness. She and Mike had often talked about having kids and the fun of watching them grow up. Now, Joanne wondered if that would ever happen. Despite John's rapt attention, she could not help but feel a touch of melancholy.

"A penny for your thoughts," John offered as the waiter placed the steaming plates on the table before them.

"Nothing special," Joanne replied and added, "This is the best-looking prime rib I've ever seen."

John momentarily studied her face and then turned his attention to his dinner. He had known Joanne long enough to understand that faraway expression in her eyes. He knew when she was not thinking of him.

They passed the meal in casual conversation and comments about the delicious cuisine. By the time they had finished the crème brûlée, Joanne's spirits had risen considerably. Unfortunately, the entertainment outside the window had ended. The family had disappeared, leaving only their footprints in the snow. The soft violin music had done much to make her feel better.

"Are you up for a little dancing?" John asked as they left the dining room.

"Where?"

"There's a disco downstairs, complete with deejay," John suggested. "The concierge told me that this is quite the night spot."

"Let's go!"

"You're not too stiff?" John asked, leading the way.

"Not when it comes to music," Joanne chuckled.

As they entered the disco, Joanne was surprised by the noise and the crowd. Everyone from their group was already there, as well as so many other people that she had to walk sideways to squeeze between them to the only empty table in the far corner. She waved at Brenda and Jeff as she passed them gyrating on the dance floor.

"Isn't this wonderful!" Brenda gushed as she joined Joanne and John at their table.

"We haven't danced since Brenda's best friend's wedding last year," Jeff commented.

Turning to Joanne, John asked, "Are you ready to try your luck dancing with me?"

"I'm game if you are. I haven't danced since the wedding in Hawaii," Joanne replied.

"I doubt that you've forgotten. You were really the best dancer there," John grinned.

"You were pretty good yourself," Joanne responded as John pulled her close and swayed to an old slow tune.

Joanne melted into John's strong arms and matched his footsteps perfectly. Memories of dancing under the stars in Hawaii flooded back, making her homesick for the island. The nearness of him momentarily filled the void left by Mike's decision to continue in the submarine service.

As an old Johnny Mathis song about a man's need to be true to the woman he loved while in the arms of another washed over her, Joanne momentarily lost her balance and stumbled against John. He was warm and wonderful and available. It would be so easy to forget and to allow his affection for her to take her away from the sadness that lingered in her life.

"This isn't right. I have to go. It's not you; it's all me. I can't do this. I'm sorry," Joanne muttered as she pushed away gently and looked into his eyes.

"I understand. Don't have any regrets for me or for Mike. You've been completely honest with me. I'll walk you to the elevator," John said, fighting the pain of losing her that stabbed at his chest.

"Okay," Joanne whispered, knowing that he needed to save face. The worst thing she could do would be to leave John standing on the dance floor. He did not deserve that kind of treatment.

Walking through the lobby, Joanne turned away from the smiling faces of the other guests of the lodge. The couples and families were so happy together that she could not bear to look at them. Her heart ached for the days when she felt light and young. Missing Mike had made her feel old and tired.

"Listen, Joanne, you've been honest with me from the beginning. I've known that you were still in love with another man, but I thought that I could change your mind. Now that I see that I can't, I won't force my attentions on you any longer. However, everyone needs friends. Let me be your friend. If you decide that it's time to move on, I won't object if you want to give me a chance to make you happy, but, in the meantime, I'm here if you need me," John stated as they waited for the elevator doors to open.

"Thanks for understanding," Joanne replied, smiling bravely.

"Is there a light at the end of this tunnel?" John asked, studying her sad face.

"I've given myself a deadline. I can't wait forever. I'll have to move on if things haven't worked out before then," Joanne replied as she stepped into the elevator.

"What's your date?" John asked, holding the door open.

"My birthday, June seventeenth." Joanne waved as the door gently slid shut.

Once alone in the room, Joanne collapsed onto her bed and cried. The man she loved was at sea, and a delightful one was within easy reach, but she could have neither of them. Instead of dancing the night away and then sleeping in her lover's arms, Joanne lay alone, waiting for sleep that would not come to ease the pain of loneliness.

Rising, Joanne reached for the telephone that

she had ignored since before Christmas. The low-battery light blinked ominously as she dialed the message center. Since all of her friends were on the trip with her, Joanne did not really think anyone would have left a message. The act of searching for them was more to take her mind from her loneliness than to see if anyone had tried to reach her.

"Two messages," Joanne muttered as she prepared to delete them. "Probably wrong numbers."

The deep voice shocked her and caused Joanne's knees to buckle. Mike had phoned, and her old habit of turning off her phone to save the battery had caused her to miss the call. Listening closely, Joanne felt chills and warmth coursing throughout her body simultaneously. Sinking to the bed, she wiped the tears that flooded her cheek. Mike was in Italy missing her and she was enjoying Christmas with her parents and skiing with coworkers. Worse, she had almost allowed her loneliness to push her into the arms of another man.

As she listened to Mike's second message, Joanne smiled. He sounded so close, almost as if she could reach out and touch him. Just as Mike mentioned the dress, the phone died.

Staring at the silent instrument, Joanne rushed to her suitcase and searched for the charger. Remembering that she had not packed it, she picked up the room phone and called the cell message center, but the message had vanished as had so many others. She had meant to report the annoying tendency to the company but had forgotten in the excitement of reporting to the Pentagon. Now, the failing equipment and her neglect had erased Mike's message.

"I'll never know what he said!" Joanne cried and burst into a fresh torrent of tears.

Falling into the pillow, Joanne sobbed until her throat ached. She had missed his call, erased his message, and almost been unfaithful to her love in one night. She felt awful and hated herself and technology.

Hours later, when Brenda returned to their shared room, Joanne pretended to be asleep. She did not want to discuss her misery again; stirring up the pain never helped. Even the greatest sadness looked more tolerable in the morning.

Chapter Nineteen

The next day, as bright sunshine flooded the lodge and glistened on the snow, Joanne quickly packed her bags while her roommate was at breakfast. She dashed off a quick note to Brenda, offering the promise of more details the next time they met. She had to go home where she could be alone and think. She had to find Mike. She did not care how many phone calls she would have to make. She had to hear his voice, see his face, and hold him in her arms again.

As soon as Joanne reached her apartment, she phoned the cell company and complained about the deleted messages. The sympathetic service representative put her on hold for what seemed like hours as she searched for a way to restore the messages. When she returned to the line, she brought unfortunate news.

"I'm sorry, ma'am, but there's nothing we can do. I know it's no consolation, but it's happening throughout the network. I'm sorry. You'll have to call your party," the service representative replied.

"I can't," Joanne cried. "He's a submariner. I can't reach him until he's in port again. I've already tried, but he must be out to sea."

After a pregnant pause, the woman said, "I'm

sorry. I've done all I can. My husband's in the Marines, so I know what you're feeling. I wish I could help, but our system can't retrieve the lost messages."

Sighing, Joanne said, "Thanks for trying. It's not your fault. It's all my fault for not having the phone turned on. I didn't expect him to call. Good-bye."

Sinking into the sofa, Joanne forced the tears not to fall. She did not have time to lament the missed calls or to wallow in self-pity. She had to find Mike. She did not know whether he was still in Europe or on the way back. At this point, Joanne only knew that she had to make contact with him.

Knowing that offices at the Pentagon were always open, Joanne slipped out of her casual clothing and into her uniform. She could do nothing from her apartment, but she might be able to find the information she needed at work. Although her current assignment did not put her in contact with submarine data, Joanne's security clearance was sufficiently high to allow her to learn the whereabouts of one of them.

The Pentagon parking lot was as crowded late on Sunday night during the holiday season as it was during the regular workweek, reminding Joanne of her preference for the Metro. However, not knowing the amount of time she would need for her search efforts, Joanne did not want to take the chance of missing the last train home. She soon discovered that leaving the Pentagon late at night would not be an issue.

"Merry Christmas! Couldn't stay away?" the guard on the desk asked cordially.

"Some places just work as magnets and pull you back," Joanne laughed, showing her ID, and added, "Merry Christmas to you, too."

"You're not the only one with that same thought," the guard commented.

"Yeah, I had to park farther from the door than I had anticipated, but I needed the walk," Joanne quipped as she waited for the elevator.

"Ate too much Christmas dinner, huh?" the guard chuckled.

"Let's just say that I didn't have this many curves before the pie, cookies, cake, rolls, and the stuffing," Joanne laughed, despite her loneliness for Mike.

"I know what you mean. Sometimes it's hard to tell who got stuffed . . . the bird or me," the guard added, laughing happily.

Although she enjoyed the casual exchange with the guard, Joanne relished the silence of the elevator. The brief ride gave her a chance to strategize her plan of attack. Rather than going directly to her desk, she decided to visit a coworker's unit to see if the information she needed might be more readily available.

Turning left instead of right, Joanne briskly walked through the well-lighted hall. Anyone seeing her would have been able to tell from the set of her shoulders that she was a woman on a mission. However, no one would have guessed that the focus of Joanne's determination was the man she loved rather than Navy business.

Arriving in her friend's unit, Joanne searched the cubicles for a familiar face. Not seeing anyone she knew well, Joanne was on the verge of leaving when she heard someone call her name. Turning, she smiled at the sight of Brenda approaching with an armload of papers.

"I'm here by assignment, not by choice, but I thought you had plans for the weekend. Didn't you go on the ski trip?" Brenda asked, accepting Joanne's offer to take some of her precarious load.

"I did, and I've returned. The skiing was great, the lodge was breathtakingly beautiful, and the company was witty, but I had to come back," Joanne replied, carrying the binders to Brenda's desk.

"Then why are you here instead of there?" Brenda asked, studying Joanne's face carefully.

"Remember the guy I told you about—the one I used to be engaged to? He phoned from Italy, and I missed his call. Cell-phone problems caused me to lose the message. I don't know where he is, but I need to find him."

"Any idea where to start? It's not easy locating one officer without a plan," Brenda said.

"He's attached to a submarine that might still be in the Mediterranean. I thought I'd start there," Joanne replied, leaning against the wall of Brenda's cubicle.

"What's the name of the sub?" Brenda asked as she pulled up a potentially helpful document.

"The *Montpelier*, out of Norfolk."

"According to this, she's still in Naples, but this info hasn't been updated since early last week. She might have sailed by now," Brenda replied.

"What's the next step? If you don't have the status of the sub, where can I check next?" Joanne asked, feeling as if she would have a long road to travel.

"You might try Carl over there," Brenda indicated with a nod. "He often has more up-to-date information than I do. I only see these reports as an FYI kind of thing. I don't really track ship movement, but he does. At least he knows about the carriers. If he doesn't have what you need, he'll know the person you should ask."

"Thanks for your help, Brenda. Something tells me that I'm in for a lengthy search," Joanne commented.

"It's hard to find a sub when it's under way, but you might get lucky. Don't be discouraged if the best you can find out is that the *Montpelier* is on the way back to Norfolk," Brenda said.

"That's okay with me. I'll be able to meet him when it docks," Joanne said.

"Happy hunting," Brenda said and turned her attention to the folders on her desk.

Joanne crossed the wide expanse of room quickly. Although her confidence had taken a hit, she hoped that Carl would have the information she needed. If he did not, a call to the base might have to be the next step, and Joanne did not look forward to taking that action. Contacting a base was always a lengthy process, requiring many checks and clearances. Finding the information at the Pentagon would be much less stressful and, she hoped, faster.

"Carl, I'm Joanne Crawford, a friend of Brenda's. I'm looking for information on the *Montpelier*. Might you have something current?" Joanne said by way of introduction.

Peering over his glasses, Carl compared the photo of Joanne that hung from the chain around her neck with her face. Satisfied that she was navy, Pentagon, and cleared for the information, he pulled up a database. Muttering to himself, he scanned alphabetically for the name of the submarine.

Shaking his head, Carl announced, "Sorry, it's not here. I don't track them but thought the info might have appeared on this report. You'll have to wait until the morning and ask Craig Peters when he arrives. He sits in the front cubicle."

"Thanks for looking. I appreciate the help," Joanne replied as she turned from his desk.

Making the return trip to her office, Joanne thought about the remaining options. She could go home and wait until the next morning on the off chance that Craig Peters would have the information she needed, or she could call the base. Knowing that she would not be able to sleep, Joanne decided to make the phone call. If she managed to track down the right person on a Sunday night during the Christmas holiday, she would have the information she needed before Peters even reported to work.

As Joanne slipped into her cubicle, she stopped for a moment to listen to the eerie nighttime silence. Although the activity in the Pentagon had not subsided, it had taken on a new rhythm so totally different from that of Joanne's workday that she could feel the hairs on her arms stand at attention. Although she was alone in her unit, she could hear the sound of soft voices, distant footsteps, and the copier machine. She wondered about the nature of the assignments that brought workers to the complex late on Sunday night. One day, she would have to ask. For now, however, her focus was Mike.

Turning to her phone, Joanne dialed the number for the Norfolk base. The enlisted man on duty answered quickly and placed her call on hold while he tried to find someone to answer her query. Although she was no further along in her quest, Joanne hoped that, in a few hours, she would hear Mike's voice again. This time, she would never let him go.

Chapter Twenty

By the time her coworkers had arrived after enjoying the holiday and the ski trip, Joanne had spent the night at her desk and on the telephone. She had phoned the Naval base in Norfolk and spoken with a representative of every department, or so it seemed, but to no avail. No one knew the exact whereabouts of the submarine or its direction.

"What do you mean that no one knows the location of the *Montpelier*?" Brenda demanded. "Someone has to know."

"They know it's no longer in Naples, and it's not in Norfolk. Where it is between those points is anyone's guess," Joanne replied with a yawn.

"Do they know when it'll return to base or where it's heading?" Brenda inquired.

"If they do, they won't say. It might be on maneuvers with the carrier group, or it might be on the way back. Either I didn't reach the right person or I don't have the need-to-know clearance to find out where it is," Joanne replied, rubbing her tired eyes.

"What'll you do next?" Brenda asked, handing Joanne a cup of hot coffee.

Taking the coffee gratefully, Joanne replied, "I've already sent Mike an e-mail that he'll read eventually. I've asked a guy named Peters in the next unit, but he's no better informed than the base. Other than that, I've exhausted all of my options. If he were in Naples or anywhere else in the Mediterranean, I'd fly to him. I'd drive to Norfolk if he were there. There's not much I can do now."

"You look terrible. You should go home and get some sleep," Brenda commented.

"I'm okay. I'm running on nervous energy. I have too much work on my desk to go home anyway. I might leave a little early if I finish ahead of schedule. Wake me if you hear snoring," Joanne said with a chuckle.

"You don't snore, at least not loud enough for me to hear you over here," Brenda replied.

"I'm sorry about leaving the note. I just couldn't face discussing Mike again. I'm just not ready for prime time, I guess. I know now that I won't be decent company for anyone until he's with me again," Joanne replied, turning toward her desk.

"I figured as much, especially after seeing John's expression," Brenda said.

"I hope I didn't ruin his weekend," Joanne said.

"John's a big boy. He'll get over it. Besides, he knew what he was getting into from the beginning. He seemed okay, but quiet. Don't worry about him," Brenda advised.

Returning to her cubicle, Joanne tried to concentrate on her work, but thoughts of Mike kept coming into her mind. Try as hard as she could, Joanne could not focus on the task for more than a few minutes at a time. The combination of sleep deprivation and longing caused her mind to run unbidden into avenues of thought over which she had little control.

By lunchtime, Joanne had accomplished half of

the work that she had planned to do that day and discovered nothing new regarding Mike's whereabouts. When Brenda popped her head over the partition wall, Joanne quickly agreed to put aside the report that she had been struggling to write and accompany her friend to the cafeteria. The walk and the change of scenery might give her the boost she needed.

The cafeteria was more crowded than usual now that holiday shopping had ended. Silently, Joanne and Brenda joined the line that moved with surprising rapidity past the efficiently displayed food. In no time at all, they had paid their bill and begun the search for a place to sit.

"Anything to report?" Brenda asked as they wove their way toward a vacant table.

"Nothing," Joanne replied, shaking her head. "I've exhausted every effort to find the elusive Mike Shepherd. I know he's out there somewhere. I'll try again tomorrow to learn his expected return to the base. Someone in Norfolk has to know. I'll probably meet the sub when it docks. I have to see him. That's probably the best way to do it."

"Good idea. Now, don't forget that we have a wedding to put on this weekend," Brenda reminded her tired friend.

"I haven't forgotten. The gown hanging in my closet has a way of reminding me," Joanne chuckled, despite her fatigue.

"Friday night . . . rehearsal and dinner. Saturday . . . wedding! I can hardly wait to see all of this hard work fall into place," Brenda commented.

Silent for a moment, Joanne mused, "'Always a bridesmaid and never a bride.' That's me."

"Don't say that! You'll have your turn," Brenda chided her friend softly.

"I know," Joanne smiled, toying with her salad. "I'm just feeling sorry for myself. It's just that yours is the second wedding I've been in since graduation. I can't help but think that all the women I know are getting married and I'm standing still."

"Just wait until you and Mike reunite. That's when you'll have your big day," Brenda said.

"If we reunite," Joanne stated with a shrug as they cleared their table and headed back to their unit. "I've made a big mistake with Mike. I never should have ended our engagement. I've missed him terribly and thought about him as much as ever. By now, he has to think that I don't really love him. I have a lot of ground to cover to make up for this blunder. For all I know, his last call was a final farewell."

Placing her hand on her friend's shoulder, Brenda replied, "You thought you were saving yourself the pain of separation. You didn't know that you really can't stop a heart from loving and missing someone by simply speaking words to end it. Love goes too deep for that."

"The Academy trained me to be an officer and forgot to teach me the fundamentals of human relationships. This is really on-the-job training," Joanne smirked.

"By the way, have you heard from John today?" Brenda asked.

"No, and I can't blame him. I don't know if I would have been as understanding as he has been. If I had been in his shoes, I would have decided a long time ago that I was more trouble than I'm worth," Joanne stated frankly.

"I don't think he minds being your safety net. Don't ask me what he sees in you. Heaven knows that plenty of women around here look better than you do at the moment with those dark circles under your eyes," Brenda teased.

Laughing, Joanne quipped, "Every woman needs a good friend like you to keep her ego under control."

"Just doing my job," Brenda chuckled, returning to her cubicle.

The ringing of her phone forced Joanne to return to her cubicle. The reality of work had a way of intruding into the most pleasant moments. In a huge complex like the Pentagon filled with hustling military and civilian employees, reality was often only moments away.

By the end of the week, Joanne had gotten caught up on her work and made progress toward organizing the next week's load. Although she had not been able to contact Mike, she had learned his return date and begun to put her plans into action. With luck, she would not have to spend too many more days without Mike at her side.

In addition to working on her own problems, Joanne had supported Brenda's last-minute nerves and assured her friend that the wedding festivities would be a huge success. On Friday evening, with Joanne locking her arm through Brenda's, they left the building together to prepare for the rehearsal and the dinner. To her surprise, Joanne actually looked forward to the evening and the weekend to take her mind from her troubles.

Arriving home, Joanne had just enough time for a quick shower and change before dashing off again. She had purchased a sparkling short evening dress in a deep topaz for the formal dinner that would follow the rehearsal. Studying her reflection in the mirror, Joanne decided that she would wear the dress on her second date with Mike upon his return. The Christmas present was still the dress of choice for the first date.

Grabbing her coat, Joanne exited the apartment. Just as she pulled the door closed, the phone rang. Fumbling with her keys, she made a mad dash to the living room, almost falling in the unfamiliar high heels.

"Hello?" Joanne shouted.

"You don't have to shout. I can hear you just fine," the voice chuckled.

"Mike! Where are you? When are you coming home? I've missed you. We have so much to talk about," Joanne blurted.

"Take it easy! One question at a time. I'm on the sub somewhere in the Atlantic. We'll return to Norfolk within the next two weeks, definite time pending maneuvers. I've missed you, too. You're right. We do have a lot to discuss. Did you like the dress?" Mike answered cheerfully.

"I loved it. It's perfect for me. I'll wear it the first night you're home," Joanne replied, laughing and crying at the same time.

"Will you wear the ring on your left hand, too? I need to know the answer to that question before I make the drive to DC. You don't have to reply now. Think about it," Mike said.

"I don't have any trouble answering now. I've thought about it ever since I first took it off. I've done nothing but think about you and us. Of course, I'll . . . Mike? Are you there?" Joanne shouted into the static.

"Yes, but . . . didn't hear . . . last part. What . . . said?" Mike replied.

"I said I'll wear the ring!" Joanne shouted.

"What?"

"Can you hear me? Mike?"

Joanne collapsed onto the sofa as the connection died. Staring at the silent phone, she waited for Mike to call back, but nothing happened. When she could wait no longer, Joanne left her apartment. Before leaving, she made sure that her calls would forward to the cell phone safely tucked into her bag.

Standing beside Brenda as they waited for the flower girl and maids of honor to rehearse their part in the wedding procession, Joanne whispered, "Mike called!"

"When?"

"As I was leaving. Actually, I had to rush inside to catch the call."

"Where was he?"

"The Atlantic."

"When will he return?" Brenda asked, ignoring her father's shushing.

"Soon. Bad connection."

"Wonderful news!" Brenda said, as Joanne started her walk down the aisle.

Almost floating, Joanne practiced the walk that would introduce the bride to her waiting public. Although she and Brenda had known each other for a relatively short time, they had become such fast friends that Brenda had asked Joanne to be her maid of honor instead of the first cousin her mother preferred. Now, walking step, feet together, step, feet together down the long center aisle of the church, Joanne was glad that she had accepted the honor. Brenda was so happy.

As the minister explained the details of the next day's wedding, Joanne found her mind wandering to thoughts of Mike's return. Although he had not heard her over the static, he was still coming home to her. Regardless of the weather, she would wear the knit dress on their reunion date even if her goose bumps developed goose bumps.

Looking down at her right hand, Joanne smiled and slipped the ring to the empty spot on her third finger, left hand. She had foolishly thought that moving it would make her ache less for Mike's return and worry less about his safety. She had lied to herself and risked losing the man she loved above all others. Mike was her soul mate and her best friend.

Suddenly, the words of the wedding ceremony made sense. "Until death do us part." She loved Mike so much that only death could ever separate them. He was her life and her heart. She breathed with him. She laughed because of him. Nothing, not even her misguided logic, could put an end to the connection between them. He had understood the reality of their love and waited for her to come to her senses. Just as one plus one made two, he completed her just as she hoped she added to him.

"Are you okay? This is only a rehearsal. What'll you do tomorrow?" Brenda asked, handing her friend the handkerchief the minister had trust in front of her.

"I'm fine. I'm so happy. The vows are so beautiful," Joanne wept, dabbing at the tears that continued to course down her cheeks.

"Maybe you should bring a larger one tomorrow," Brenda quipped in a whisper.

"I'll need a whole box of them," Joanne replied.

"Save a few for me," Brenda instructed. "I'm sure I'll dissolve as soon as I see Jeff standing here waiting for me."

"Why don't men have to rehearse?" Joanne asked as they turned for the recessional.

"I guess it's because they have a shorter entrance. I just hope Jeff won't drop the ring," Brenda commented with a chuckle.

As the wedding party followed the bride and the stand-in groom to the back of the church, Joanne smiled happily. She had never been one for displays of emotion, but that night was different. The wedding vow had really touched her. She needed the release that only tears would bring. If she had not needed to look her best for the next day's festivities, Joanne would have rented an old tearjerker movie, opened a box of tissues, poured a glass of wine, and had a good cry. She had held back the tears of loneliness for too long.

Leaving the minister to lock up the church and join them later, the wedding party made its way to the groom's parents' house that had been transformed into a wonderland complete with sparkling crystal and glistening silver. Jeff was an only child whose parents had wanted to host a rehearsal dinner that everyone would remember. They had rolled up the carpets, hired a deejay, and arranged for a caterer to cook and serve the splendid meal. Although Jeff had not participated in the rehearsal itself, the spotlight of the dinner shone brightly on him.

"You've got to go to some lengths to beat this," Joanne whispered to Brenda as they sat together at the dining table.

"Oh, I have. Just wait until tomorrow. This is terrific, but my parents must have mortgaged their home. The reception is over the top," Brenda replied.

Feeling really happy for the first time in months,

Joanne responded, "I can hardly wait. I'm really looking forward to this shindig."

Studying her friend's face, Brenda said, "You look great. Love really agrees with you."

"Yeah. I just hope I'm not in for a huge letdown. I hope I didn't misunderstand the broken transmission," Joanne replied shyly and turned her attention to the salmon with raspberry sauce.

"Don't worry. I'm sure you didn't," Brenda responded, patting Joanne's hand lightly.

While Joanne enjoyed the rehearsal dinner feast, Mike joined the other officers in the mess. They had come to enjoy the relaxed camaraderie of living in close quarters. They joked in the manner of friends, although none of them had known each other before being assigned to the *Montpelier.*

"What'll you do when we get home, Mike?" one of his roommates asked.

"Shower and then drive to DC to see Joanne," Mike replied with a laugh.

"A shower sounds good to me. A nice long one with plenty of water and time to enjoy it," his roommate commented.

One of the other officers added, "I'd like a steak. The food's good on this sub, but I want a steak with all the trimmings, asparagus, a big salad and chocolate mousse for dessert."

Another interjected, "I'm not interested in food. I just want to hold my wife in my arms and my kids on my lap. It's been a long time."

Smiling, the captain said, "This lengthy trip has been rough on all of us. I'm a veteran of twenty years of sub duty, but I still miss being at home. It's especially difficult at holiday time. I'd like to thank you for your service. It's been a good cruise. Give my compliments to your men."

Mike returned to his room, eager for time alone to think about his future. Luckily, his roommates had duty, affording him a few precious solitary moments in the little room they shared. Privacy and time to think were the things he missed the most about life on the submarine. He hardly had any time to himself. When he was not on duty, he lived in close proximity to other officers. Even after four years at the Academy, he needed to have time alone to think.

Taking advantage of the precious moments, Mike lay on his bunk and thought about Joanne. The connection had been horrible, but at least he had been able to hear her voice for a few minutes before the transmission failed. He had been luckier than most of the others whose phones would not transmit from that distance. He would have liked to have heard her response to his question, but that would have to wait until he reached Norfolk.

Mike was going home. He had endured the longest underway of his short career in the submarine service and was glad to be leaving the boat for a while. Unless something unforeseen occurred, he would not have another long underway for at least six months. During that time, if all went well, his life would enter a new phase.

He had taken Joanne's love for granted, too. Mike had assumed that she would understand his long absences and be able to live with the fear of danger because she, too, was an Academy graduate. He had been mistaken. She had been badly shaken by the submarine's near-disaster and unwilling to tolerate more uncertainty. Mike had made a mistake that almost cost him the woman he loved.

"Watch over?" Mike asked, struggling to rise from his bunk.

"Your turn, buddy," his roommate replied.

"I didn't sleep a wink," Mike replied and stretched.

"You'll see Joanne soon enough," his roommate said. "It's different being on a sub than at school, isn't it? It's a hard transition."

"Yeah. It's not being able to control anything about my life that's so rough. As a student, I complained about the loss of liberty at the Academy, but now I know that I missed the big picture. This is so much more restrictive. At least at the Academy, I could see the sky between classes."

"We had a lot more freedom then, too," his roommate replied.

"You're not kidding. We had most weekends free," Mike agreed, straightening his uniform.

"We had time for our girlfriends then, too," his roommate interjected.

"We spend a lot of time together," Mike observed. "We sat across the table at chow calls. She sat beside me in many of our classes. Joanne studied with me at night."

"Those were the days. At least you're going home with good news," his roommate yawned.

"I almost don't believe it. I thought the days at the Academy were restricting. They were mild compared to being under way," Mike commented. "Sorry for keeping you up. You must be sleepy. I'm almost out of here."

"I doubt that I'll get much sleep. One of the JGs said that he didn't on his first long underway. He said that he wanted to go home so badly that he was too charged up to sleep. I can hardly wait to see my girl," Mike's roommate stated as he settled into his pillow.

Walking the narrow corridors, Mike made his way aft to the nuclear power plant that gave life to the vessel. Checking the gauges and nodding to the crewmen who watched them, he took his watch station. He hoped nothing would happen that would delay their trip home. He needed to see Joanne again, to hold her in his arms, and to convince her that she meant more to him than anything in the world, including his military service.

Chapter Twenty-One

The abbreviated phone conversation with Mike forced Joanne into more frantic action. She knew he was on the way back to Norfolk and, with luck, to her. She had so much to do, so many arrangements to make, and so much work to finish before meeting him at the base.

As soon as she arrived at the Pentagon, Joanne submitted her leave slip. She did not know if her unit supervisor would approve it and did not care. She would be in Norfolk when Mike returned even if she had to face disciplinary action later.

Sitting at her desk, Joanne discovered that knowing that Mike would soon be in her arms had heightened her level of concentration. She had to meet the deadlines for the reports before her departure. If she did not, she would let down the rest of the unit. Joanne wanted to follow Brenda's example; her friend had closed out all of her work prior to leaving for her honeymoon. If Brenda could do it with all the pressure of a wedding on her shoulders, Joanne could do it, too.

Joanne missed Brenda terribly. She wanted to be able to share her excitement at going to see Mike with someone, but her friend would not return until the next week. By then, the initial energy would have settled into a dull roar as the demands of work took precedence over the excitement of the pending reunion.

Not wanting to eat alone in the huge cafeteria, Joanne took to visiting Pentagon City, the shopping mall connected to the complex by the Metro line. Walking the bustling corridors provided a way to burn off energy as well as shop for the spring fashions. Also, she did not want to see John. Joanne felt so happy that she could not face the thought of watching his brave smile when he learned of her plans and reunion with Mike. She knew that John's feelings for her were real and hoped that he would find someone who would be able to return them.

Treating herself to a slightly longer than usual lunch break, Joanne entered a bridal shop that had only recently opened in the mall. Inside, in addition to the traditional gowns with their voluminous skirts, Joanne found sleek, close-fitting gowns with thin straps and slenderizing lines. She had not allowed herself to think of making wedding plans since breaking off the engagement with Mike. Now, with him returning and the ring securely on the third finger of her left hand, Joanne could dream again.

"Would madam like to see anything in particular?" the saleswoman asked with a broad smile.

"This one, please," Joanne replied, fingering the silk of a creation that matched the one she had carried in her mind since a little girl.

"A very good choice for a woman with a trim figure. There's no point in hiding your assets under yards of unnecessary fabric. I'll be just a minute," the saleswoman replied as she placed Joanne in a dressing room and slipped into the back.

Breathing deeply, Joanne tried to stop her heart from pounding. Twice, she had accompanied brides as they shopped for their gowns. Twice, she had eyed lovely creations and turned from them to look at bridesmaid's dresses. This time, she would not have to force her eyes away from the heavenly lace and silk. She saw no reason not to try on one. After all, she was an engaged woman with a wedding to plan and a fiancé who was steaming home to her. At least, Joanne hoped that her reunion with Mike would be as wonderful as she imagined. She did not know if she would be able to survive the disappointment if it were not.

Slipping into the cool fabric, Joanne stepped in front of the wall of full-length mirrors. Her heart stopped. The gown was exactly like the one in her dreams. It fit her as if tailored to her measurements. The soft cap sleeves hugged her shoulders while the lace insert at the bust and waist accentuated her figure. The gown kissed her hips and thighs before fluttering in tiers of lace that gradually fanned into a gentle train.

"It's amazing. The gown is an almost perfect fit. Never in my years as a seamstress have I seen a woman look so lovely in a gown. I will only have to adjust the buttons on the sleeves," the seamstress gushed.

"It is lovely. I've seen it in my imagination so many times that I knew it would fit without even trying it on," Joanne said softly.

"This would make a perfect veil," the saleswoman added as she placed the simple short silk veil with its tiny headpiece onto her head.

Joanne barely breathed as she surveyed the transformation from Navy officer to bride. The ecru of the gown brought out the healthy tones of her skin and brightened her eyes. She looked lovely. All she needed was strappy sandals to complete the ensemble.

"It's perfect, but I'd like to bring my mother to see it. Write down all the specifics while I change," Joanne stated.

"This is a new sample, madam. You're the first to try it on. We can hold it for you until Monday so that you can bring your mother to the shop. Otherwise, we will have to order the gown and need at least a six-month lead time," the saleswoman replied.

"No, that's fine. I doubt that I'll be able to fit into her schedule on such short notice. Besides, a summer wedding fits my plans perfectly," Joanne replied, steeling herself against the hard-sell tactics.

As Joanne changed into her uniform, she took one last look at the gown. It was perfect, and she wanted it. However, until she had the chance to speak with Mike, she did not want to jinx their reunion. Although he had spoken of the ring and his love for her, they had not seen each other in months. Joanne feared that they might have been living with dream images that no longer applied. They had both grown during their separation. The gown would wait.

Returning to her desk, Joanne plunged into her work. She had much to do and little time to accomplish the task if she wanted to stick to her plan of leaving for Norfolk in one week. As it was, she would have to work all weekend to finish the reports that would fall due during her absence. However, this time, she did not care about the loss of liberty. A weekend of leisure was a small price to pay for a lifetime in Mike's arms.

The week passed slowly with Joanne filling most of the minutes with the minutiae of work. She was among the first to arrive and the last to leave every night. If Brenda had not returned from her honeymoon, Joanne would have found the long hours torturous beyond belief.

Over lunch in the cafeteria on Thursday, the day before her departure for Norfolk, Brenda advised, "You really should prepare yourself for all possibilities. The sub's return might be delayed. Mike might have changed. You might discover that you've changed toward him. You haven't seen each other in ages. Anything could have happened."

"I'm prepared. I've had two weeks to prepare," Joanne replied firmly.

"I just don't want to see you get hurt. Anticipation is often more than the reality. Both of you have experienced life differently and haven't been able to process any of it together," Brenda said, studying her friend's set expression.

Shrugging her shoulders, Joanne replied, "I know. Mike's life has been so totally different from mine that there's no way I can fully understand it. Living in that confined space with only men for weeks would drive me nuts, but he likes it."

"Does he know about John?" Brenda asked.

"No, I don't see any particular reason to tell him," Joanne responded. "Nothing happened with John. He was and, hopefully, will always be a good friend. I wasn't attracted to him in a romantic way. I couldn't be. Mike was on my mind the entire time."

"What if their paths cross one day? John knows about Mike. Maybe you should put them on even ground," Brenda suggested.

"Maybe one day, I'll tell Mike about the great guy who comforted me in my loneliness and tried to win my heart. It'll make an interesting bedtime story when we're old and gray," Joanne chuckled.

"Speaking of John, here he comes," Brenda stated.

"The most beautiful women in the entire complex! How did I get so lucky?" John laughed as he sauntered toward them.

"You're such a flatterer, but I'll take it. I'm an old married lady now and need all the compliments I can get," Brenda joked.

"Marriage has transformed you into an even more stunning woman," John replied, bowing from the waist.

"Oh brother!" Brenda moaned.

Laughing, John turned his attention to Joanne and asked, "How've you been? I haven't seen you in a while."

"I've been busy. I'm leaving for Norfolk after work tonight to meet Mike when his sub comes into port," Joanne replied, watching John's face for a reaction.

A slight stiffening of his shoulders provided the only clue to his feelings as John asked, "Then I guess everything's right with you."

"I'll know after I see him," Joanne replied.

"At least you didn't have to wait until June to wear that dress," John interjected.

"I'll wear it next week even if I have to pile sweaters on top of it," Joanne chuckled at his memory.

"Good luck. Fair winds and following seas," John said as he walked with the ladies to the Navy corridor.

"Thanks, John. You've been a great friend to see me through this turmoil," Joanne said, standing at the intersection of their halls.

"It was simply a blip on your radar. See you when you return," John said as he waved good-bye and vanished into his unit.

"He's a great guy," Joanne commented. "I know he'll find the right woman one day. I just wasn't it."

"He will. Guys like John don't go unnoticed for long. Now that he's made it clear that he's interested in settling down, he'll find someone in no time. I hope you haven't cut him loose too soon," Brenda said as they returned to their cubicles.

"I haven't. It never would have worked anyway. I wouldn't have wanted to rebound into marriage," Joanne stated.

"Maybe not, but John would have provided you with a little warmth and companionship on cold nights until you found someone else. He was willing to settle for that in the short term," Brenda said as she sank behind the partition.

"I know, but I couldn't string him along. What if I never get over Mike? I've heard of women who spend their entire lives pining for one man. Maybe I'm one of them," Joanne replied, leaning over Brenda's partition.

"You're too young for that. Besides, I wouldn't let you do it," Brenda replied. "I would have introduced you to some of Jeff's friends. You would have found an acceptable man among them."

"Is that what I'd have to settle for—acceptable? No, thanks anyway. I think I'd rather go it alone than marry just anyone so that I wouldn't be alone. Alone isn't so bad. If I can't have Mike, I think I'll stay to myself for a while," Joanne said, sighing.

"It's your choice. Just don't put yourself on the shelf because of Mike's decisions. He's living his life. You need to live yours," Brenda advised, scrolling through the data displayed on her computer screen.

"I will. This meeting with Mike will provide the resolution I need . . . one way or the other," Joanne responded as she turned her attention to her afternoon's work.

For the millionth time since deciding to meet Mike's submarine, Joanne hoped that she was not making a mistake. She worried that Brenda might be right about the effects of time and distance on their relationship. They might find that their love could not withstand the stress of separation. Regardless of her fears, Joanne had to find out. She could not be happy with anyone else until she knew the reality of her relationship with Mike. They had to either move forward or end it forever. The ring on her left hand might prove a misleading statement of a future that might not ever happen.

Immediately after work, Joanne headed the car down Route 95 in the direction of Norfolk. Determined to reach the base before ten o'clock, she had packed a few energy bars so that she would not have to stop along the way. She was so energized by the possibility of seeing Mike the next day that she did not feel the fatigue from a long day at the office.

Joanne had not heard from Mike since the fractured phone call. She had phoned the base but could not find out if the submarine was on schedule to return that weekend. Even her contact in the Pentagon did not have an up-to-date schedule. The sub had completed its maneuvers and was expected back in Norfolk as originally planned. Like all the other wives and girlfriends, Joanne would have to wait on the dock to catch a glimpse of the man she loved.

By the time Joanne reached Richmond, she was so sleepy that she had to stop. The trip to Fredericksburg had taken two hours in the crush of traffic. The next leg to Richmond had taken even longer. With hours of driving ahead of her, she could no longer stay awake. Checking into a hotel, she surveyed the room, phoned her parents, pulled back the covers, and immediately fell asleep. Norfolk would have to wait until the next day.

The next morning, after a quick breakfast, Joanne turned the car once again to Norfolk. Singing along with the music, she felt the distance separating her from Mike shrink with each rotation of the wheels. As the distance markers ticked off her progress, Joanne felt her pulse quicken and her heart beat faster.

The closer she came to the base, the more Joanne could envision herself standing outside the gates that separated the families from the submarines. She saw herself waving and shouting Mike's name as the crew and officers of the *Montpelier* appeared. She could feel her arms wrap around his neck and her happy tears of reunion wash his face. Joanne could almost smell the sweetness of his skin as the hum of the tires carried her closer to the man she loved.

Arriving at the base, Joanne encountered the first obstacle to her success. The incidents of September 11 had tightened security, making it impossible for her to gain access to the yard. Despite explaining to a disinterested MP on the gate that her fiancé was an officer on the *Montpelier*, Joanne failed to gain access.

Moving her car to the short-term parking outside the gate, Joanne sighed in frustration. She had traveled the long, boring road to find Mike without anticipating the security issues that would keep her from him. Rather than head back to DC, she tried again—this time with her government ID in her hands.

"May I help you, ma'am?" the sentry asked with a little grin of recognition.

"I forgot to mention that I'm Navy. Will my Pentagon ID give me access to the base?" Joanne asked.

"Do you have official business here, ma'am?" the sentry inquired as he studied the ID that Joanne thrust into his hands.

"Yes. I'm here to meet Ensign Mike Shepherd," Joanne replied, stretching the purpose of her personal business into that of the government.

A tiny chuckle escaped the sentry as he said, "Unless he's with you, ma'am, your ID won't do much good on this base. It's access-based on need only. I'm sorry."

"Has the *Montpelier* returned? You could phone him. He could meet me here," Joanne suggested, trying to break through the necessary restrictions.

"I'll try, ma'am. Just a minute," the sentry replied as he walked toward the guardhouse.

As Joanne waited for what seemed like hours, she studied the drab structures just inside the gate. The base, like all the others she had ever visited during her time at the Academy and since graduation, consisted of buildings constructed in the standard government-issue gray that seemed to remove all life and personal choice from the premises. In the spring and summer, the now-empty flowerpots would add the only spots of color other than those of the flag that flew prominently inside the gate.

Looking at the colorlessness of the yard, Joanne wondered at her ability to thrive in such an environment. Strangely, she had done well at the Academy and in each of her assignments despite the lifelessness of the surroundings. She supposed that most military personnel took comfort from being together rather than from the ethos of the establishment.

"Sorry, ma'am," the sentry stated, returning Joanne's ID. "The *Montpelier* hasn't returned. It's expected back tomorrow."

"I have to be on that dock when it arrives. What should I do to establish need?" Joanne inquired.

"Ma'am, unless you can get your name on the list before tomorrow morning, there's nothing anyone will be able to do for you," the sentry replied, saluting sharply to end the conversation.

Joanne drove away with her mind whirling. Her name had to be on the list if she wanted to greet Mike as he stepped from the submarine. Knowing that Brenda would be hard at work despite it being Saturday, she decided to phone her friend for assistance.

"Hey, Brenda," Joanne began, "I'm in Norfolk, and I need help. What can you do to get me on the admit list down here? I can't gain access to the base without it."

"I was wondering when you'd call. I should have thought of that. It's not enough to flash a Pentagon ID anymore. I'll make a few calls and get right back to you," Brenda replied.

"Thanks."

"Stay there. I'll do anything to put this romance on the right track," Brenda chuckled.

The strong wind rattling the car windows reminded Joanne that it was still winter, despite the more temperate weather of the South. Needing a place to wait, she drove down the street until she saw a coffee shop. Pulling the collar of her coat close, Joanne entered the Starbucks, ordered a mocha grande, and sat down to wait.

In a matter of minutes, Brenda called back with

the news, saying, "It's done. My friend around the corner phoned Norfolk with the information that you'd be arriving late tonight and need access to the base tomorrow. The kicker is that you'll have to arrive in uniform, not that cute little dress Mike bought for you in Naples."

"I'd wear Academy-issue white works if that baggy, saggy uniform would give me access to Mike," Joanne laughed. "You're a lifesaver."

"Not at all. It's the least I can do for the course of true love," Brenda replied, teasing gently.

"If I fail to convince Mike that I love him, it won't be because I didn't try or have the right support," Joanne added.

"Navy women have to stick together. All's fair in love and war . . . and sometimes it's hard to tell them apart," Brenda laughed.

"Wish me luck. If the inauspicious start I've had today portends anything, I'll need it," Joanne commented as she ended the call and finished her coffee.

Now, all Joanne had to do was to wait for the *Montpelier*'s return. Waiting was the hardest part. She had not done it well while at the Academy, always impatient for the next project or opportunity. With Mike only hours away, Joanne found that the waiting game progressed with the speed of a turtle.

After checking into the hotel, Joanne decided to tour the city, since she had nothing better to do. Everywhere she looked, she saw Navy uniforms. It looked as if the town existed to support the fleet, which it probably did, since the Navy was its largest employer. Anchors dotted the parks as flowers would in other cities. Navy insignias, replicas of famous vessels, and military collectables filled the shop windows. Even the clothing had either a Navy

or seagoing focus. Not since graduation from the
Academy had she seen a town that displayed its loy-
alty to the fleet more profoundly.

Wandering the city, Joanne spotted mothers with
their children, retired couples, and government
employees going about their routines. None of
them would have guessed that she was Navy from
the faded jeans, heavy sweater, tennis shoes, and
peacoat that she wore. They might have thought
that she was a college girl, but no one would have
thought that she was a woman waiting for her fiancé's ship to return to port. If all went well the
next day, Joanne would walk hand-in-hand with
Mike down the same streets. If it did not, she would
pack her bags and head home to DC.

While Joanne waited for the hours to pass and
her ensign to return, Mike was busy with the last of
the tasks on his certification sheet. Knowing that he
had been granted a week's leave that would start
as soon as he returned to port, Mike had gone without sleep the last few nights in an effort to complete the packet and free himself from the ordeal
while in DC with Joanne. He wanted nothing to interfere with his time with her. They had much to
discuss, so many plans to make, and a future to
begin.

Stretching, Mike sighed and thought about
Joanne's smooth skin and sweet face. He had
missed her and could hardly wait to hold her again.
After the aborted telephone call, he had decided
not to take any chances that she would slip through
his fingers or have second thoughts about their relationship. He would drive to DC, meet her at the
Pentagon, and beg her to marry him in front of her

coworkers and friends. He had learned that happiness for him was having Joanne in his life. Without her, he did not feel complete.

"Finished?" Mike's roommate asked, returning to their small room.

"Done and done in. I'm beat," Mike replied.

"When's your watch?"

"Not until later. I'm crashing right now," Mike responded.

"The captain says that we'll arrive in Norfolk at 0630. It'll take a couple of hours to clear, but, after that, we'll be free."

"Good. I should be on the road by 0830," Mike commented sleepily. "Joanne will really be surprised to see me when I show up at her door. The secretary said that her unit would be working this weekend. I can hardly wait to see her face."

"I sure hope you won't be the one who's surprised. I know a guy who popped in on his girl only to find her with another man. She thought he was still out to sea. Surprise!" Mike's roommate stated.

"That won't happen to me," Mike said with confidence based on years of knowing Joanne.

"That's what I thought," his roommate replied softly as sadness covered his face.

Mike's snoring was the only response. Shrugging his shoulders, his roommate stripped down to his BVDs, flopped on top of his bunk, and instantly fell asleep. He had done his duty for the ship and his friend. The rest would take care of itself.

Chapter Twenty-Two

The ringing telephone jarred Joanne awake. Sitting straight up, she rubbed her eyes and momentarily wondered where she was. As she reached to answer it, she looked around the messy hotel room and remembered. She was in Norfolk waiting to see Mike.

"Hi, Mom. What's up?" Joanne asked as she stretched and tried to unknot the muscles in her neck from sleeping on a too-soft mattress.

"What happened? Aren't you in Norfolk? Mike just called. He's at the Pentagon looking for you," Mrs. Crawford stated.

"What? What time is it? He can't be there, 'cause I'm here," Joanne sputtered, searching for her watch.

"It's ten-thirty. His sub returned early, and he drove straight here. Where are you? How did you miss him? I thought you had planned to meet him on the base," Mrs. Crawford said.

Moaning, Joanne responded, "I did, but the sentry told me that his sub wouldn't arrive until noon. I had it all planned so beautifully. I guess I overslept. I arranged for a wake-up call that didn't happen. I'd planned to throw myself into his arms as soon as he passed through the gate. I even got my name on the list so that I could meet him. Please give him my address. Tell him to meet me at my apartment. I'll call the super and make the arrangements. I'm on my way home now."

"Don't drive like a crazy person. He'll wait. He's waited this long for you to get your act together. Another few hours won't matter," Mrs. Crawford advised sternly.

"I'll be careful. Just don't let him get away," Joanne replied frantically.

Joanne grabbed her cell phone, punched in the number of the apartment complex, and continued packing her clothes at the same time. After she gave the instructions to the super, she took a quick shower and dressed in record time. Checking the closet and drawers one last time, she rushed to the lobby. Dashing across the parking lot, she tried to phone Mike but could not reach him. She left a frantic message on his voice mail and tossed her bag into the car. In less than thirty minutes, Joanne was on Route 95 heading home.

Mike's shipmate had been right about surprises; they often backfire. Wandering the halls of the Pentagon, Mike had finally found Joanne's corridor and her unit. He had not expected her to join him in Norfolk and had decided to surprise her at work. The surprise had been on him as Brenda told him that Joanne had taken leave in order to meet his submarine at the base. His early arrival and quick departure meant their paths got crossed up.

Now, Mike had time to himself and no one with whom to share it. For the first time in months, he did not have to stand watch, share a tiny space with another man, sleep in confined quarters, or listen to the eerie sounds of life on a submarine.

For a week, he could do as he wished. And he planned to spend every minute with Joanne, if she would have him. However, he would have to find her first.

As he returned to his car, Mike looked up at the clear late-winter sky and breathed deeply. The air smelled sweet and light, with only birds passing overhead to mar the view of the scattered clouds. He had missed the sky and the smell of natural air. The air in the submarine clung to his nostrils and clothing with a unique heaviness. Smiling, Mike thought that this was air the way it was meant to be, despite the whiff of gas fumes.

Mike took the long route to Joanne's apartment, passing through Rock Creek Park so that he could see the trees. He had missed the winter spectacle of ice and snow. He had returned from the Mediterranean as the last traces of the season were melting.

Parking the car, Mike slowly walked to the apartment building. Since he had plenty of time, he gazed at the pansies and early daffodils in the garden. While at the Academy, Joanne had tried to tell him that he would regret joining the submarine service, but he had not understood her meaning until the long underway took him far from home. He missed not only people but seasons and smells. He missed the sight of clouds in the sky and birds in flight. He had taken so much for granted until under way. Not even liberty in Italy could diminish the loneliness for home, for the States, and for his girl. Living the submariner's life had made Mike realize the importance of the little things.

Mike unlocked the door to Joanne's apartment and entered. Tossing his duffel bag against the wall, he surveyed the apartment. It looked like Joanne. Not at all frilly like other women but stylishly bright and cheerful. He liked it and decided that living with her taste in décor would be an easy job. The deep teal leather living-room sofa and chairs appealed to his preference for sturdy furniture. Joanne had even decorated the bedroom in shades of blues and greens in man-pleasing plaids. Nothing was too frilly or overdone.

As Joanne's new kitten rubbed against his ankles, Mike wandered into the kitchen. He had not taken the time to eat and was starving. Now that he had time on his hands until Joanne arrived, Mike decided to eat a late breakfast, sharing some of the milk with the tiny kitten.

By the time he cleaned up the dishes, Mike had begun to feel the fatigue of the long underway and the lack of sleep on the submarine. Knowing that Joanne would not arrive for hours, he stretched out on the couch and covered himself with the throw. Full and comfortable, he quickly slipped into a deep sleep with the purring kitten lounging happily on his chest.

Joanne, however, was not relaxed. Her worst fears had become reality. She paced the roadside, alternating between anger and anxiety. She had only herself to blame. Her parents had repeatedly reminded her to check the tires and oil in her car, but she had ignored the advice. Riding the Metro to work had almost made the car obsolete. Now, waiting for the mechanic in dirty overalls to finish his job, Joanne wished she had listened.

"I'm sorry to be a nag, but can you work faster?

My whole life depends on getting home," Joanne said again.

"Lady, I told you that I'm working as fast as I can. It takes time to change a tire. Why don't you help yourself to one of those sodas in the cooler? The trunk's open. It'll give you something to do," the mechanic said, nodding toward his truck.

"I know I'm bugging you, but it's important that I get home as fast as possible. My fiancé's in town, and I have to be there. I haven't seen him in months. We're in the navy and can never coordinate our schedules," Joanne stated, twisting her hands helplessly.

Standing his full height, the man replied, "Lady, if I could fix this flat and get you on the road I would, but I can't because you keep talking to me. Stand over there, and let me do my job. These lugs are stripped. It's taking longer than I thought. It's not my fault that you got this blowout. Drink your soda and leave me be."

"All right, but hurry. Please!" Joanne repeated as she left the man in peace.

"Women!" the mechanic sputtered and returned to the shredded tire.

Joanne paced the roadside and sipped the soda without speaking. She dared not disturb the man again for fear that he could quit and leave her without help. When the tire had blown, she had gripped the wheel and prayed that she would not run off the road. Now, Joanne prayed that she would continue her journey quickly and find Mike waiting for her at her apartment.

"It's done," the mechanic said, wiping his hands on the spotted overalls.

"Thank you. You don't know how happy you've

made me," Joanne gushed as she rushed toward her car.

"Just do me a favor and buy new tires. The donut will get you home but not much else. I'd rather not get another call from you," the mechanic advised, packing the jack in her trunk and slamming the door.

"Don't worry. I'll take care of it. I don't want another blowout. Thanks again," Joanne replied and added. "I'm sorry for being such a nag, but . . ."

"Your fiancé's in town. I know. Drive carefully," the mechanic responded.

The sun had set and the evening turned cold by the time the mechanic waved Joanne on her way. Blending into the heavy traffic heading north on Route 95, she pressed onward. Her head pounded from the anxiety of waiting and the fear of missing Mike. Her stomach ached from the slightly stale peanut-butter crackers that had served as her dinner. However, despite the bumper-to-bumper traffic, Joanne was determined that nothing would keep her from her apartment and future.

Joanne parked her car in the darkened lot and sprinted into the building. Rather than wait for the elevator, she dashed up the three flights to her floor. She swore under her breath as her fingers fumbled with the key. Throwing open the door, she rushed inside.

"Mike?" Joanne called as she searched first the living room, then the kitchen, and finally the bedroom.

Only silence and the yawning cat greeted her. Tears of frustration and futility burned behind her eyes. If only she had anticipated his early arrival, Joanne would have met Mike at the base. If only she had bought new tires, she would not have had to wait for AAA to fix the blowout. If only she had not ended the engagement in the first place, Joanne would not feel so miserably unhappy and helpless now.

Closing the door, Joanne stopped and stared. Taped to the back she found a note in Mike's ant-sized scrawl. Peering closely, she read, "I waited, but you didn't come. You'll know where to find me if you want me. Mike."

Joanne closed her eyes and sighed. Mike was gone and she did not know where he was or if he would return. Her head pounded from stress and lack of a decent meal. She felt angry and frustrated and hurt. Worse, she did not know what to do next.

Phoning her mother, Joanne said, "He's not here."

"I wonder where he's gone? I gave him your message and told him to wait for you," Mrs. Crawford said.

"It took forever for AAA to come and fix the tire. I only just arrived. I guess he couldn't wait forever," Joanne stated bravely.

"Didn't you call him?" Mrs. Crawford asked.

"Yes, but he had turned off his cell phone and didn't answer my home number. This is a mess," Joanne cried, fingering her hair in frustration.

"If he loves you, he'll return," Crawford advised gently.

"What if he doesn't come back? What if he's had enough of the drama? Maybe I should go look for him," Joanne commented, striding the length of the living room.

"Where would you look? You don't even know where he'd go. Mike could have checked into a hotel or driven to his parents'. He might be in a bar somewhere. Where would you start?" Mrs. Crawford asked.

Stopping in her tracks, Joanne said, "I know where he went, or at least I think I do. I'm going out. I'll forward my home-phone calls to my cell phone, and I'm taking it with me. If he calls, ask him to meet me."

"Where?"

"He'll know. We always said we'd meet there," Joanne said as she grabbed her keys and ran from the apartment.

The evening was cold and clear as Joanne headed the car away from the Washington area along the crowded beltway. The bumper-to-bumper traffic looked as if everyone were trying to escape DC for points north and east. Joining them, Joanne began her journey toward the bay and Mike.

Darkness had completely enclosed the Annapolis area by the time Joanne reached the Academy gate. The quiet town and even more silent Yard offered little promise of success. Most of the midshipmen seemed to have retreated into the dorm for shelter and study.

Driving through the gates, Joanne searched in vain for a parking space in the visitors' lot before heading to the midshipman store parking area at water's edge. Never-ending construction restricted parking to seniors and staff only. Despite the designation, seniors had to park away from the dorm. More than once, Joanne had covered the distance from Hospital Point to the instructional buildings and the dorm in record. That starry night was no different.

The silence on the Yard would have been frightening if Joanne had not spent four years passing along the grounds on nights just like that one. She was accustomed to the sound of the water lapping at the seawall and the sight of the sailboats pulling at their moorings. Even in the low light of the campus, she could see the familiar sights and the few cold midshipmen as they made their way from the library or labs to Bancroft Hall, the dorm that housed all four thousand of them.

The yard had not changed, and Joanne felt as if she had never left. She remembered each crack in the pavement and every tree and bench. Despite having been stationed in Florida, Hawaii, and the Pentagon, Joanne had returned to the "boat school" on the bay for solace . . . and Mike. She only hoped that he had done the same.

Taking the shortcut up the stairs and past the barbershop, Joanne jogged around the corner and down Stribling Walk. The glow of the lights from Bancroft and Tecumseh Court made the brick path passable although still very dark. The trees along the walk cast eerie shadows as their branches tried to intertwine and block the view of the night sky.

Nodding at the midshipmen who passed on their way to the dorm, Joanne quickened her steps. Her breath made vapor clouds as she tried to breathe deeply and compose herself. She had triumphed in serious situations as a midshipman and hoped that she could do it again. She had commanded fellow midshipmen and turned officers' commands into reality. In the months since graduation, Joanne had earned outstanding evaluations on her projects and proven herself to be a valuable member of the team. However, this was real life, her personal life. She would need all of her skills and training to triumph this time.

Now, with the chapel dome in sight, Joanne realized that her hardest task lay ahead. She was no longer fighting for the good of the corps but for herself. She would need all of her negotiating skills to convince Mike that she loved him despite the missteps that had separated them and threatened to destroy their relationship.

Standing across the street from the chapel, Joanne studied the silent building lit in floodlights that made the copper dome shine golden in the night. The white marble glistened and the doors beckoned her to enter. She had spent so many hours inside for service, glee club concerts, and meditation that the chapel had become her favorite place on the Yard. It was there, listening to the Navy hymn "Eternal Father, Strong to Save" once Sunday as a visiting high-school senior, that Joanne realized without a doubt that life as an officer in the Navy was what she wanted more than anything. Now, standing with her hand on the doorknob, Joanne knew that making a life with Mike meant even more.

The aroma of freshly waxed wood rushed to meet her as Joanne pushed open the chapel door. Inside, the marble walls were silent, the candles on the altar extinguished, and the lights dim. Yet one tall white candle flickered in the breeze. The eternal candle in front of the window depicting the midshipman burned as it did every day and night.

Joanne walked quietly; her shoes barely made a sound on the marble floor. Reaching the midway point, she stopped and turned toward the stained-glass image of a midshipman in the window. For years, that figure had symbolized hard work and dedication to Joanne and her mates. Now, the midshipman had taken on a deeper meaning. His solitary walk was theirs. With luck, Joanne would soon not walk alone.

"You knew I'd come here, didn't you?" came a voice from deep inside the pew to the left.

Joanne looked in the direction of the speaker but could see no one in the flickering candlelight. However, she knew who it was without seeing him. Looking away from the voice, Joanne concentrated on remaining calm. She needed all of her training for the moments that would resolve her fate and her future.

"I thought you would. I would have. We met here more than once when we were mids," Joanne replied without taking her eyes from the flickering flame.

Chuckling, Mike commented, "This place helped us focus when times got tough and our resolve wavered. Will it work its magic tonight?"

"I hope it will. I think we can talk out our problems," Joanne replied, not moving from her spot facing the window.

"Where should we start?" Mike asked, moving closer. He longed to touch her but did not want to confuse their thinking. They needed clear heads more than passion at the moment.

"I think I should begin," Joanne began softly.

"Okay. I'm listening," Mike said, leaning against the pew.

Without turning from the window, Joanne spoke softly, saying, "I owe you an apology for the way I acted after the sub accident. I panicked and made a rash decision. I acted like a civilian, not an officer. You were right in saying that I had faced danger and hadn't flinched while I was in flight school. I didn't even see the danger. But when you were aboard that maimed sub, I lost it. I forgot that we're trained to live with and survive danger. I forgot to be strong. I forgot to be navy. Instead, I threw out my training and became an emotional wreck. I pressed you to become someone that you're not. I wanted you to put aside your dreams because of my fears. That's unfair. I shouldn't have done that. I should have understood your needs. I should have remained calm. I'm sorry."

Mike watched Joanne's struggle with her emotions and wording. He wanted to help her, but he sensed that she had to cover this ground without his help.

Mike had to trust Joanne to persevere though this blip in their radar just as she had worked through so many other tough spots standing in the same place in the chapel. He longed to hold her, but he would have to wait.

"Apology accepted," Mike replied softly.

"Don't let me off so fast, Mike," Joanne said firmly. "I let you down and myself. I love you and allowed love to become a wedge between us. The beauty of love is in understanding the needs of the other person, not making demands. Love is accepting the career decision of the other person. Love is being there for the other person. I didn't do that."

"You were frightened. It's understandable," Mike interjected.

"I loved selfishly and turned away from you," Joanne replied, shaking her head. "What can I say? I'm a selfish person. I was afraid that you'd find yourself in danger in the future. I didn't want to feel that scared for another person ever again. I didn't want that level of pain and worry. I was only thinking of myself and of what I couldn't bear."

Reaching toward her and then withdrawing his hand, Mike said, "I might have reacted the same way if I had been the one left behind. It's hard to comprehend what's happening to the one you love when you're not experiencing it firsthand."

Wiping a stray tear, Joanne responded, "That's no excuse for what I did to us. I thought that putting distance between us would stop the feelings, but it didn't. Breaking off our engagement didn't stop the worry and only added to the pain . . . yours and mine. The pain of missing you has been greater than the worry about your safety."

"I survived and eventually understood," Mike commented. "You did what you thought was right."

"I was a silly fool," Joanne declared angrily. "I compared every man I met to you and found them woefully lacking. None of them has your charm, your wit, your sense of humor. They're nice people, but they're not you. I wasted our precious time. I turned away from you when you needed me."

"That's in the past. I got over it," Mike replied, studying her profile.

Shrugging her shoulders helplessly, Joanne said, "I was wrong, and I want to make it up to you if you'll let me. I said I'm a selfish person. I want it all. I want our old life back. I want you. I can take the separation and the pain as long as I have you."

Just as he had done so often while they were midshipmen, Mike stood quietly as Joanne wrestled with her emotions and desires. He watched her search for the right words with the chapel and the window as her inspiration. Now, it was his time to speak.

Standing next to her, Mike said, "You're right, you were selfish, but so was I. I wanted the career I've always dreamed of having, and you wanted me to stay on land. Nothing we studied here, no forestal lecture, and no career counseling prepared us for the toll that distance and worry can exact on a relationship. I guess this is why the chaplains urged us not to marry until after we'd finished the first tour. Yes, you were demanding and selfish and, don't get angry, a little cowardly. Life got tough, and you couldn't see it through."

Turning to face him, Joanne asked, "Can you forgive me?"

"There's nothing to forgive. You were just showing your love, but we both need to remember that love has to be flexible," Mike replied, pulling Joanne into his arms.

"Where do we go from here?" Joanne asked, feeling safe for the first time in months.

"We continue as if this blip never happened," Mike replied, kissing her lightly. "I've grown a lot during our separation and learned that I don't like not having you in my life. We never stopped loving each other even after you broke our engagement. That bond still existed. I could feel it when I fell asleep and when I woke up. I thought about you during maneuvers and wanted to share the details with you. You were with me as I wandered the streets of Rome. In my mind and heart, you shared gelato and penne with me. You walked under the Tuscan sky and held my hand in vineyards. I visited every single museum and church I could find. You were with me every step of the way."

Holding him close, Joanne said, "Oh, Mike, I wish I could have been there. That's the hardest part of the separation, not being able to share the things we experience and think. I would have liked to have shown you Hawaii and gone sightseeing with you in Italy. But I'll do better the next time you're under way. I promise."

"There won't be another underway, Joanne. I've been granted a transfer to meteorology. I'll begin training after my leave expires," Mike stated softly.

"You love subs. Do you really want to do that?" Joanne asked, studying his face for signs of regret.

"I love you more," Mike commented. "That's what I realized while I was under way. Being away from you is too hard on me. I want to wake up next to you every morning and go to sleep with you in my arms every night. I want to share my life with you in real time, not store up memories for later. I want us to be a part of the past, present, and future. Life isn't fun without someone to share it."

"Oh, Mike, after my blunder, you still love me?" Joanne cried.

Holding her face in his hands, Mike replied, "You're my heart and soul. I can't help but love you. From the moment I saw you on our first day at the Academy, I fell in love with you. I loved you when you were covered in slime. I loved you when you were dripping wet after a swim meet. I loved you at commissioning with the new ensign bars on your shoulders. You've become such an integral part of me that I don't know where I stop and you begin. I'm incomplete without you."

Joanne dissolved into unaccustomed tears. Mike had said everything that she had longed to hear since she first realized that she loved him so many years ago. However, their training and military duty had all but convinced her that she would never hear those words or know that level of completeness. The military life had almost made her forget the tenderness and longing that can exist between a man and a woman.

"I love you so," Joanne muttered, kissing his lips and cheeks. "I almost died when I heard the news of your sub. I was selfish, but it was selfishness with a good motive. I couldn't bear the thought of losing you to the sea. I'm Navy, but I'm a woman who doesn't want a rival. I'd almost forgotten that part of my life. I'm sorry, but I love you so much."

"There's no one else in the world for me but you," Mike stated, holding her close.

For a few moments, Joanne and Mike heard only the sound of their breathing. The silent chapel seemed to embrace them and block out all intrusions, protecting them from anyone who might enter. Even the Navy with its regulations and duties could not pull them apart.

"What'll we do now?" Joanne asked, studying Mike's handsome face.

"What'll we do? I seem to remember that we've booked this place for the twenty-fourth of June," Mike chuckled.

"We're getting married? I won't have to be a bridesmaid again?" Joanne laughed, hugging him close.

"You'll be the star of the show. No more bridesmaid for you. You'll be a married lady . . . a matron of honor," Mike replied, as they walked toward the rear of the chapel and the door that led into the night.

"I can't believe it's finally happening. I guess it's true that the window has magical powers. No more mauve gowns for me," Joanne laughed as she took one last look at the midshipman window and stepped into the night.

"I don't get it," Mike confessed, missing the joke.

"Mauve's very popular for weddings these days. I've worn it twice in less than six months. The next time I dress for a wedding, I'll wear ecru satin and lace," Joanne quipped happily.

"Then it's a go?" Mike asked with feigned seriousness.

"Of course, I want to marry you as planned. I can't think of anything I'd rather do," Joanne replied, laughing softly.

"Then why do I hear hesitation in your voice? Second thoughts maybe?" Mike asked, trying to see her eyes in the moon glow.

"It's just that we haven't seen much of each other for a long time. Maybe we should get to know each other first. Our life together is so uncertain," Joanne suggested tentatively.

"What's to know? I love you; you love me. Done," Mike stated simply.

"That's true, but I still have questions. Where will

we live? Will your meteorology training last long? Where will you be stationed after you've finished? Will we be separated again? I don't know any of that. I'm not unsure about us. It's the details that I don't quite understand yet," Joanne replied, as they walked toward the midshipman store parking lot.

"Fair enough. I've had time to work out the details, but it's all news to you. I'll get an apartment. We'll live there until after I finish the training. It's an eighteen-month master's program at the University of Maryland. After that, I've asked for reassignment to Hawaii. Everyone says I should get it since I've already stated that typhoons and ocean storms are my interest. You can return to the intelligence office there. I thought it was about time that you showed me around the islands," Mike chuckled as they stood in the glow of the streetlight.

"Hawaii! I never thought I'd return so soon. I didn't believe that old wives' tale, but throwing that lei into the water definitely worked. You've planned everything. I'm impressed," Joanne laughed happily.

"You're not the only one who's good at working out details. Any more objections?" Mike asked, placing both hands on Joanne's shoulders.

"No, none. I'm so happy," Joanne replied, kissing him lightly.

"From this moment on, it's fair winds and following seas for us," Mike commented, throwing his arm around Joanne's shoulders.

As Joanne and Mike walked toward the seawall for a last look at the dark water, the chapel bells began to peal the navy hymn. For the first time, they did not fear the dangers of the sea, knowing that they had each other. As long as they held on tightly and believed in the power of love, life would offer only smooth sailing.

Epilogue

The carriage swayed slightly as the pair of white horses trotted regally through the streets of Annapolis and through the Academy gate. Tourists waved as the bride and her family smiled and chatted happily. The sun shone brightly, and a gentle breeze from the bay fluttered Joanne's veil.

The footman in red livery alighted, helping first Joanne's father and then her mother to descend the carriage steps. With her parents smiling proudly, Joanne accepted the man's hand and gently eased from the carriage. The yards of heavy silk unfolded around her feet, hiding the delicate blue garter that she would later remove.

Angela Crawford pressed her daughter's hand and smiled through her happy tears. She remembered the joy of her wedding day. She had been a beautiful bride, but not as stunning as Joanne. Joanne's natural beauty sparkled through the sheer fabric; her smile tried to out-dazzle the sun.

With her father standing at her side, Joanne looked at the chapel dome. The shining bronze had beckoned her to worship and to reflection many times during her college days and since graduation, grounding her during times of distress. Today, she came to the edifice feeling as if she would float down its long aisle. For the first time, she would stop only briefly at the midshipman window before turning her attention to her handsome officer. She would not want to keep Mike waiting.

Waving to the last straggling guests as they rushed up the stairs, Joanne linked her arm into her father's. She held the huge bouquet of white calla lilies and roses in her gloved hand. Her father smiled and assisted her up the steps as the fugue the organist played drifted toward the open door.

"I'm ready, Daddy," Joanne declared with a brilliant smile.

"No second thoughts? No worries?" her father asked.

"None. I've dreamed of this day all my life. It's exactly as I planned it," Joanne replied, smiling.

"And Mike?"

"Like with all couples, we'll have our ups and downs, but you and Mom set the example on weathering them. Marriage is hard work, but Mike and I will always have 'fair winds and following seas,'" Joanne said as the wedding march began.

"Then it's anchors aweigh," Mr. Crawford announced, placing one last kiss on his daughter's cheek before straightening her veil.

"Sir, yes, sir," Joanne replied sharply, resting her hand on her father's arm as they stepped through the chapel door.

Joanne beamed at the sight of the handsome officer flanked by the chaplain and his best man. The swords at their sides sparkled in the bright sunlight that streamed through the chapel windows. Mike's face broke into a smile of delight as he watched her walk toward him. Joanne was the most beautiful bride he had ever seen. The congregation agreed and whispered remarks of appreciation as she floated toward him. No one seemed to notice the momentary pause and the gentle nod as she passed the midshipman window.

As the chaplain intoned the ancient rite, Joanne's father placed her hand in Mike's and joined his wife in the front pew. From that moment, the bride and her groom would have to make their own way in life. From the expressions of love and happiness on their faces, no one doubted that they would have anything but smooth sailing.

About the Author

Born in Washington, D.C., Courtni Wright graduated from Trinity College (D.C.) in 1972 with a major in English and a minor in history. In 1980, she earned a Master of Education degree from Johns Hopkins University in Baltimore, Maryland. She was a Council for Basic Education National Endowment for the Humanities Fellow in 1990. She has served as a consultant on National Geographic Society educational films on the practice and history of Kwanzaa, the history of the black cowboys, the story of Harriet Tubman, and the African American heritage in the West.

Ms. Wright's writing career covers multiple genres. Her first romance novel, entitled *Blush*, was published under the Arabesque imprint in September 1997. Since then, eleven other titles have followed. Holiday House published her children's books, *Jumping the Brook*, selected for the Society of School Librarians International's list of "Best Books of 1994"; *Journey to Freedom*, named a "Teacher's Choice" book by the International Reading Association; and *Wagon Train*, an acclaimed favorite. Her venture into Shakespearean analysis, entitled *The Women of Shakespeare's Plays*, was published by University Press of America.

She lives in Maryland with her husband, two Pomeranians, and a cat. She is the proud mother of a naval officer stationed aboard a submarine.